AND THEN IS HEARD NO MORE

AND THEN IS HEARD NO MORE

A ROXANNE CALLOWAY MYSTERY

RAYE ANDERSON

Doug Whiteway, Editor

Signature
EDITIONS

Cover design by Doowah Design.
Photo of author by Michael Long.

This book was printed on Ancient Forest Friendly paper.
Printed and bound in Canada by Hignell Book Printing Inc.

We acknowledge the support of the Canada Council for the Arts and the Manitoba Arts Council for our publishing program.

Library and Archives Canada Cataloguing in Publication

Title: And then is heard no more / Raye Anderson ; Doug Whiteway, editor

Names: Anderson, Raye, 1943- author. | Whiteway, Doug, 1951- editor.

Description: Series statement: A Roxanne Calloway mystery

Identifiers: Canadiana (print) 20210136901 |

Canadiana (ebook) 2021013691X |

ISBN 9781773240886 (softcover) | ISBN 9781773240893 (HTML)

Classification: LCC PS8601.N44725 A639 2021 | DDC C813/.6—dc23

Signature Editions
P.O. Box 206, RPO Corydon, Winnipeg, Manitoba, R3M 3S7
www.signature-editions.com

To all the great and inspired theatre artists I have known.
May you continue to light up our lives.

1

MARGO WISHART AND her friend Roberta Axelsson reached the Winnipeg city limits at 7:45. They had tickets to the theatre and were cutting it fine. Margo was annoyed. She had been invited to a pre-show reception for the Friends of Prairie Theatre Centre. It was the season opener and the city's rich and famous would be there. She'd heard that the lieutenant-governor for Manitoba would be putting in an appearance. They'd be lucky to find a parking spot and get to their seats before the play started.

It was October fifth, a bright fall night. No wind, a huge full moon and the end of harvest season. A couple of farm vehicles had been chugging slowly homewards after a long day in the fields, filling more than half the highway with their massive bulk and it hadn't helped that Roberta had taken her time to get ready. She'd been deliberating over a bundle of coloured scarves when Margo had arrived to pick her up.

"We do want to look our best!" she had crowed. "It's going to be an event!"

Roberta lived on the outskirts of Cullen Village in the Manitoba Interlake. She had bought four acres of land and an old wooden farmhouse that spring and spruced it up with bright paint, but that was as much as she could afford. "It's a work in progress," she liked to say.

They stood in her mud room. Margo sighed with impatience. She had had season tickets to PTC as it was called, back when she was married to the university's dean of education and had lived in town. She had let her subscription lapse since she divorced and moved to her lakeshore house three years ago. The drive home from Winnipeg to Cullen Village took almost an hour and on a cold, dark prairie winter night, in blowing snow or on icy roads, it could be difficult. She'd thought she'd buy single tickets, when a play appealed to her and the weather forecast was good, but somehow she didn't get around to it.

Now, here she was with complimentary tickets to the big opening night of the season and they were going to be late. It was frustrating, and she was going to be embarrassed. She reached into the box of scarves and seized a length of mauve chiffon and a textured tangerine shawl. "These will do. Put them on! We have to go!"

"Okay, okay!" Roberta obliged but she didn't really get it. She lived her life at a leisurely pace and hurrying was not something she was used to. Margo still had one foot in the working world. She taught art history, part time, at the university. Women artists, especially the ones who worked with fabric, had become her area of expertise. She'd been asked to write an article for a Canadian theatre journal about a costume designer who would be working at PTC this season. She had visited already, met Carla Hansen, head of wardrobe. Thus, the invitation. She had been thrilled to get it. When she'd been married, she had gone to these occasions often enough that she had sometimes thought of them as a duty. Now this one was a rarity, a scarce treat. She'd checked that her former husband and his newer, younger wife wouldn't be attending. They weren't. She had been looking forward to this evening. She bit her lip. She should have known Roberta would be late.

By this time, she was driving down city roads. She pulled into a side street that led directly downtown, to where the theatre was located. There, she lucked out. Someone was pulling out of a parking spot in front of a restaurant, one block over from their destination. She tucked her Honda SUV into the space; they hopped out and ran, with two minutes to spare.

Prairie Theatre Centre was housed in a custom-built grey concrete slab. It was faced with Tyndall stone, a local limestone studded with marine fossils that reminded the people of Winnipeg and its surroundings that the land they lived on was an ancient lakebed. The building had no windows on the street side and resembled a bunker, but bright lights beamed from the front doors. Margo was relieved to see people still standing around talking, drinks in hand, in the lobby. The audience hadn't gone in yet.

The house manager, elegant in a tailored suit and bow tie, caught her eye as they handed over their tickets. "Dr. Wishart!" he greeted her. Margo had been introduced to him, just two days before. She couldn't remember his name, then was glad to spot the name badge on his lapel.

"Hello, James! We got here just in time."

"You're in luck." He wore a professional smile. "We're delayed. You've got time to run upstairs for a quick drink." He indicated a doorway to the right. *Private Reception, Friends of PTC* said a sign on a stand beside it. "There's a coat rack inside." And there was. The room at the top of the flight of stairs glittered with celebrities. Margo surveyed the crowd. She recognized the mayor and a couple of well-known politicians, a local magnate who donated generously to the arts; a well-known CBC personality was chatting to the theatre's marketing director. Roberta spotted the food table and made a beeline for it, helping herself to a glass of wine en route. Up here, in this privileged eyrie, it came free. Margo was driving. No wine for her tonight.

Professor Thom Dyck waved a hand. Thom was a colleague. He ran the theatre department at the university and had introduced her to the PTC staff. He was also on PTC's board of directors.

"Glad you could make it," he said. "They're running late tonight. It's not like them." They watched as Tamsin Longstaff, PTC's general manager, detached herself from a group of donors and went to talk to James, the house manager, who was hovering at the door. They left together.

"They can't find Gerald," Thom explained. "That's the reason for the holdup. He always opens the show." Gerald Blaise had been artistic director at PTC for over twenty years. It was his habit to stroll onto the stage on each opening night, affability oozing from every pore, and welcome the audience to "his house." "He's never missed, not once, and this is the season opener. Hasn't been seen all day. They haven't a clue where he's got to."

Roberta joined them, crumbs at the corners of her mouth. In one hand was wine glass. In the other she held a plate on which sat two chocolates, handmade by a local chocolatier specially for the occasion, with the PTC logo imprinted on the top. She offered one to Margo. Margo declined. Thom looked inquiringly at Roberta, colourful, untidy, decked out in her bright scarves and homemade earrings, rings on almost every finger. Margo introduced them.

"I just met the head of the Humane Society! Isn't that great?" Roberta enthused and popped one of the chocolates into her mouth. Animal welfare was a cause that was dear to her. She had sold her old farmhouse to Mo Magnusson, a young woman who had inherited a lot of money after the violent death of her mother. Both Margo and Roberta had been involved in the investigation into that murder, earlier that year. Now Mo was setting up an animal rescue and Roberta was an enthusiastic volunteer. They were interrupted by an announcement. They should take their seats. The play would begin in five minutes.

"Wonder if Gerald's shown up, or if they're going to go ahead without him," said Thom, downing the remains of his drink. "See you later!"

Margo and Roberta had barely made it downstairs and found their seats when the lights dimmed and Tamsin Longstaff strutted onto the stage. She was tall and thin and she wore very high heels. She lacked Gerald's relaxed bonhomie but smiled broadly and was crisply professional. Gerald was unavoidably detained, she said, and was sorry he couldn't be with them tonight. A curious murmur ran through the auditorium but that soon subsided. The audience had no reason to be concerned. Tamsin kept her comments brief. She made all the necessary acknowledgements to sponsors and the like, stepped out of the spotlight and exited, stage left. The lieutenant-governor and her husband made their entrance, they all stood for the playing of "O, Canada," and the play began.

Margo and Roberta settled back into their comfortable, red plush seats to enjoy it. The script was brand new, a Winnipeg story written by a local playwright, based on the life of a woman who had been one of the leaders of the Winnipeg General Strike back in 1919. Margo had worried that it might be didactic but the writer had injected wit and humour into the dialogue and a dash of romance besides. Many of the actors were also local, familiar to the audience. It was a popular choice and the crowd was enthusiastic as it emptied into the lobby at intermission. Roberta scooted to the washroom. There would be a lineup there in no time. Margo watched the playwright being congratulated by Thom Dyck and others. He was smiling bashfully but was obviously pleased with the response. Professor Dyck looked happily engaged.

"Margo!" Carla Hansen pushed her way through the crowd. "Here you are. What do you think of it?" Margo knew it wasn't the play as a whole that she was referring to but what the actors were wearing. Carla and her crew of sewers and cutters had built the period costumes. She prided herself on making sure that everything worn on stage looked authentic, especially for an historical piece like this. The fabric, the hats, the shoes all had to look just right. She herself had dressed for the occasion, in a long skirt, blouse and jacket that managed to look Edwardian as well as modern. A tall woman loomed behind her. She reached out a large hand.

"Sadie Williams," she introduced herself. The voice was deep and sonorous. Sadie had been Sam Williams up until five years ago. Samuel, not Samantha. The hand was perfectly manicured, the nails a tasteful pearly pink. Crystal bracelets dangled from her wrists and her rings sparkled. The dress she wore was pink silk with an overlay of lace to match. More crystal hung at her ears. She made her clothes herself, or hired one of the sewers who worked in the many theatres where she worked to run them up for her. "Can't find a thing to fit. Shoes are an absolute bitch," she'd been known to complain. Margo was thrilled to meet her. Sadie had just arrived in Winnipeg as the costume designer for Shakespeare's *Macbeth*, next play up, and she was the person Margo wanted to write about.

Carla pointed a glass in the direction of Tamsin Longstaff, huddled between a woman in an elegant blue dress and two men in suits.

"See that?" she said. "Tamsin's with the board executive, trying to figure out what to do about Gerald. That guy she's talking to is Frank Moran, he's the chair."

"They should have called the police already," Sadie growled. "It's a no-brainer. Gerald would choke rather than miss his own season opener. But I suppose they don't want a fuss. Not on opening night. Has Tamsin talked to Budgie yet?"

"Budgie?" Margo asked.

"Annabel." Annabel Torrance was married to the missing Gerald. They were a theatre couple. Annabel was her stage name, chosen with care, an upgrade from Ann, the one she'd grown up with. She was presently in Regina, acting in a play at that city's Globe Theatre. She would finish on Sunday, then come back to Winnipeg in time to start rehearsals for *Macbeth* on Tuesday. She was going to reprise the role of Lady Macbeth. Gerald was scheduled to direct.

Many people in the theatre community believed that plays were often chosen at PTC with Annabel in mind. Not that she wasn't good. She was. Critics and audience alike were looking forward to discovering what she'd do differently, as a much older Lady Macbeth than she had been when she'd last done it at

PTC, twenty years before. They were surprised that the company had decided to resurrect this one. But if you were going to do a Shakespeare play, *Macbeth* was known, and Gerald was going to direct it himself. Budgie was capable of pulling off surprises to delight her audience. She could be relied on to be formidable onstage.

"She's been called Budgie since theatre school. Looks a bit like one, don't you think?" A framed photograph of Annabel, when she'd done *Cat on a Hot Tin Roof*, hung on a wall nearby. Margo suppressed an urge to smile. It was true. She had seen Annabel perform many times on the PTC stage. Her little face had a slightly hooked nose and thin lips but still looked attractive. It was amazing what some artfully applied makeup could do.

"They called her earlier. She hasn't heard anything from him." Sadie waved to someone she knew, across the crowd.

"Won't she be worried? And doesn't she have to perform at the Globe tonight?" Margo asked.

"Budgie will tough it out." Sadie raised perfectly arched brows above three shades of coral eyeshadow.

"Gerald was at the preview last night," said Carla. "Gave some notes then left, not long after ten. The caretaker heard his cats howling this morning. He has a spare key. Went in and fed them." Gerald was partial to Persians. He had two. "Said his car wasn't in its space downstairs." The condo was in a converted warehouse just across the back lane from the theatre. "So, he must have gone out last night. Or this morning." Roberta's arrival interrupted them. Margo was glad to see her back. She wanted to introduce her to Sadie and Carla. She knew they were hoping to use hand-dyed fabric for the witch costumes for *Macbeth* and Roberta spun and dyed yarn. Soon, they were deep in conversation about natural dyes and the colours they produced. The subject of the missing Gerald Blaise never came up again before it was time to take their seats for Act 2.

Margo and Roberta didn't stick around long after the end of the show. There was to be a party and they were invited but they needed to hit the road and get back home to the lakeshore. Roberta had chickens and ducks to tuck in for the night and a family of foster kittens snuggled up with their mother in her spare room, and Margo needed to pick up her dog, Bob, from her friend Sasha Rosenberg's house.

They talked about the play and the people they had met on the moonlit drive home. Carla had said she wanted to "pick Roberta's brains" some more about natural dyes and how they worked. She wanted to see some samples. Margo hoped that might result in some work for Roberta, who was always strapped for cash. She was looking forward to coming back into the city on Tuesday to sit in on the first day of rehearsal for *Macbeth*. Now, Roberta had been invited too. That was going to be fun. They barely thought at all about the missing Gerald Blaise.

2

TOBY MALLESON, DIRECTOR of marketing, walked into Tamsin Longstaff's office at Prairie Theatre Centre at 10:05 the following morning and closed the door behind him. That was a bad sign. Tamsin sighed.

"What's happening about Gerald?" Toby asked, standing in front of the closed door, his arms folded. Toby was elegant. He ironed his shirts. Today he was dressed in various shades of cream and taupe with a crimson tie. His head was shaved, he sported a faint, dark stubble, and he was frowning. "His absence was noticed, Tamsin. I've got calls and messages from all over wanting to know why he wasn't there last night."

Tamsin took off her reading glasses and swivelled her chair around to face him. She was going to have to deal with this, like it or not. "The reviews are okay?"

"Yeah. Well, better than okay. They'll do. What do I say about Gerald?" Toby was not to be distracted. "Have you talked to the police yet?"

"Sit down, Toby," Tamsin replied with the calm demeanour of a woman well used to putting out brush fires. In their business, they happened daily, although this one was bigger than usual. She had left the post-show party shortly after midnight and made it back into the office before eight, hoping for news about their missing artistic director. There hadn't been a word.

"Don't worry," she said, with what she hoped was a reassuring smile. "There will be a perfectly good explanation, you'll see. He'll show up in time to start rehearsals on Tuesday. He's bound to."

"Tuesday?" Toby sat down as instructed, on the other side of Tamsin's desk. "This is Friday, Tamsin. He's been gone almost thirty-six hours now and you're talking Tuesday? He could be dead in a ditch somewhere. Mugged. Maybe he's had a heart attack and he's lying in a hospital bed somewhere. Suffering from amnesia." His voice had risen. Toby had initially studied theatre. He could be a bit of a ham.

Tamsin shook her head. Close up you could tell that she was closer to sixty than forty, although she did a good job of concealing it. She was never seen without lipstick, her hair was a natural-looking brown with highlights, cut in a flattering layered bob, and her nails were perfect scarlet ovals. Her staff sometimes wondered how she managed to type at lightning speed without chipping them, but she did.

"Calm down, Toby, please. And listen. Gerald is probably perfectly safe. He's just gone away for a few days."

"Gone away?" Toby sat back, looking puzzled. "At the beginning of the season? You've got to be kidding! People want to talk to him about the new play. And the actors for *Macbeth* will start arriving on the weekend. They'll all want to speak to him. Where's he gone to?"

Tamsin wished she hadn't been awake half the night asking herself the same questions. "I don't know," she replied. "And yes, there's work to do. You're not the only one picking up the pieces, Toby. We'd all best get on with it." She put on her glasses again and turned towards her computer.

"Whoa!" Toby snapped. "What do I tell CBC? They're screaming for an interview. And they're not the only ones. You're not calling the police because you know he's gone away? Did he tell you? Is he on vacation? Taking a few days off before he has to go into the rehearsal hall and direct Budgie in the Scottish play? You've spoken to her, right? What's she got to say about this?"

"It's Budgie that told me," Tamsin explained patiently. She rocked back in her chair, giving up any hope of getting back to the grant proposal she was working on. "She says he's done it before. Taken off like this. Twice, actually. First time he went off to Mexico with a twenty-one-year-old straight out of theatre school. Second time it was a weekend in Muskoka with a marketing intern. Budgie suspects a student from U of M this time. A girl that was in that summer course he taught for them. It's what he does when he's under stress, she says. It's a safety valve. He'll come back."

"So that's what I tell the media? Our AD has taken off to some spot unknown to let off steam with some kid less than half his age before he has to direct a play with his wife in it?" Toby rolled his eyes. "Did you tell the board that?"

"No, I didn't," Tamsin replied. "And you'll keep all that to yourself, thank you." She looked at Toby over the top of her glasses and thawed a little. "Come on, Toby, you know what to do. Be vague. Make something up. He's had to go away for personal reasons. Family. Private stuff. Imply that some relative's dying or something. Stall. It's no big deal. They'll all have lost interest by tomorrow."

"Has anyone tried to get hold of the student?"

"No, we haven't." Tamsin didn't know who the girl was and hadn't had time to find out. "Look, Toby, I've got a meeting at eleven and I've got to get this grant done. Do what you have to do."

"Okay." Toby pulled himself out of the chair and stepped towards the door. Then he turned. "What if you're wrong?" he said. "What if Budgie's got it all wrong? What if he really is in some kind of trouble?"

Tamsin mustered another smile. "Gerald?" she said. "Come on, you know how he is. He always lands on his feet."

BUDGIE TORRANCE OPENED her eyes and peered at the bedside clock. 11:14. She'd gone out after the show last night, with some of the cast and crew. Late-night Italian food and a couple of drinks, then back to the hotel. Thick drapes kept the room dark and she'd hung the DO NOT DISTURB sign on her door. She switched on a light, pulled over some extra pillows, reached for her phone, then glanced though her messages. Gerald still hadn't shown up. There was one from Tamsin. The board was asking awkward questions. Was she sure Gerald was okay? That he'd be back in time to start rehearsals on Tuesday?

Another was from Toby Malleson: "WTF, Budgie, the *Free Press* and radio stations are asking where G is. What do I say?" Another, from Larry Smith, the caretaker at their condo in Winnipeg, complained that Gerald hadn't said he was going away. The cats had been meowing loudly so Larry had gone in to check. They were hungry. Gerald hadn't left food and litter for them. And he hadn't arranged with Larry to have them fed. That made her swing her legs out of the bed and sit up straight. Gerald might have taken off in a snit, but not take care of his cats? Never.

She padded to the washroom to pee. Then she looked at herself in the mirror. She hadn't taken off her makeup last night before she fell into bed. She looked like an aging raccoon. She put a coffee pod into the machine and pressed the start button. Had she got it wrong? Was Gerald really in some kind of a fix? She had been so sure. She always knew when Gerald had a new conquest in his sights. She could see him start to preen. Sure sign. Took more trouble than usual over what he wore, brushed his hair a lot, had a certain gleam in his eye. She didn't mind. She was used to it. It was kind of cute. Funny, almost.

They'd agreed years ago that they would pursue their own amatory interests. It worked for them. She had her own fun. They gave each other some slack. They'd been married close to thirty years and they had each other figured out. The kid from the university (she was pretty sure it was her. She'd watched the two of them together in the kitchen at a party in Thom Dyck's house a few weeks back, the girl all big-eyed and adoring, him leaning in a bit too close) was no big deal.

The coffee was ready. She went to the little fridge where she kept necessary supplies, found a carton of milk, poured some into her mug and stirred. She took a sip and sat at a small, round table. "Still," she thought.

She and Gerald had had a row on the phone last weekend, about *Macbeth*. She hadn't wanted him to direct it himself. Maybe she shouldn't have let him know that. But it was true. She'd wanted Nathan Simkin to do it. Budgie was dying to work with him. Nathan was young and would bring some fresh new ideas to the production, she was sure of that. But no, Gerald wanted the job for himself. Same old. It was bad enough that he'd chosen *Macbeth*, again. Been there, done that. She was itching to have a go at one of those big roles that had been written for and about men. She'd be a great Richard III, but no. Back to the lady, and it was going to be so old hat. He was yammering on about earth tones, organic shapes, all that old crap. She had seen the designs. Lady M in medieval drapes.

"No," she had retorted. "This will not do." She'd ranted on about how hackneyed it was, a cliché. She'd actually told him he was stupid. "She's been married to Macbeth for maybe twenty years?" she'd said. "And in those days girls got married off when they were fourteen." Budgie was the same age as her husband but she could get away with looking like she was much younger with the right look and some flattering lighting. "She's still mad about the guy." At least he'd had the sense to hire that cute Danny Foley to play Macbeth. That would help. But the nun-like headdress wrapped around her head would age her and make it more difficult to convince the audience that she was sexy.

Gerald had gone huffy on her. He did that sometimes. Tried to guilt her out. Muttered about how she didn't share his vision.

"What vision, Gerald?" she had replied, dripping acid. "You haven't dreamed up an original concept in years. Maybe you never have." He'd hung up on her then. She hadn't cared. She'd have a quiet word with Sadie Williams, the costume designer. Sadie would get it. She was smart. She'd make sure that Budgie looked presentable.

So she hadn't been concerned about Gerald. Why would she? They'd had worse arguments before, way worse. He'd come around like he always did. But now he'd done a disappearing act. He hadn't done one of those in years, before they ever came to Manitoba, when the jobs he'd had were much more precarious and life was more stressful. He'd settled comfortably into being AD at Prairie Theatre Centre. His contract was coming up for renewal this year. Was he worried about that? She didn't know. She hadn't been around much to be able to pay attention. She'd been away most of the summer, at the Shaw Festival in Ontario, then here, in Regina. She'd been in Winnipeg for a couple of weeks in August, but that was it.

Gerald had never missed the opening of a play at PTC before, far less the one that opened the season. He loved openings, working the crowd, the festive atmosphere, the excitement. Nevertheless, it was possible. He'd have known that Tamsin and Toby would cover for him and she, Budgie, wasn't around to stop him. But go off and neglect to make sure that Tarquin and Delilah were provided for? That didn't make sense. He adored those cats. Budgie looked at the bedside clock again. It was now 11:47. Winnipeg was an hour later than Regina. Gerald had been gone a day and a half. Should she call Tamsin and tell her to speak to the police? But what if he really was just off on some stupid dalliance and the press got hold of that? It would cause such an unnecessary scandal. She reached for the hotel phone and pressed the number for room service. She'd order breakfast first and have a shower, then she'd make up her mind.

THE SUN SHONE brightly down on Cullen Village. Margo Wishart looked out her window at the silvery lake, shimmering all the way to the horizon. The trees were golden and bronze, the air was still, not a hint of wind with winter on its breath. Not yet. Skeins of geese had been flying west all morning, honking their way towards harvested fields where they would forage all day before coming back to roost at the lakeshore before nightfall. By now, October, there were thousands of them. Someday soon the snow line would reach Cullen Village and they would take off, one big clamouring V after another, heading south. They wouldn't be back until spring. But not today. Today was glorious. She should phone Sasha Rosenberg and suggest a dog walk. Margo was feeling guilty because she'd taken Roberta Axelsson to the theatre last night and prevailed upon Sasha to dog sit. Sasha had been good about it. "Not a problem," she had said, taking the dog leash. "Enjoy yourself."

Margo knew Sasha would have loved to go, but she had needed to make a choice. The invitation she had received was for herself and a guest. Only two tickets, and when she had called the box office to see if she could purchase a third, they were sold out. Opening night of the season, of course they were. She had wanted Roberta to meet the wardrobe staff, so she had made her decision. She reached for her phone. She would invite Sasha for lunch, to make amends.

"No big deal," said Sasha. "But since you're offering, how about we go to the café at The Locks? We can take the dogs with us and eat outside."

Margo was surprised. "They do hot dogs, Sasha." That was what the café was famous for. Sasha tried, sometimes, to keep kosher.

"And burgers," Sasha retorted. "Fries." They did, huge helpings of homemade potato fries. Sweet potato fries too, and poutine, the Canadian classic, fries with cheese curds and gravy. "Lenny can have a sausage." Lenny was her basset hound. He ate everything. And so it was decided. An hour or so later, they set out in Margo's car, both dogs in the back, past stubbled fields, dotted with large round hay bales, and regimented rows of sunflowers, their faces turned to the south, following the noonday sun.

The big Red River flowed north from Winnipeg, dammed before it entered the lake at its southernmost point. Locks at the side of the dam allowed boats to navigate their way to lower water and the pool formed at its foot was a great place to catch fish. Boats bobbed on the surface and pelicans gathered to swoop and dive into the water. Margo had brought along her camera. She might get some good shots.

The café at The Locks had been a fixture for decades. Day trippers liked to drive out from the city along the scenic road by the river. They'd stop to eat and walk along the shore to watch the birds and the people fishing. This was a Friday and the kids were in school. It wasn't too busy. Margo and Sasha sat at a wooden picnic table in the warm fall sun and stuffed themselves on fried food. The dogs had their share too. A walk was definitely required before they headed home.

They strolled to the locks, the dogs on retractable leashes, long enough that they could explore, Margo's camera slung around her neck. There were a few boats out on the water and some people were fishing on each shore. Big, white pelicans congregated on rocks that jutted out into the pool. Margo opened up her camera.

"Here, give me that leash," said Sasha, taking it so that Margo's hands were free. The dogs were ambling along, sniffing out unfamiliar territory. Cars were parked on the roadside at a spot just past the dam. There was a paved pathway and a guard rail. From here you could get a good view. Margo watched a bird swoop in to land on the water near others, roosting on the rocks. She snapped it just as the webbed feet spread out to land and the big, black tipped wings spread to break its flight. She got a good shot.

"Hey, guys!" she heard Sasha say. The dogs had wandered onto a small parking lot, stretching their long leashes. They seemed to be interested in a shiny red Audi. Bob was straining to reach the back of the car and Lenny was at the back fender, trying to get his front paws up on it, sniffing at the trunk. "Leave that!" Sasha pulled on the leashes. They resisted. "Wonder if someone left their catch in their car?"

"Maybe," said Margo. She was more interested in watching another pelican hovering over the water, as if it was ready to dive.

"Lenny doesn't go for dead fish." Sasha was walking towards the dogs, reeling in the leashes. "Unless it's rotten and he can roll in it." Margo got the shot she wanted, covered the lens on her camera and walked closer to take Bob's leash.

"Someone could have been hunting," she said. "Maybe shot a deer?" This was hunting season. Geese and deer were favourite targets. "Nice car," she commented. "Looks brand new." They pulled the dogs back onto the pathway and began to walk back to where Margo's Honda was parked in front of the café. "We've got time to get back to the village and take these two to the dog beach. They need to get some real exercise. Run off those wieners." A section of beach at Cullen Village had been designated dog friendly. Bob and Lenny could romp along the sand, off leash. Bob loved to swim. Lenny did not.

The rest of that beautiful afternoon unfolded as it should. Towards its end, Sasha walked her hound back home and Margo put on the kettle in her house by the lakeshore. She took out her phone. It wasn't long past four. There was still time to call Carla Hansen at the theatre. Margo hadn't seen her to thank her properly for giving her the complimentary tickets after the play ended. Carla answered. She was in the costume room, cutting fabric, she said.

"I'm interrupting you," said Margo.

"That's okay," Carla replied "It's been a crazy afternoon. The police have been here. Tamsin finally called them. About Gerald not showing up. They'd like us all to stop what we're doing and let them search everywhere but we can't. Tamsin ended up yelling at a sergeant. We all heard her. Tamsin never yells. She must be really worried. Anyway, Gerald's definitely not been seen since he left after the dress rehearsal on Wednesday night. He must have walked out the back, towards the condo. There's no camera on the back door. Hardly anybody uses it. You know they live in that

restored warehouse just across the back lane? Him and Budgie?"
Margo didn't.

"The police aren't saying anything but a couple of our techies
went over there this morning, just to check in with the caretaker
and see if he knew anything. He's been feeding the cats. Can't
believe Gerald went off and left them. Purebred Persians. They're
his babies. He's nuts about them. Anyway, his car's gone, so they're
going to look for it. Shouldn't be hard to find. Budgie bought it for
him for his sixtieth. An Audi. It's red."

Margo was about to sip her tea. It didn't make it to her lips.

"I have to go, Carla," she said, already wondering who to call.
"See you Tuesday. And thanks again for the tickets." Margo hung
up and scrolled through her contact list, looking for the number
for the RCMP detachment at Fiskar Bay, just north of Cullen
Village.

Constable Ken Roach answered her call. Sergeant Gilchrist
wasn't available, he said. What was this about? Margo remembered
Constable Roach, from the murder case earlier that year. He was
stern, terse and authoritative. She didn't want to talk to him.

"I'll call back tomorrow," she said, and hung up. Then she called
Roberta Axelsson. Roberta had Corporal Roxanne Calloway's cell
phone number. She'd been given it by Roxanne in February, when
Roxanne was investigating that old murder case out of Fiskar Bay
and it had looked as if Roberta might be in danger. Margo would
get the number from Roberta and call Roxanne directly. Roxanne
was in the RCMP's Major Crimes Unit. She could take care of this.

3

"ANOTHER COP HAS just gone into Tamsin's office. This one's in plain clothes." Nell Bronson, stage manager for *Macbeth*, walked backwards into the wardrobe room at PTC, eyes still focused on what was happening down the corridor. Carla Hansen stood at a large table cutting up fabric with practised ease. Sadie Williams sat at a table by one of the large windows ranged along one wall, building headdresses for the three witches in *Macbeth* on Styrofoam moulds, trays of buttons and feathers ranged in front of her. A box of fake autumn leaves.

"Said she was from the RCMP," Nell continued, closing the door behind her and turning towards one of two comfortable chairs that Carla provided for actors while they waited for fittings. Nell wore typical stage management gear: old, worn jeans, a grey sweatshirt with a Winnipeg Jets logo, comfortable sneakers with quiet soles.

"How come you know that, Nell?" Carla stopped cutting, scissors poised in mid-air.

"Because she told me, Carla," Nell replied smugly. "When I showed her the way upstairs. A sergeant. Calloway, Galloway, something like that. Got red hair."

"Wasn't RCMP yesterday." Sadie hauled herself out of her chair.

"No. Those guys were all city police. Shall I put on the kettle?"

There was a table in a corner nook, provided with a collection of mugs, a coffee maker, a kettle and all that was required to make tea, including a teapot. Police had been poking around yesterday afternoon. They had mainly talked with Tamsin and Toby

Malleson. One of them had been in Gerald Blaise's office, not for long but enough to send a nervous shiver through the theatre staff. Toby had gone around, confiding in everyone.

"I've asked them to be discreet," he had assured them all. "They're going to put out an alert about the car and not mention Gerald by name. For now. If the car shows up somewhere like the airport they'll know he's just taken off somewhere for a few days." All the interruptions had taken up precious time. Now they were in, working on Saturday morning, catching up. There were a lot of costumes in this play.

Tamsin had trotted back and forth to the photocopy room the day before, keeping an eye on things as she went.

"She does it deliberately," Nell complained. "PTC could afford to buy her a printer of her own but it gives her an excuse to walk around and see what's going on. Had a Canada Council grant to submit but their website was down and she was going to have to courier a hard copy. Priority, she said, and there was me with all my lists." She had a stack of them, cast members, contacts, rehearsal schedules. "Then the cops kicked me out so they could inspect the place."

She wasn't fooling anyone. There was nowhere else Nell Bronson wanted to be but at the theatre when she was working on a show. Carla and Sadie too. Now Nell reached for a box of tea bags. "Thought I'd have the place all to myself on a Saturday morning. Is there any ginger and lemon in here?" The kettle began to boil.

"Couple of board members were in yesterday, talking to Tamsin. She's got her hands full." Carla continued to carve up the fabric.

"So, what are they going to do if he doesn't show up?" Sadie passed a mug to Nell, helped herself to one and sank into the other chair. She dwarfed it.

"Well," Nell drawled, obviously in the know and dying to tell. "Thom Dyck, the theatre prof, the one that's on the board, is on standby for Tuesday. He can manage to run a read-through, we hope. Tamsin's got calls in to Edmonton and Toronto, trying to find out who's available, just in case. I had Chinese with Tamsin last night. Told me herself."

Carla put down her scissors once more.

"Do we know why it's RCMP now?" she asked, folding up the pieces she had cut. "Have they found something out of town?"

"Gerald? He never leaves the city," Sadie scoffed. "He hates small towns. And the countryside. Doesn't go outside if he can help it, not even in the summer. Swims in pools. Indoor ones. And goes to the gym. That apartment of theirs doesn't even have a balcony."

"Maybe he's shacked up in a hotel somewhere. Hecla. Riding Mountain. Having a cozy weekend with Lisa Storm before Budgie gets back." Nell grinned over the top of her mug.

"You reckon? Is that why he cast her?" Carla leaned against the big cutting table. Lisa Storm was to play the First Witch, the youngest one.

"He's been fussing over her costume. Wants her to look sexy and attractive." Sadie herself was dressed to kill today, in a short blue skirt, mauve tights and pale blue stilettos with little bows pasted on the front. "That explains it!"

"You bet. She's in the same play as Budgie? Gerald's usually more careful."

"But the RCMP?" Carla persisted. "What are they here for?"

TAMSIN LONGSTAFF HEARD the news that Gerald Blaise's car had been found, with a body in the trunk, quite calmly. Her eyes widened, her nostrils flared as she inhaled deeply, and her crimson lips compressed into a small, round O. She had worked with Gerald for fifteen years and he was still missing. The body might well be his. But, for now, she assumed her normal, controlled presence. She realized that there was a need for a police presence but her first concern was that operations at the theatre should not be disrupted.

"We have an audience arriving for a matinee at two, and another performance at eight this evening. The same tomorrow. Monday is a dark night."

She noticed a puzzled look flicker across the face of the woman in front of her—the Mountie, not that she looked like one with her well-cut cap of red hair, neat black jacket and pants, laundered white blouse. Maybe things were finally changing in that venerable Force.

"Theatre talk. The lights are off. We're closed. Night off," she explained. "Our production crews have this weekend off, although I see our wardrobe department is at work today. We're starting to build a new show. Rehearsals begin on Tuesday. Gerald was supposed to be directing it. We're going to have to find someone to replace him, if he really is dead." She frowned and tapped a long fingernail on her desk. "Have you spoken to Gerald's wife yet? Annabel Torrance. She's working at the Globe in Regina."

Roxanne Calloway had learned that already. Larry Smith, the caretaker at Gerald Blaise's condo building, had been helpful and informative. The RCMP were already making an initial search of the apartment, looking for any signs of a scuffle or blood.

Roxanne had arrived at The Locks the evening before, an hour or so after Margo Wishart's call. The car had been locked but the licence number indicated it was definitely Gerald Blaise's missing red Audi. It had taken time to call for assistance, get permission to open the trunk and, once the body was discovered, for the medics to arrive and declare death. It had been dark. The technicians had worked by floodlight, examining the body in place. There had been a lot of blood in the trunk. The throat of the man inside had been cut. The provincial medical examiner had taken possession of the remains, but the Ident Unit would be continuing now, on site, in the morning light. So far, they had found nothing else of interest.

"Looks like he was killed elsewhere," Corporal Dave Kovak, who led the Forensic Identification Unit, had said to Roxanne.

"Then driven out here. It probably happened in the city, but it looks like you'll be stuck with the case."

The City of Winnipeg Police Service took care of all crimes committed within the city limits. Where the body showed up determined whether it was their case or not. Outside the city, it became the responsibility of the RCMP. That had annoyed Inspector Schultz, Roxanne's supervisor.

"Should be their case, dammit," he'd almost spat with annoyance, "and now we've got it. It's going to be on my budget. How come you're involved, anyway?"

She'd received a call. A tipoff. She'd followed up on it. Sir.

She'd had a date last night, with Inspector Brian Donohue, also in the RCMP. Roxanne was in the Major Crimes Unit. Brian worked mainly on cybercrime these days and, as an inspector, spent most of his time behind a desk. She'd been going to go over to his place to watch a movie. Her son, Finn, was at her sister's house, sleeping over. She and Brian both had kids. It was hard to get a night together and she'd had to pass. She could have left the scene in the hands of the Forensic Identification Unit and made a report. But if she did, the case might be assigned to someone else. This was too interesting and an opportunity that Roxanne intended to seize. She was sure that Brian, under the same circumstances, would have done the same. He'd worked in the Major Crimes Unit before his promotion. He got it. So she had texted. SORRY. WORK CAME UP. CALL LATER. It had been into the early hours of the morning before she had left the crime scene, too late to make that call.

"Someone from the RCMP in Regina has gone to speak to Ms. Torrance," she now told Tamsin Longstaff. "Are there other relatives in Winnipeg? We need someone to identify the body."

Not that there was much doubt as to who it was. The police knew what Gerald Blaise looked like. His photograph was everywhere at PTC, in the theatre programs, in framed photographs that lined the walls. There was one right beside the door in Tamsin's office, of her and Gerald receiving an award, all smiles. Gerald was a celebrity in Winnipeg, certainly in the arts community. His face showed up regularly in the arts news and on social media. Tamsin sat back and ran her fingers through her hair. "There's no one. He and Budgie were both only children and they didn't have kids of their own."

"Budgie?"

"Oh, sorry. Annabel. It's what we all call her." Tamsin's phone kept vibrating. That could be Budgie herself. She sat up straight again. "If you need me to, I'll identify him," she said, tight lipped.

Brave lady, thought Roxanne. She had noticed that Tamsin had not asked how Gerald had actually died or wondered who might have killed him. She had rolled straight into figuring out practical solutions to immediate problems. She recognized that it was one way of coping.

"Thank you," she said. "I'll let them know we're coming. In an hour?" Tamsin nodded but her eyes had already strayed back to her computer screen. She wanted to get back to her own job. "Could someone show me around the building for now?" Tamsin looked relieved.

"Nell Bronson, one of our stage managers, is around. I'll ask her to give you the backstage tour."

Roxanne had never been behind the scenes in a theatre before. A labyrinth of corridors led to different areas. The "shop" was at the back of the building. It was where they built and painted scenery and was connected to the stage via large hydraulic doors. Roxanne scanned the room. There were tools ranged on wall racks, including sharp knives and cutters. The paint area had big sinks and a drain in the floor. There was even a hose hooked up to a wall spigot. It would be so easy to carry out a murder here. Protective clothing hung on pegs and a fan extractor removed toxic substances from the air. The smell of blood could have been eradicated at the flick of a switch. Double doors at the back of the shop led to a loading dock, outside, on the back lane behind the theatre. It would have been simple to drive up, load a body into the trunk of the car and drive off. There were even dollies at the back door for transporting heavy items.

"There's surveillance out here?" she asked the stage manager. Nell Bronson seemed a sensible sort, hair cropped short, casual clothes, a woman in her forties. She'd been stage managing for over twenty years, she had told Roxanne.

"Sure," said Nell.

"How many entrances?"

"To the building? There's the front door, to the lobby. Box office is open there until eight-thirty if there's a show on. It has a twenty-four-hour camera. The stage door has one too. It opens onto the parking lot, east side of the building. Did you come in that way?" Roxanne had. She'd needed to buzz in. "There's a fire exit back of the lobby, only opens from the inside. No camera there. And there's another exit, from the office area upstairs, that comes out just to the right of here, onto the lane." She pressed a button beside one of the large doors and it rolled up revealing the lane outside. Roxanne peered out. The wall was blank concrete but there was a row of small windows, high above. A door with a single step down could be seen further along it.

"Gerald used that one a lot," said Nell, her hands tucked into the pockets of her jeans. She nodded across the lane to a red brick building. A doorway was almost exactly opposite. "He lived over there, right? He and Budgie have a condo." The building had once been a warehouse. It had been converted years before.

"And there's no camera?"

Nell shook her head. "Guess not."

Gerald Blaise could have entered or left the building where he worked at any time without anyone knowing.

Nell led Roxanne back into the shop and through a side door onto the stage. It was pitch black inside. "Stay where you are. Don't touch a thing." She hit a switch and work lights came on. Roxanne looked around. Black drapes separated the stage from the backstage area. There were tables with items used in the present production, each one in a labelled spot. "Props," said Nell. They walked out onto the stage. It was set up for the evening's performance, with furniture in place. It all looked quite ordinary in plain light. Roxanne looked out into the auditorium. She had sat there once last year. Her sister had brought her to a play. "Just over eight hundred seats," Nell informed her. "See up there?" She pointed to a row of windows up behind the seating. "That's the control booth. We call the show from there."

"Call it?'

"Light cues. Sound. Entrances. You know."

Roxanne didn't. Was she going to have to learn some of this theatre jargon? "Everything's very neat and tidy," she commented.

"You bet. Dead organized. Pedro, the director of production here, is a freak for cleanliness, and safety. Everything in its place."

That could be helpful, Roxanne thought as she was led out of the stage area at the other side, past racks of stage lights to a vast room that Nell Bronson called the rehearsal hall. It soared up two stories and was painted entirely black. Metal pipes criss-crossed the ceiling. The grid, Nell called it. Some big black lamps were bolted to them. A row of drapes covered windows along one wall and lines were taped out on the floor.

"The floor plan for *Macbeth*," Nell explained. "It's the exact same size as it will be on stage. Different colours for different scenes." She turned to face Roxanne. "Did Gerald off himself?"

"I don't know." Roxanne looked at her in surprise. It was highly unlikely. Someone had closed the trunk lid on the bleeding body that was inside it.

"But he's dead? For sure?"

"I can't say. Not yet. What makes you think he could be suicidal?"

"I didn't say he was."

"You thought he might be." Nell Bronson went to a cupboard and looked through papers on a shelf, avoiding answering. She handed a couple of sheets to Roxanne.

"That's a floor plan of the building. We give it to actors so they don't get lost while they're here. And this is next week's rehearsal schedule."

Roxanne took the papers and waited. Nell hoisted herself onto a table and sat, looking at the floor, before she spoke.

"Look," she finally said, "I've worked with Gerald on and off for years. He's okay most of the time but sometimes he's not. Things get him down. Like most of us, right?" She shrugged her shoulders.

"What kind of things?"

"Well," said Nell, "he gets edgy sometimes before we start on a new show. One that he's directing himself. And this one, *Macbeth*, there's a lot riding on it. Expectations, you know? Gerald's always farmed out the Shakespeare plays that we've done to other directors but he decided to do this one himself. And he usually directs comedies. He was a bit more uptight than usual. He'd have been fine once we actually got into rehearsals and started working on it. So, if he didn't kill himself, what happened to him?" Her frank gaze homed in on Roxanne once more.

"I can't tell you that right now." Roxanne looked straight back at her.

"Jesus Christ. Someone's done away with him?" Nell's mouth fell open. "With Gerald? He can be a bit of a jerk sometimes but who would want to kill him?"

"We don't know that that's what has happened," Roxanne replied. But that wasn't true. She knew that someone had definitely killed Gerald Blaise.

UPSTAIRS, IN HER office, Tamsin Longstaff was talking to Budgie Torrance on the phone.

"Are you coming home?" Tamsin asked.

"How can I?" Budgie responded. She snuffled, like she actually had been crying. "I can't abandon the show so close to the end."

"Budgie," Tamsin reasoned. "You have a matinee in a couple of hours. How are you going to go on? Can't someone cover for you?"

"Never." Budgie's voice turned steely. "I shall do it." Tamsin could hear Budgie assuming the role of brave trouper as she spoke. "It's best I do it. And maybe it will keep my mind off what's happened to poor Gerald."

"They don't know it's him yet, for sure." Tamsin tried to sound reassuring.

"Don't be ridiculous!" Budgie snapped back. "Of course they bloody know. The stupid idiot's gone and got himself killed, hasn't he? What did they do to him?"

"I don't know." Tamsin didn't. Sergeant Calloway hadn't said how the person whose body was in the car had died and Tamsin hadn't asked. "So, you'll be coming home on Sunday night as planned?"

"Got a plane at six, right after the matinee." Budgie paused to blow her nose. "Tamsin," she asked. "Who's going to direct *Macbeth* now?"

"Not sure yet," Tamsin replied cautiously. "You're still planning to do it? I can cancel the contract if you need me to, under the circumstances."

"I certainly am doing it! People are looking forward to it. They've bought tickets. How can I let them down? And Gerald would want me to, wouldn't he?"

"Okay." Tamsin was relieved that she didn't have to find a new Lady Macbeth. Not that there wouldn't be a lot of actors eager to take it on. That wouldn't have been a problem, but there were few of Budgie's calibre. It would take someone exceptional to replace her.

"You know Nathan Simkin?" Budgie prattled on. "You should talk to him. He'd be fantastic." Tamsin knew what she was getting at. Gerald had complained to her that Budgie wanted Simkin to direct instead of himself over a boozy dinner one evening not long ago.

"Not available," she fired back. She didn't know if that was the case but she wasn't going to ask him. She had ideas of her own. And she couldn't believe what Budgie was saying. Was she in shock or something? She'd just found out that her husband of over thirty years might be dead, possibly murdered, and here she was, angling for Tamsin to hire the director of her choice, the one she wanted to replace Gerald?

"Budgie," she said, changing the subject. "What do we do about the cats?"

"Oh, fuck the cats!" Budgie burst into tears. "I don't know," she babbled. "Put them in a kennel or something. Ask Larry, the caretaker. He'll know what to do with them. I've got to go now." She was still sobbing as she hung up.

Tamsin put in a call to Stratford, Ontario. Jazz Elliott had just wrapped up a show there. It was almost certain that PTC needed another director for *Macbeth*. Jazz was available. She could fly in on Sunday, be in Winnipeg to start work on Monday. Tamsin would confirm later tonight. Jazz was going to cost but she'd be good. And she could cope with Budgie Torrance, no trouble at all.

Roxanne Calloway showed up in her doorway. "You ready?" she asked. Soon they were seated in Roxanne's little RAV4, turning into traffic, heading towards the morgue.

"I have to warn you," said Roxanne. "It was a brutal murder. His throat was cut."

Tamsin Longstaff swallowed. "Well, at least it would have been quick," she said.

4

AT 2:00 PM the Saturday matinee audience at PTC watched the current play begin, oblivious to the real drama being played out around them. By the time the curtain came down there was an obvious police presence. The body found at The Locks had been identified as that of the theatre's missing AD. All areas not involved in the ongoing production had been taped off. The cast were directed to enter and leave the theatre via the lobby. They could access their dressing rooms, the green room—the actors' lounge—and the stage itself. That was all. The front-of-house staff were confined to the lobby, the box office and the auditorium. Not that they ever wandered further. Many of them were volunteer ushers or students working the bar and concessions in return for some cash and free theatre tickets.

The actors were asked to gather in the green room after the show. Tamsin Longstaff broke the news that Gerald Blaise had been found dead. They were stunned into an unusual silence, then one voice asked, "How did he die?"

"We won't know until after the autopsy," Roxanne Calloway told them. She wasn't ready to tell them that their boss's throat had been cut. She knew that word of Gerald's possible murder would be flying around on social media as soon as they were done if she did.

Toby Malleson fielded a deluge of calls and messages. His office, upstairs, was still accessible, as was Tamsin's. The board room had been offered to Roxanne as a place where she could conduct interviews for today, but right now the cast occupied their own space, seated together on saggy chairs and sofas, still wearing their costumes.

They had last seen Gerald on Wednesday night, after a dress rehearsal with a preview audience. He had met with them after, on the set. He'd told them how happy he was with their work, how sure he was that the play would do well. He'd patted the director on the back and shaken the playwright's hand. He'd said that he was looking forward to opening night and that he'd see them all then. And off he'd gone, just after ten. They'd never imagined it would be the last time they would see him. Two of the actors were weeping on one another's shoulders. They'd liked Gerald, they said. He was a good guy.

"We are treating this as a suspicious death," said Roxanne. That needed to be said, although it was obvious. "Our Forensic Identification Unit will be examining different areas of this building over the next day or two. We need your cooperation." They were attentive. Lips stopped quivering, tears were wiped, noses blown.

"Someone killed him? You've got to be kidding," said an older woman, one of the actors. One of the stage management crew already had her phone in her hand and was tapping a message out into cyberspace. *Macbeth* was known to be an unlucky play in the theatre. That was why it was referred to as the Scottish play, never by name. And here it was, living up to its reputation, before they even started rehearsals. That was good fodder for a tweet.

Upstairs, Pedro Diaz, director of production, was in Tamsin Longstaff's office. He was not a happy man.

"What do you mean, the shop's sealed off?" Pedro was not tall but he was broad enough to fill Tamsin's doorway. "Shit, Tamsin, I've got deliveries coming in Monday morning. We have to start. This is a big build coming up." Tamsin sat back in her chair.

"That might change," she said. "Jazz Elliott's going to direct."

"You got Elliott?" Pedro walked right into the office and sat down. "New design, you think?"

"She's flying in tomorrow. Wants to meet with the designers soon as. So, we'll see. And with a bit of luck the RCMP will be out of your hair by Monday." She leaned forward. "You could make yourself useful, if you want to stick around. After you've made the rest of those calls." Pedro had to talk to all his technical crew to let them know about Gerald's death, if they hadn't already heard. Nell Bronson was on another line already, speaking to the incoming cast and crew of *Macbeth*. "You should go meet the corporal in charge of forensics. You might find what they're doing interesting and they might be glad to have your help."

She'd pushed the right button. Pedro was a curious guy. That was why he worked in theatre. Every new set that was built for a play was different. He enjoyed the challenge. And he also liked to be seen as practical and responsible. An hour later, he stood in the middle of his shop, directing traffic, making sure those cops didn't make too much of a mess. He watched as they dusted their powders around and shone their infrared lights. There were plenty of fingerprints. One of them got quite excited over by a sink.

"Nah," he told him. "Our carpenter sliced his finger a couple of days ago." He knew all about his building. Only he, Gerald and Tamsin had master keys that opened everything, he said. The other staff were given keycards with limited access to the places they needed to go. No one knew where Gerald's keys were, one of the cops told him.

"Tamsin's the keeper of the keys," Pedro said to Corporal Kovak of the Ident unit. "She'll have a fit if Gerald's master has gone missing."

All the surveillance videos that were available had been examined. Gerald did not show up on either of the tapes for Wednesday night. Dave Kovak shook his head when Pedro told him about the back door that had no camera, the one opposite the entrance to Gerald Blaise's apartment.

"So we don't know when he actually left the theatre?" he said.

At around 5:00 pm, Winnipeg time, another matinee performance ended on the stage of the Globe Theatre in Regina. Word about Gerald's death had travelled fast. It had made the national news already. Annabel Torrance walked onto the stage to take her bow and the audience sprang to its collective feet. The rest of the cast left her standing solo in the middle of the stage, her hand on her heart, her head bowed. Someone tweeted out a photo. #showmustgoon.

"Look at this, Tamsin. What was it she said to you?" Toby Malleson was poised, thumbs ready.

"Gerald would have wanted me to."

"Great!" Toby retweeted. Tamsin wished this day would end. Her board chair was insisting that the executive meet with her tomorrow. She could just imagine the look she'd get from under Frank Moran's hooded eyelids when she told them how much she was having to pay Jazz Elliott to come in and direct at short notice. And she had no idea how Gerald's death would affect box office sales. Or if they could find someone good to act as interim artistic director at such short notice.

She needed time to think about Gerald. The image of his face, drained of blood, the clotted wound running ear to ear, lurked at the back of her mind. He'd bled out into the trunk of the car, she'd been told when she had asked.

Who would have thought the old man to have so much blood in him, she thought, remembering the line from *Macbeth*. She shuddered. She could use a stiff gin and tonic. She spotted the red-haired RCMP sergeant walking past her office door, got up and stuck her head out into the corridor.

"Hey, Sergeant," she called. Roxanne Calloway turned.

"Want to go eat?" said Tamsin. "I've got to be back for eight to talk to the audience before the evening show but I could call Oliver's and see if they've got a table."

Roxanne was glad to agree. She'd never eaten at Oliver's and she was hungry. Maybe she could combine business with pleasure.

She had just talked with Inspector Schultz by phone. She needed a team right now, she had insisted.

"There's that new McBain girl," said Schultz. "You've worked with her before, right?"

Roxanne was glad that he'd mentioned Izzy. She had been a constable out in the Interlake until a couple of months ago and had assisted on the murders Roxanne had solved in February. She herself had suggested that Izzy apply to work in the Major Crimes Unit.

"You can get her started and we'll see who else we can spring once we find out how big a case this is," Schultz added, managing to sound magnanimous. That was ridiculous. Izzy would be great out in the field, investigating, but Roxanne also needed a third person to act as file coordinator. Schultz was not to be swayed. There were other cases to investigate. It had been a busy year. An expensive one. Resources were stretched right now. He'd talk to McBain, let her know. Tell her to check in with Roxanne.

OLIVER'S WAS JUST around the corner from PTC, a restaurant of long standing, with red upholstery and white tablecloths. Half an hour later she had a glass of merlot at her elbow and Tamsin Longstaff had sunk most of her gin.

"You've been over to the apartment?" Tamsin hadn't bothered to look at the menu. She ordered prime rib of beef, rare. It was what she always ate here.

Roxanne had. Gerald and Budgie's apartment was on the third floor, with windows looking out across the river on one side, towards the back of the theatre on another. It had high ceilinged rooms, exposed beams and polished wood floors. The couple had shared a bedroom and the en-suite bathroom, but they also each had their own study. Budgie's was papered with posters and photographs, going all the way back to the start of her career, when she was playing minor Shakespearean roles at Stratford, Ontario, and contemporary plays in Toronto. Pride of place was given to a large photograph of her in a famed performance of Euripides' *Medea*. She looked fierce in it. She had collected memorabilia, fans and masks and shawls. They hung off chairs and mirrors and a large screen. A whole wardrobe contained costume pieces.

Her desk, however, was reasonably well organized. Writing materials were sorted into boxes and drawers. There was no sign of any electronic device. She'd probably taken all of them with her to Regina. There was a filing cabinet, covered by a bright shawl. All the contracts she had worked had their own folder, filed by date. She had kept programs, photos, reviews. A file for the role of Lady Macbeth was up front in the top drawer.

Gerald's room, on the other hand, was messy. He was in charge of the household accounts. He had kept them in a hanging file rack. He'd still worked with paper. There was a pile of bills lying on top, going back two or three months, but it looked like they had all been paid. A stack of arts magazines and a sculptured statue lay on a small table beside a big leather armchair, a reading lamp behind it. Two walls were lined with bookshelves full of scripts and books about the theatre. Paintings hung on every available space. His desk was large, of old polished oak, littered with notepads, doodles for stage sets, scribbled notes about *Macbeth*. His phone, like his keys, was missing and his wallet had been found, empty, on the floor of his car. It was possible that Gerald had been mugged, robbed and killed for a cellphone and the contents of his wallet, but why had his car been found thirty kilometres out of town at The Locks?

The living room was elegant, with more artwork on the walls. There was no spare room for visitors to sleep over.

"He has a cleaner come in every Thursday," Larry Smith, the caretaker, had told her. She had been here last week, as usual. That was too bad. That was the day after the presumed murder. The cleaner had been efficient. The apartment was shiny clean. The cats looked on, balefully, one from a perch on the back of a sofa, the other from a cushioned chair. They were both blue Persians, with thick grey fur and orange eyes. "They're worth thousands," said Larry. "Budgie will probably sell them. Too bad, Mr. Blaise really liked them."

The kitchen was well stocked with rows of spice jars and a full wine rack. There was a shelf of cookbooks.

"Who liked to cook?" Roxanne asked.

"That was Mr. Blaise." Larry referred to Budgie by her first name but not Gerald, Roxanne noticed. "He often had friends over for dinner. On the weekends, mostly."

"While Ms. Torrance was away?"

"Suppose so." Larry looked at his feet and scuffed his toe on the polished floor.

"Anyone special?"

"Oh well," said the caretaker, his hands deep in his pockets and his shoulders up almost to his ears. "I wouldn't know about that." She had waited to see if he would say any more. He hadn't.

"Gerald had many friends?" she now asked Tamsin.

"Sure. Lots." Tamsin looked across the table at her, an arugula leaf poised on the end of her fork. "Gerald liked people. It's one of the things that made him good at his job." She popped the arugula into her mouth.

"He was? Good at his job?"

Tamsin had progressed to a glass of shiraz. She'd have to stop at that, she had said. Had to go back to PTC tonight, to make a pre-show announcement. Couldn't wobble onstage in front of an audience. She sounded like she'd like to drink some more.

"Gerald was a charmer," she said now, cutting into a slab of pink meat. "He was great with the board. Kept the audience happy. He'd lasted twenty years in the job."

"And that's unusual?"

Tamsin chewed, swallowed and drank a mouthful of wine before she answered. "For an AD? Most of them move on after ten, twelve years. Gerald might have stayed on too long. But there's not many jobs in Canada he can move up to, after PTC."

"He planned to? Move on?"

"Word was he'd been fishing." Tamsin put down her knife and fork and considered before continuing. This close, Roxanne could see dark circles under her eyes and the lines at the corners and between her brows. "But nothing, so far."

"He was paid well?"

"Better than most. His contract was coming up for renewal. He'd have been under review this year. I don't think they'd have upped his salary by much more."

"But he would have been renewed?"

Tamsin looked wearily at Roxanne over the top of her wine glass. Perhaps exhaustion and alcohol had made her drop her guard. And grief. Or worry.

"I don't know." Tamsin shook her head. She pushed her plate away, half finished. She sat back in her chair and looked at Roxanne, head leaning to one side.

"Confidentially?" Then she shrugged. "Someone's going to tell you anyway." She caught the server's eye and pointed to her coffee cup. "Gerald was getting past his best-by date. I know a few of the board thought that. Some critics had hinted. And the funding bodies were quite clear that he'd been playing it too safe for years."

"Too safe? How?" Tamsin waited while their coffee was poured. She put two spoonfuls of sugar in hers. Roxanne was surprised. The woman was thin, even by Roxanne's standards. She herself was often criticized for being too skinny. Tamsin stirred her coffee.

"Well, when he came here, to PTC, the company was in trouble. The AD before him was an experimenter, thought of himself as an intellectual. I wasn't here but I heard all about it. The plays he chose were serious and the audience didn't understand half of them. Ticket sales went down, they were losing money. So after four or five years of that, Gerald arrived like a sunbeam. That's what one of the older board members called him. She told me, 'Gerald made our audiences smile again.' He gave them comedies straight from Broadway. Musicals. *A Christmas Carol*. Lately, a lot of plays based on famous novels or films. When I started on this job, he'd been here for five years already and the audience was lapping it up. Gerald liked to make people happy."

"Would anyone have wanted to replace him?"

"There's always people want his job." Tamsin downed what was left of her coffee and patted her mouth with her napkin. "But why bother killing him? Easier to poison the ear of a couple of important board members and make sure he didn't get his contract renewed. It wouldn't have been difficult. But there would be no guarantee that whoever did that would get to succeed him. There would be a competition for the job. A national one. Will be."

After dinner, they walked around the corner to the parking lot. Tamsin ducked into the theatre at the lobby entrance.

"I suppose we'll be seeing you again soon?"

She would. Roxanne walked to her car. Izzy McBain had texted her already. ON YOUR TEAM! YEAH! START TOMORROW? She would call Izzy as soon as she got home. She was just pulling out of the lot when her phone buzzed.

"Detective Sergeant Cooper Jenkins, Winnipeg Police Service," said a deep voice. "You're investigating the missing theatre guy, right? The one with the red Audi?"

"I am," she replied.

"We've got a kid here you might want to talk to. We think he stole that car."

5

ROXANNE AND IZZY McBain arranged to meet up at a restaurant near the Manitoba Youth Centre. It was 10:00 am, Sunday morning, and the place hadn't filled up yet with the post-church brunch crowd. Izzy was sitting near the front desk when Roxanne arrived. She sprang to her feet, a welcoming smile on her face, blonde hair pulled back into its usual ponytail. Roxanne had last seen her seven months before, in Fiskar Bay, when Izzy was a regular RCMP constable. She'd transferred to the Major Crimes Unit only a month ago and been stuck at a desk since.

"This is just great!" she enthused, "My first real case in the MCU and I get to work with you again. Did you swing it?"

Roxanne hadn't. It was sheer luck and timing that had brought them together once more. Izzy filled her in on the latest news from the Interlake while they ordered coffee. She and Matt Stavros, who had worked alongside them, were still seeing each other. He had been wrangling for months with an insurance company about replacing the house on his aunt's old place. Construction had started, finally, and Matt had decided to go to law school. He'd just started last month. They were renting an apartment together, near the university.

The coffee arrived. Izzy had ordered a lemon pastry. She ripped a piece off and popped it into her mouth. Sergeant Gilchrist, her old boss, was planning to retire soon. Izzy hadn't wanted to stay in the Fiskar Bay detachment without him or Matt Stavros there.

"Roach has been a real jerk since I went back on patrol," she said. Roxanne wasn't surprised. Constable Ken Roach had a mean streak. He'd been annoyed that Izzy had been chosen to be part of the MCU investigative team back then instead of himself. He wouldn't hesitate to be vindictive. And Izzy had developed a taste for more interesting cases. She had done stellar work on the investigation into the death of Stella Magnusson. Both Roxanne and Brian Donohue had supported her application to Major Crimes. Roxanne was glad to have her on her team. Izzy hadn't changed a bit.

She told her how the case had gone so far. They were due to interview a kid called Zeke Sinclair at eleven. A city detective sergeant was going to meet them there. A rumour had been flying around a junior high school in the North End that Zeke had driven a fancy red car out of the city and when he and his buddies had opened the trunk they'd found a dead body. They'd closed it up and run. The phys. ed. teacher had overheard the kids talking and called the police. Zeke had promptly disappeared, but then he had been picked up, taking part in a raid on a liquor store early Saturday evening. His gang had run in and grabbed bottles, then raced back out into a mall. An old guy sitting on a bench had put out his cane and tripped him. Zeke had landed in a heap of broken glass and spilled vodka. The security guys had grabbed him.

"The city DS says Zeke has two older brothers who both use knives," Roxanne said. "The oldest one's in jail right now but the other one is on the loose."

"You think the brother might be your killer?" Izzy wiped her sticky fingers on a paper napkin. "He mugged the theatre guy and then got his little brother to get rid of the car? And the body?"

"That's something we need to find out." Roxanne pushed back her chair and reached for her jacket. DS Cooper Jenkins was already waiting in the front hallway of the Youth Centre, grey haired, lean, wearing a leather bomber jacket. You could tell that he was a cop. He had that watchful look. He was just there to make the introductions, he said.

"I'll let you two ask the questions."

Roxanne smiled. He wanted to listen in and find out what was going on, more like.

The workers at the Centre had found Zeke Sinclair a sweatshirt and jeans to replace his booze-soaked ones. They were too big, making him look even smaller than he was. A Band-Aid covered a spot on his forehead where he had collided with a piece of broken glass. He sat opposite them, a youth worker at his side, three police opposite him. Too much, Roxanne realized. One small brown boy, three white adults. She should have come alone. But Zeke acted like he wasn't intimidated.

"You two are cops?" he sneered at the two policewomen. "Don't look like it."

"I'm Sergeant Calloway. This is Constable McBain. We're from the Major Crimes Unit of the RCMP."

"Mounties? Where's your horses?"

"Out back." Izzy nodded in the direction of the window. "Hers is silver and mine is brown." She'd snagged a beige sedan from the carpool at HQ. It wasn't her style. The kid snorted and pulled the heel of one foot up onto his knee, trying to look relaxed. Cooper Jenkins looked bored.

"So, you stole an Audi?" Roxanne asked. "On Thursday?" This kid didn't look big enough to look over the steering wheel, or reach the pedals.

"What Audi?"

"A red one. The one with the body in the back." His foot went back down onto the floor. The toe of his sneaker tapped.

"His throat was cut," Roxanne continued.

"Hey," said the kid. "Wasn't me. Wasn't none of us."

"Who was with you, Ezekiel?"

"Zeke." Brown eyes peered out at her from under lowered brows.

"Your brother, Isaiah, uses knives, doesn't he? That's what he's inside for, right?"

"So, he couldn't have done this one," Zeke fired back.

"Where's your other brother? Jeremiah?"

"Dunno." He pulled his head down between his shoulders, snail-like. If he knew, he wasn't going to tell.

"We need to talk to him." Cooper Jenkins' gruff voice cut in.

"So, go find him," the kid retorted.

"Zeke." Izzy McBain adopted a more conversational tone. "Why don't you tell us how it happened?"

"What happened?" he challenged her.

"All the kids in your school are talking about it." She shone a big smile on him, teasing him like a jokey, older sister. "About how you drove the Audi out to The Locks. Great car to drive, eh?" Zeke rubbed his hands on his knees. He turned to the worker beside him.

"I'm thirsty. Can I have a Coke?"

"Later," said the guy. Zeke looked back across the table at the police. He sank deeper down into the baggy sweatshirt, his hands in his pockets. He thought for a moment.

"Okay." He spoke directly to Izzy, ignoring Roxanne and DS Jenkins. "We found the car. Thursday morning. Other side of Main, in a parking lot."

"You skipped school?"

"Who's *we*?" Roxanne interjected.

"Not sayin'." He bristled again. Roxanne decided she should leave Izzy to do the questioning. Izzy had grown up with brothers. Talking to a young boy came naturally to her.

"What parking lot?" Izzy sounded curious rather than demanding. She got results.

"The one beside that theatre place."

"With the keys still in it?"

"Yep. Right in the ignition. Can't have been there long. Someone else would have taken it if we hadn't."

"What did you do then, you and your friends?"

"Took it for a ride, didn't we? There was some money in the glove box. Spare change. Gas tank was almost full. We went up Main Street and right on out of town. We were going to get hot dogs."

"And did you?"

"No. We didn't park it right outside the hot dog place, y'know," he told her. Roxanne and Coop Jenkins had become invisible to him. "There were too many people sitting there watching. Thought it would look funny, us kids getting out of a car like that, so we left it further along. In a parking lot beside the river, past the dam, where all those big white birds are. Opened up the trunk, just to have a look. Didn't know what to do then, when we saw that dead guy inside. We closed the car up and left it there. Walked up onto the bridge, the one across the river. All the way over to the other side. Hitched a ride back home."

"And you got one?"

"Sure. Farmer-type guy with a big old Buick. Dropped us off, back on Main."

"Did you know who it was? In the trunk of the car?" Roxanne interjected again.

"No. No way. There was blood. Lots of it. Never knew he was cut though," he blurted out, caught off guard. That part of his story might actually be true.

"If we take you for a ride downtown, Zeke, can you show us exactly where you found the car?" Roxanne asked, trying for a tone more like Izzy's.

"When do I get my Coke?"

"When you get back."

The look he gave Roxanne was that of a world-weary old man. She could see what Zeke Sinclair would look like when he was sixty-five. If he lived that long.

The worker went to fetch coats. They signed Zeke Sinclair out for an hour.

"I can leave you girls to it?" asked the DS. Izzy and Roxanne exchanged a look. Don't react to that, it said. But Cooper Jenkins noticed. He was smirking as he strode away.

They piled into the brown car from the RCMP carpool, Zeke and his worker in the back.

"Hope nobody I know sees me driving around with you guys." The boy peered through the dirty window as they drove into the downtown area, closer to his home turf. "How come you drive this boring piece of shit?"

"Not mine," said Izzy.

Shortly after, she pulled into the theatre's parking lot. There were few cars in it, but the Ident truck was parked near PTC's stage door. It was the weekend. All the surrounding office buildings were closed and there were few shops nearby. The lot wouldn't fill up until the next theatre audience arrived.

"So where was the red car, Zeke?" Roxanne left Izzy to do the asking again.

"In the middle. Second row." The boy pointed.

"In the morning?'

"Yeah. Tennish."

Roxanne got out and looked. It had been four days since the body was found and she couldn't see any sign of blood but there might still be traces that Ident equipment would pick up. She called Dave Kovak. He came out of the stage door, still in his protective gear. That caught Zeke Sinclair's interest. He wound down the window to look. Ident would have to check the whole parking lot, Kovak said. It would need to be taped off.

"People are going to be arriving in an hour or so to see the afternoon show, Roxanne. There's not enough parking around here. They're going to be so pissed off."

"Her name's Roxanne?" Zeke Sinclair said to Izzy from the depths of the back seat. "Whadda they call you?"

"Constable," said Izzy. She laughed. Zeke Sinclair grinned back.

"What did you do with the car keys, Zeke?" Roxanne asked as they drove back to the Youth Centre. "The ones to the Audi?"

"Threw them off the bridge."

"Did you throw anything else off the bridge? Like a cellphone?"

"No, Roxanne," he said, mocking her.

"How about we stop and get you a Slurpee on the way back?" said Izzy.

"No thanks," said Zeke. He wasn't accepting any favours. The blonde chick might be kinda fun but she was still a cop.

They dropped Zeke and his worker off back at the Youth Centre.

"Too bad," said Izzy. "He's going to grow up just like his brothers."

Roxanne thought about her son, Finn. It was still the weekend. Maybe she'd go take him and his cousin, Robbie, out to a movie, or bowling. Take some time off and do the mom thing this Sunday afternoon, while she could. Give her sister a break.

"We're done for today, Izzy. Go home and say hello to Matt for me. I'll see you first thing tomorrow morning."

"Matt's got his nose stuck in his books," Izzy said. "I'll go back to HQ and do my report." And off she went, ponytail bobbing behind her, an eager bunny.

TAMSIN LONGSTAFF WAS glad that Sergeant Calloway hadn't shown up that Sunday. It was one less thing to deal with. PTC was still crawling with forensic technicians. By 1:00 pm they'd taken over the parking lot. The matinee audience complained that they had trouble finding places to park. She and Toby Malleson had needed to go down to the lobby and help soothe irritated theatregoers. The start of the show had been delayed until they were all in their seats. Toby had said he'd do the pre-show announcement, so she could scoot upstairs and put on some lipstick before the board executive arrived.

"Can you book me into the hotel, please?" Budgie Torrance had pleaded on the phone, playing the martyr, as well she might. It was less than four days since her husband had died. The police had left fingerprint dust all over her apartment and the cleaner didn't work weekends. But Jazz Elliott had also insisted on staying at the same grand old hotel as Budgie.

"Going to be with you for almost six weeks so I might as well be comfortable. And I do like eating in that Palm Room," Jazz had said. Tamsin was in no position to argue. She needed Jazz, and Jazz knew it. Jazz's plane wasn't getting in until midnight and she'd take a cab to the hotel, no problem. And Budgie liked to eat breakfast in her room, then she'd be checking out. With a bit of luck, they wouldn't run into each other. Tamsin hadn't told Budgie that Jazz would be directing, yet. She wanted to do that in person.

Frank Moran, QC, presided at the head of the board table. How was it going, he asked? The police had found nothing of interest so far, Tamsin informed them crisply. No evidence of blood at the theatre, so it was possible that the actual murder hadn't happened here. There had been minimum staff working on the weekend, so the police still had to interview some people.

"Will they be talking to me?" he asked, as if he was joking. "Any suspects so far?" None that Tamsin knew of. Gerald's body would be autopsied some time during the week. He would probably be cremated, but Budgie had asked if they could conduct a memorial service in the theatre, when the time came. The executive thought that was a good idea. The right thing to do. There would be a big turnout. And they would, of course, donate the use of the space.

"How is she doing? Budgie?" The elderly board secretary was a fan. "Is it true that she's going to carry on working and do Lady Macbeth?" She was. "She's so brave." The secretary wasn't alone in her admiration for Budgie. Online ticket sales had gone up after the picture of Budgie onstage at the Globe had showed up on people's Twitter feeds.

"Glad there's some good news coming out of this." The board chair was examining the financial pages Tamsin had provided. "Can we manage without an interim artistic director until we get a job search under way? Make up for some of what this is costing us?" Frank Moran always kept a close eye on the bottom line.

"Gerald was working on next year's season," said Tamsin. "He wanted to get the Canadian rights to a couple of new American plays. They're in demand so they need to be nailed down right now. And we don't have Alison anymore."

Alison Beck had been their administrative associate. It had been her job to make sure all the scheduling and contracts were in order before a season was finalized. She'd spent a lot of time negotiating with agents and actors. Alison had been smart and good at her job but they had let her go, end of the summer. She'd become a bit too opinionated. Was pushing for Gerald to do more local work, had a play in mind, thought it brilliant. Gerald had disagreed. He'd chosen the historical play about Winnipeg instead. Alison had dug in her heels.

"That one is too cozy," she had insisted. "We need to do edgier work." And it wasn't just that. She'd had this idea that they should do *Othello* instead of *Macbeth*, with women in the lead. Budgie would play Iago. She'd gone ahead and mentioned it to her over a couple of drinks one night and Budgie had been enthusiastic. But it was soon clear that that wasn't going to happen and Budgie had let Gerald know how disappointed she was, for days. Alison had overstepped her mark and it was time for her to go. As usual it was Tamsin who had had to deliver the bad news. They had advertised the job but hadn't hired anyone yet.

"Do the police know about that?" asked Moran, as if it was significant. Alison Beck? From what Tamsin had heard, Alison had placed most of the blame for her firing on Tamsin. She might have wanted to kill Tamsin, but not Gerald.

"I can't take on Gerald's workload as well as my own," she said firmly to the executive members. "We have to hire someone."

"Of course, Tamsin," the secretary bleated. She had white curly hair and a long nose. "But we could appoint an artistic advisory. Thom Dyck could chair it."

Artistic direction by committee? That was worse. They would argue forever, then compromise, never a good solution. There were windows at the end of the boardroom. It had started to rain outside. That would wash away any blood in the parking lot, if there was any. Tamsin hoped that it would turn out that Gerald really had been mugged, by someone she didn't know. The guys in the shop had overhead some of the cops talking so she knew that was an option they were investigating. And she hoped that Gerald had died far away from here. That that red-haired RCMP sergeant and her cohorts would find the killer soon and this would all be over. Then the police would be gone out of her hair and she could get on with the rest of her job.

She ushered the board members out of the room. It had been a long meeting. Frank Moran squeezed her arm as he left. The audience was leaving, she could hear the babble down in the lobby. The tragedy that gripped the rest of the theatre didn't affect them in the wake of a good performance, that was one good thing. The corporal who ran the forensic unit was walking down the corridor towards her, a young woman at his side. She was round-faced, with pale blonde hair pulled back off her face, looked Icelandic, but she also had inherited Slavic cheekbones and eyes.

"Constable Isabel McBain," Corporal Kovak introduced her. "She's with the Major Crimes Unit. Joining us to work on the case." Izzy had finished her report double quick and decided to do some investigating on her own.

"Really?" Tamsin said. "Why don't you come into my office, Constable? There's someone I should talk to you about." It wouldn't hurt to let the RCMP know about Alison Beck.

6

JAZZ ELLIOT, ROXANNE Calloway and Izzy McBain converged on Prairie Theatre Centre shortly after nine. Jazz had walked from the hotel. She stomped up to the stage door. Roxanne had expected someone spiky and, well, jazzy. Instead she saw a plump little person, a felted hat pulled down over her head, a snub nose set between large, red-framed glasses and round cheeks. The rain had stopped, the sun was out and the temperature had dropped. Snow flurries were forecast, this early in October. Jazz had come prepared. She wore winter boots, ready for whatever Winnipeg's notorious weather might throw at her. She carried a bulging bag with knitting needles protruding from the top in one hand and a briefcase in the other. When she removed her coat inside the building, she revealed a baggy hand-knitted sweater in patches of different colours. It reached almost to her knees. Under it, her leggings were black and her socks were purple with yellow stripes, also hand knitted.

"I get to see Tamsin first," she insisted, after they had introduced themselves. "Won't be long." She wasn't. Tamsin had emailed her the set and costume drawings for *Macbeth* the day before.

"No way," she'd emailed back. "Get me a meeting first thing with the designers."

Her design team waited for her in the boardroom. Sadie, for costumes; Colm, who designed sets; and Randy, whose speciality was lights. The tech crews were on hold. Pedro Diaz had cancelled the lumber delivery. He knew it wasn't going to be used. Jazz would change everything.

Soon Izzy was ensconced in what had once been Alison Beck's office, her own laptop open on the desk. She'd been charged with interviewing the staff that had just returned from the weekend. She'd thought she'd take the opportunity to look around Alison's old workspace, but it had been cleared. She told Roxanne that Tamsin Longstaff suspected Alison Beck.

"You went to PTC yesterday and talked to the staff?"

"Sure, I did. Wasn't going to waste a whole afternoon," Izzy had responded. Roxanne shouldn't have been surprised. She knew Izzy liked to act on her own initiative, to follow her nose. Still…

"You need to tell me what you're up to," she said.

"Sure." Izzy did not sound contrite.

The Ident Unit had taken Gerald's laptop in for further examination.

"We need it," Tamsin Longstaff complained, frowning at Roxanne over the top of her reading glasses. "He was working on the plays for next year. We have to know who he's been talking to."

"So do we," Roxanne replied. "We'll get it back to you as soon as we're done." She didn't say exactly when that would be. "A Mr. Moran wants to meet with me later today. He's on your board of directors, right?"

"Chairperson," said Tamsin. She rifled through a file drawer and pulled out a sheet of paper. "Here you go. Board contact list." Then she added another. "And you might find this useful." It was a glossary of theatre terms. Roxanne glanced down it. Flats. Flies. Prompt book.

"Ghost light?"

"Ah." A flicker of pain flashed across Tamsin's face like she'd been slapped. "A single light bulb, left on a stage all night, so people can see their way. The dead and the living. The techies have rigged one for Gerald, in the wings, stage right. Where he liked to stand and watch the show sometimes. So that he can find his way home, if he's looking. Theatre people are a superstitious lot, Sergeant. Some people say that this theatre's haunted. Some bricks from an old vaudeville house that used to stand here were incorporated into the building and they say that a ghost came with them. Don't let anyone catch you whistling around here. And don't you dare use the name of that next play we're producing inside our walls. It's bad luck."

"Too bad Gerald Blaise's apparition can't just pop up and tell us who killed him," said Roxanne.

She had scheduled a meeting with Annabel Torrance for eleven. Since the boardroom was no longer available, she'd take the opportunity to have a good look through Gerald's office herself. She might not find anything that had been missed but it might help her get a handle on what had made him tick.

JAZZ ELLIOTT WAS in her element, punctuating everything she said with her hands, as she sat at the head of the board table. They should forget those designs they had done for Gerald. This production needed a rethink. Sadie Williams sat on her right, Randy and Colm on her left. They all had notepads in front of them but for now she talked, they listened.

"It's the eighties. Restructuring the economy on the backs of the poor. Hard-headed guys in suits. Scaffolding and walls. When Macbeth falls so do the walls he's built, like Berlin."

"November 1989, Jazz." Colm was a stickler for detail and he was not happy. He was a local designer. He'd worked for Gerald for years. Wood and canvas were his thing. He'd been looking forward to painting castle battlements and trees.

"Right," said Jazz. "End of an era. It's when technology comes into its own. We could use projections, like TV newsreels. Computer printouts. Fax memos."

"Great!" Randy the lighting designer's face brightened. "What about sound?"

"I'm working on getting someone. Anyone local that you'd suggest?" Gerald's concept hadn't needed an ambitious soundscape. He hadn't hired a sound designer. Jazz thought otherwise.

"How do the women fit in?" asked Sadie Williams. "The Lady? The witches?"

"It's when difference feminism happened. Women being strong in their own right, you know? So that's what I think the witches are up to. They work for the Macbeths, but they're using female knowledge to undermine the boss. The gentlewoman in the sleepwalking scene is the second witch. The young one's ambitious, a computer whizz. She runs their communications, summons up pictures on a screen for Macbeth to look at."

"The visions that they show to Macbeth?" asked Randy.

"Exactly. The third one is old and bitter, had to play the subservient secretary too long, she's out for revenge. And since we've got an older Lady Macbeth, we'll make her a political wife who gets cut out of the game as Macbeth centralizes his power around himself."

"Suits with skirts. Shoulder pads?" Sadie was doodling already.

"And helmet hair. Bright colours for the women, think Maggie Thatcher and Nancy Reagan."

"With sober colours for the guys? Got it."

They settled in to make some concrete decisions. They had to have something they could present to the cast and crew tomorrow, first day of rehearsal. The actors would arrive looking for a wall covered with drawings, so they could see what their costumes would look like. And usually there would be a maquette of the set. They wouldn't see anything like that for a week yet.

ANNABEL TORRANCE ARRIVED at the stage door by taxi just before eleven. She towed a suitcase and looked weighed down by sorrow. As she progressed through the building she was met with hugs and kisses. Condolences were whispered, noses blown. It took time. Eventually she arrived at Gerald's office door, where a red-haired woman was rifling through Gerald's filing cabinet.

"Who are you?" Budgie demanded. "And what do you think you're doing here?

"Sergeant Calloway of the RCMP," Roxanne replied. "We had an appointment at eleven. I'm sorry for your loss."

"You're a Mountie?" Budgie eyed Roxanne's street clothes. They weren't very exciting. Grey sweater, white shirt, dark grey pants, but they fitted well. This slim, redhaired woman was not her idea of a typical RCMP officer. "I suppose you do have to snoop."

Budgie peeled off a blue wool coat. Under it, she herself was dressed in black, relieved only by a soft grey scarf. A fitted black sweater, short skirt and tights. She wore knee-high boots with heels. Jet earrings dangled from her ears. Her only rings were her wedding band and a large, shining diamond. Her hair was cut short and tinted a tasteful soft blonde, her makeup immaculately applied. Her eyes were rimmed with black liner. It wouldn't get smudged. Budgie was past crying.

Tamsin appeared in the hallway behind them. She looked at Budgie's suitcase.

"You've checked out of the hotel?" she asked.

"Definitely." The police had finished searching her apartment and she wanted to go home, she told them with a wistful sigh. The cleaner was cleaning up any mess they'd made. She'd promised she'd be done by noon.

"Leave the suitcase there, Budgie," Tamsin said, turning to go. "In the office. And lock the door. You two can talk in the green room. It's comfortable and you'll be more private."

"Thank you, Tamsin, you're so kind," said Budgie graciously to Tamsin's receding back. She did it well. She had played the Queen onstage here last year. Roxanne was glad not to have to interview Gerald Blaise's widow in his old office. She followed Budgie downstairs. Budgie unlocked the green room door with a key. Was Pedro, the production manager, wrong? Did Gerald Blaise's wife have a master key that gave her access to the rest of the building? And if she did, who else?

They found Jazz Elliot inside, ensconced in a fat armchair, knitting, her design meeting over. Her feet, in her woolly socks, were up on a footstool and a teapot sat on the table in front of her. Her cup was old china with a saucer and a teaspoon.

"Go away, Budgie," she said. "I've got first dibs."

"Tamsin said we could use this room." Budgie sank into a chair opposite. "I'm going to be interviewed by this lovely police person. I hear you're going to be our new director?"

"I know who you wanted," growled Jazz. "Nathan Simkin. But you're stuck with me, so suck it up. And go find somewhere else to talk."

"You're only knitting," Budgie retorted. Jazz looked up through her glasses. They magnified her eyes. The corners of her mouth turned down.

"I think while I knit," she said, articulating each word. "And I have this whole production to figure out, double quick. I need quiet space. Without interruptions." She switched her baleful gaze to Roxanne. "Haven't they given you an office, Constable?"

Roxanne stretched out a hand. "Sergeant Calloway," she said.

"And the office she's using is Gerald's old one." Budgie drooped sadly as she said it. "We can't possibly talk there." Her whole body sagged. Jazz put down her knitting. She grudgingly shook Roxanne's hand.

"All right, you win," she said. She stuffed needles and wool back into her bag. "I'll go find somewhere else." And soon she padded off in her stocking feet, bags in each hand.

"Wonder if that's still hot." Budgie recovered from her woeful demeanour instantly. She reached out and lifted the teapot lid. "Oh good, there's enough for both of us." She took Jazz's place in the big armchair and draped one booted leg over the other, waiting for Roxanne to fetch mugs and clear away Jazz's used cup and saucer. "It's actually quite good that Jazz is going to direct the Scottish play," she smiled, all charm now. "She's very good."

Roxanne was not distracted. "You and Gerald Blaise have been together a long time," she began.

"We have." Budgie smile turned sad but sweet. "We met at the National Theatre School in Montreal. I was eighteen, he was twenty. We got married after we graduated, in Toronto. Right at the beginning of our careers."

"You moved to Winnipeg twenty years ago?"

"We did."

"You like living here?"

Budgie looked surprised. "In Winnipeg? Well, I'm not here much. We share the condo." She stopped. "Shared," she corrected herself with dramatic emphasis. "But I was on the road most of the time. We actors are gypsies, Sergeant."

She didn't look like one. She was too polished, well turned out, in good shape. She must work out regularly. If Gerald was sixty, she would be fifty-eight.

"I do one gig here most years, early in the season, so I'm gone for January and February, when it's frigid out. Gerald always found me something worth doing. But I do two or three plays elsewhere. I'm a favourite at Stratford in the summer and I sometimes do the Shaw Festival, like this year. And there's always *Hilltown*." That was a TV program, a family saga set in the foothills of Alberta. Roxanne didn't subscribe to TV anymore, she watched Netflix when she had time. But she did recollect that Annabel Torrance played the matriarch of the family in that show. She was famous for it and she'd been doing it for years.

"It pays very well," said Budgie. "But it all means that I'm away a lot. Gerald and I always made sure to book time off together, though. Usually in May, June, when things are quiet. We liked to go to New York, or London. Catch up on what's new. See a lot of plays." She adopted a nostalgic look.

"So Gerald lived alone most of the year?"

"He wasn't alone, dear. He had his cats. He was devoted to them." She unfolded her legs and leaned forward. When she got closer, Roxanne could see that her skin was traced with fine wrinkles. That well-applied makeup covered purple circles like bruises under her eyes.

"Look, Sergeant." Budgie laced her fingers and wrapped her hands around her knees. "Our marriage was a partnership, right from the start. Gerald was free to pursue his own interests." She smiled up at Roxanne from beneath etched brows. "And so was I. We agreed to be discreet. We didn't have to tell all or anything like that. But we trusted each other that ours was the relationship that counted. It worked for us. Always did. It was never a problem."

"Did Gerald have a recent interest?" Roxanne asked.

"Oh, probably." Budgie raised one perfect eyebrow. "They've been getting younger as he grows older." She drooped again, remembering that Gerald himself wasn't going to be growing older any more.

"None of them ever became difficult? When he tried to end their relationship?"

Budgie's little mouth rounded as she thought. "You think one of them could have attacked Gerald because he said that they were done?" She covered her mouth with her hand. "I don't think so. Gerald always made it quite clear that the arrangement was temporary. And the way he died. That was so brutal. Someone would have to be insane to do that. And very strong. Don't you think?"

Roxanne wasn't going to reply to that. It was possible. Had one of Gerald's "interests" lashed out at him with a sharp knife in a fit of rage?

"You kept separate finances?" she asked.

"Absolutely," said Budgie, settling back into the chair, seeming more relaxed now that the subject had shifted away from that of her dead husband. "We split the condo costs. Gerald paid the utilities since he was here most of the time. We both did quite well. Gerald had his salary and I make a tidy little bit."

"Gerald's contract was coming up for renewal?"

"It was. Not that it would have been a problem. The PTC audiences love him. So does the board."

She spoke with conviction. Did she really believe that or was she just pretending? Acting?

"Did he ever think of moving on?"

Budgie laughed a little laugh. It sounded slightly forced. "Of course he did! He'd be tempted by a job on the coast, or Toronto. But really, Gerald loved it here. He walked into PTC twenty years ago and this company fitted him like a glove. And Gerald didn't mind the winter. He stayed indoors. He'd have been here for another five years at least."

"And then he'd have retired?"

"Goodness, no. People like us never retire, Sergeant. We go on until we drop."

If they were allowed to, Roxanne thought. If they were hired. It might be true for Budgie. She was always in demand. She'd probably end up as one of those grand old dames of the theatre, still acting when she was eighty. But Gerald? What lay ahead for him once this job ended, and his salary along with it? At sixty years? Was that one of his problems? And could it have led to his murder?

"Gerald was well-liked, Sergeant," Budgie insisted. "No, he was loved." She couldn't imagine anyone who would want to do him harm. She had last seen him three weeks ago. He'd come to Regina for the opening of her play there. She hadn't seen him since.

When they went back upstairs, Budgie put on her coat and lifted the handle to her suitcase, preparing to drag it across the back lane and enter the apartment she had shared with her murdered husband. Toby Malleson came to her side and wrapped an arm around her shoulders.

"Want some company going over there, Budgie?" he asked.

She reached up and pecked him on the cheek. "Thank you, Toby. You are so considerate." She left, her hand tucked into Toby's arm. He took the suitcase from her and pulled it behind him.

Izzy McBain beckoned from her assigned office. "Gerald Blaise played around," she said, when Roxanne had closed the door behind her. "Younger women."

"I know," said Roxanne.

Izzy reached onto the desk behind her and produced an eight-by-ten-inch photo, black and white, of a pretty, fair-haired woman. An actor's headshot. "Lisa Storm," she said. "He was emailing her. She's acting in the play. The one coming up. They're very friendly emails. And it's not only pretty young girls."

She clicked and a different photo came up on her laptop screen. She turned it towards Roxanne. "This is Timothy." Roxanne saw a man, late twenties, maybe thirty, shirt open to the waist, well-muscled, curly brown hair, a tan. "Gerald Blaise really liked him."

Tim Baldwin wasn't pretty. He was gorgeous.

7

TIMOTHY BALDWIN MIGHT have film star good looks but he wasn't an actor. He sculpted, and was beginning to be noticed by art critics, internationally as well as in Canada. There had been an article about him in a Canadian arts magazine last year, and he'd won a couple of significant awards. His studio was on Denman Island, off the B.C. coast. According to his emails, Gerald Blaise was planning a visit to Vancouver in November, after *Macbeth* opened, with a weekend trip to the island. Budgie had said that she and Gerald took holidays together every year, but it seemed he went on other trips, on his own. Had she known about this one? Did she know about the beautiful Tim?

Meantime, Roxanne was scheduled to meet with Frank Moran, at his office, high up in a downtown building. He was a senior partner in his firm. He occupied a prized corner spot. His secretary hung up Roxanne's coat and asked her to wait. Before long, she found herself on the opposite side of a large desk. The chair in which she sat was leather and large. His was high-backed, studded, with padded arms. His desk was clear of paperwork. There was a leather mat, a carved wooden box containing pens and pencils, a telephone and a reading lamp. He had a computer but it sat off to one side, in a corner, on its own designated desk. All a bit old-fashioned, Roxanne thought. About fifteen years out of date. But all big and powerful looking.

"How is the investigation going, Sergeant?" he began. He wore a sober grey suit. His tie had insignia dotted across it in a diagonal pattern. Was it his old school tie? Or university? "Shall we be getting some results soon?" he continued, without waiting for an answer to the first question. Was this why she had been invited to meet with him? To interrogate her about the murder case before she decided to question him? She wasn't surprised at how direct he was. He had a reputation for being formidable in court.

"Nothing so far. It's possible the victim was assaulted on the street. But there's no evidence of blood where the car was found so we think he may have died elsewhere, then the car was driven to the theatre parking lot. Which means that the killer knew who Gerald Blaise was."

"Gerald was a public figure." Frank Moran placed his elbows on his desk and steepled his fingers in front of him. "He had been robbed. His wallet was empty, right?"

Who had told him that? He had connections, of course he had. Was he checking out her investigation, via his friends on the golf course or at the squash club, some of whom might be her superiors, from high up in the ranks of the RCMP? Roxanne shifted uncomfortably in the big chair, built for a large man, not for a woman her size. Her feet barely reached the floor.

"It was." She kept her voice even. Best to stick to the facts.

"And there would have been credit cards? A driver's licence? With his name on it?"

"We would expect so."

"Well, then." He opened his hands and spread them expansively. Problem solved. If the death had been the result of a robbery, the theatre need not be the actual crime scene, and that was his main concern. "Too bad the body was found where it was," he continued. "Out in the country. The city police would have been better equipped to pursue this inquiry. They hear what's happening out there, on the street." He looked at her down an aquiline nose. A patrician nose. "Don't you think, Sergeant?"

"The city police are assisting us." Well, that was almost true. One of them had given them a contact. She slid forward and planted both feet firmly on the carpeted floor. It did mean that she was perched on the edge of the chair, but that couldn't be helped. She felt less like Alice down the rabbit hole. "We're following a lead but it's a weak one. It's possible the murder was committed by someone Gerald Blaise knew and made to look like a mugging. You could help us, yourself, by answering some questions."

Frank Moran sat back in his seat and smiled. Was he mocking her for trying to take over the role of questioner?

"Fire away, Sergeant." His eyes slid from meeting hers down her body, as far as her breasts, and up again. She couldn't believe it. The QC? And here she was, alone with him. It had happened quickly. Had she imagined it? She sat back again and crossed her legs.

"Everyone at the theatre insists that Gerald Blaise was well-liked. They say nothing wrong about him. His contract was up for renewal. Was he about to lose his job?" She tried to sound firm, assertive. It seemed to work. The lawyer considered before he spoke.

"It's likely that he would have had to go. You figured that out for yourself or someone told you?"

There he went again, turning a statement into a question. And managing to sound condescending.

"Why would he have to go?" she countered.

Frank Moran's eyelids lowered, like those of an inscrutable Buddha. "His time was up." He shrugged. "He'd had twenty years in the job already. His work was becoming stale. He was serving up the same kind of plays, ones that would keep audiences amused. Safe plays. Tedious. Predictable." He leaned forward onto the desk again, getting closer. Roxanne stifled an urge to push herself further back. "Some of us like our theatre to be more stimulating. Confidentially, Sergeant, some people thought he shouldn't have been renewed last time. Certainly not for five years. I wasn't on the committee. There were a couple of ladies who had influence. They liked Gerald very much. They made sure he got his contract."

"If he hadn't been killed," she said, "and he'd lost the job, would he have found other work?'

"Probably not." Moran raised one speculative eyebrow. "You do know that Gerald had money, don't you? He was independently wealthy. He could afford to retire."

"We are examining his finances," she said, hearing herself sound defensive. "It takes time. Our resources are limited."

"Ah, well." Frank Moran smiled his urbane smile, back in control. "Let me help you with that." He sat back into his chair again and looked down his long nose. "You've been in the apartment, right? Seen the artwork on the walls? Gerald was a collector, Sergeant. There's a Wanda Klassen in his living room. He got that years ago, when he first came to Winnipeg. He has many pieces that are quite valuable. You met Annie Chan when you were working on that case in the Interlake, didn't you? He's got a painting of hers too."

So he had been checking out Roxanne's work record? Of course he had.

"Sales of those have gone through the roof, now that she's really famous. They're fetching six figures. Gerald told me himself. He could sell that alone and live off the proceeds for a while." The lawyer looked like he was enjoying himself. Why had no one mentioned this before? And why hadn't she noticed? She'd barely looked at the paintings hanging on the walls in Gerald Blaise's condo. She remembered the expensive Persian cats. The new Audi. It was obvious that Gerald had money.

"Was he paid well?"

Frank Moran laughed aloud. "In theatre, in Canada? You must be joking. His mother came from an old Toronto family," he explained. "An elderly aunt died and left him everything. Including a house in Rosedale. Gerald sold it, ten years ago. You can imagine what he got for it."

She had no idea but she knew it would be lots. "Was he buying work from a sculptor called Timothy Baldwin?"

"I haven't heard about him." Finally, she'd asked a question he couldn't answer. He waited for her to explain who Baldwin was. She didn't oblige. She continued to ask her next question.

"He had relationships outside his marriage. Did you know about that?"

"There were rumours. But Budgie had the odd fling too. It happens. He knew how to conduct a relationship like that without it becoming a scandal. Many men do."

And he scanned her body again, down then up. There was no mistaking it this time. Here she was, in an office with a closed door and this man, one who was well regarded in the legal community, was playing that old game with her. The sooner she got out of here the better.

"I don't know who he was involved with right now, if that's what you're asking me," he continued.

He knew he'd made her uncomfortable, she was sure of it. It was there in the patronizing tone of voice, in the hint of amusement. He probably wasn't the slightest bit interested in her. He was just letting her know who was in charge, using sex as a weapon.

"We have some leads we are following regarding that. Thank you for your help." She got to her feet and reached across the desk to shake his hand, eager to end this conversation.

"Keep me apprised of the situation, Sergeant. We're all here to help."

She beat him to the door, but he reached it in time to rest his hand on her shoulder as she left the room.

"Best of luck," he said. "I'm sure I'll be seeing you soon, at the theatre."

She caught a funny look in his secretary's eyes as she lifted her coat off its hanger. That woman knew what he was like. That Mr. Frank Moran, QC, used his sex and his status to intimidate women. And maybe he went a lot further with others than he had with her. He'd probably been getting away with it for years.

You didn't get to be a female sergeant in the RCMP without having to deal with a fair amount of unwanted attention and intimidation. You learned how to avoid trouble and shut up about what happened sometimes. She knew she'd been lucky. She'd become Jake's girl early on when they were both training for the RCMP at the Depot. She remembered clearly what happened one day when another trainee had grabbed her ass in a hallway. Jake had been right behind her. He'd hauled the guy off into a washroom and soon the word was out that you didn't mess about with Calloway. She was taken. But was that what it took, physical protection from another man? Since Jake had died, she had had a different kind of protection, the respect that came from being the widow of an officer who had died in service. She was off limits. Not that that would last forever. Jake had been gone four years. Now she was seeing Inspector Donohue. She wasn't sure that the Force had figured that out yet, but it would.

And she had rank now. She wasn't as vulnerable as a lowly constable. But still. And what had the lawyer actually done? A pat on the back wasn't harassment. There was just that look, up and down, measuring her with eyes that made her feel dirty. Twice. She shuddered. She hoped she could avoid being alone with Frank Moran in future. At least she had gleaned some important information. She reached her car, got inside and called Ident. They had checked out Gerald's Audi, Dave Kovak told her.

"Wiped clean. All of the outside and inside." And the empty wallet. Not the inside of the trunk, or inside the glove box, but the prints there were all the same ones, probably Gerald's own. The kid who drove and took the cash from Gerald's glove box must have known to wear gloves. If that part of the story was true.

They had had a quick look at Gerald's bank balance. He'd had statements lying around in his study. He had more than two million dollars stashed away.

"I just learned about that," Roxanne said. "He inherited a lot of money." Maybe that was the motive for his murder, she thought as she drove away.

A voice rang out from her speakerphone. "Hi Sarge, Detective Sergeant Jenkins here." It was the city cop who'd told her about Zeke Sinclair. "You got time to talk?"

"Sure."

"Are you near Main? Coffee?"

TWO RIVERS MET in the middle of Winnipeg. It had been a meeting place for millennia, the reason that the city existed. It was trendy now, with outdoor stages, small shops. In the summer you could walk along the riverbank. When it got colder and the water froze, there was a skating trail that ran further than any other in the world. She could use a coffee. Why not?

She met Jenkins there, in a coffee bar. They ordered their drinks and found a table near a window, looking out onto a plaza. In the distance you could glimpse the river. It was only 4:00 pm but the sky was grey and the lights were lit. They flickered on the surface of the water.

"You have some new information?" Roxanne asked.

"A kid got beat up at Zeke Sinclair's school today. During the lunch hour." Jenkins reached for the paper coffee cup. His fingers were nicotine stained. "Got cut as well. It's bad. He's in Children's Hospital."

"A friend of Zeke's?"

"Yep. And the brother Jem's on the loose."

"You think he cut him?" He nodded.

"As a message to the rest of those kids to shut up. And they have. No one's talking. They're all shit scared. Swear blind they know nothing."

"Why are you so sure that Jem Sinclair's responsible?" she asked.

A corner of his mouth lifted in a lopsided smile. "It's his style. He's mean like that. It was deliberate. That kid's scarred for life.

And I'll bet he was the one that told the whole school about Zeke finding the body in the back of the car. He's not too bright, his teachers say. And he likes to talk a lot."

"So, Zeke's story was true up to a point? You think he's covering for Jem?" said Roxanne. "That Jem's the murderer?" Outside the window of the café, big snowflakes were starting to drift down.

"Maybe. He could have tried to rob the guy. It went wrong, he killed him. Stuffed him in the trunk. Then he told Zeke to dump the car somewhere."

"Zeke told us he found some money in the glove box. And he said they got a ride back to Winnipeg from a guy in an old Buick."

"Well, forget that." Deep creases appeared in the corners of Cooper Jenkin's eyes when he looked amused. "A car was stolen from the golf course just down the road from The Locks later that afternoon. Showed up in a parking lot in the North End next day. Those kids probably drove themselves back to the city."

"Maybe Zeke didn't throw the keys off the bridge, either." Roxanne drained the last of her coffee. "Okay, I'd better speak to Zeke again. Or his brother."

"Zeke's not going to tell you anything that will get Jem into trouble. And Jem will be hard to find." Jenkins stood up. "I'll keep my ears open. Let you know if I hear anything." He zipped up his jacket. "They've got an aunt. Tracy Ross. A Mama Bear. She might know."

The Bear Clan had been created by local residents to walk the streets of Winnipeg's North End, looking out for people in need of help.

Jenkins reached into a pocket and pulled out a notepad, then a pen. "Call this guy. He'll know when she's on patrol." She watched him write a name and number on the pad and hand the piece of paper to her. He looked at her, frowning. "Talk to Tracy or Zeke first. Don't go near Jem on your own," he warned.

"That's okay. I know how to be careful." She took the paper from him.

"Okay then. See you, Foxy." He started to walk away.

"Excuse me?"

He turned, a mocking look on his face. "Good name, eh? Suits you."

She watched him go. He took a pack of cigarettes from his pocket as he went, an old, worn cop, cynical from years of dealing with bad stuff. One of the guys. She knew the type well. It wasn't the first time she'd been given a nickname. The guys in the Fiskar Bay detachment had called her Spiderwoman.

But Roxanne felt patronized. First Moran and now Jenkins. She didn't need his advice and she resented his assumption that she didn't know how to take care of herself around difficult suspects. She'd dealt with those before. She knew she didn't have the heft of some of her male colleagues, but she was fit and she was fast. And sometimes being smart worked. She'd check up on Zeke again. She'd like to know if he'd lied about throwing away Gerald's keys. Maybe they were still in circulation. But she wasn't going to spend much time chasing up this lead. She thought it much more likely that Gerald Blaise had been killed by someone who knew him very well, and knew that he was wealthy.

She emerged into a winter wonderland, snow sifting down from a heavy sky, sparkling in the light that lit the plaza, shoppers walking fast, heads down, laden with packages. There was no wind, but it was going to get colder. She'd better get home before the city started to ice up. Pick up her son from her sister's house. Call Brian Donohue. Maybe he could tell her something about Detective Sergeant Jenkins of the City of Winnipeg Police Service. That might be useful.

8

THE TEMPERATURE ROSE above zero with the morning sun. Ice melted and evaporated from the roads. The highway was bare as Margo Wishart drove into Winnipeg, her friend Roberta Axelsson once more at her side. It was Tuesday morning, first day of rehearsal for *Macbeth,* and Margo was excited. She'd never been to a first reading of a play with professional actors and she was eager to find out what had happened with regard to Gerald Blaise's death. It was public knowledge by now that his body had been found outside the city and she knew exactly where. Roxanne Calloway had texted her to thank her for the tipoff, for letting her know about the red Audi parked at The Locks.

When they arrived, they found the rehearsal hall at Prairie Theatre Centre thronged with actors and stage crew. There was much hugging and kissing going on. Chatter about how awful it was that Gerald had died the way he did, but wasn't it great that they were going to be directed by Jazz Elliot. There was no sign of Jazz herself yet, or of Annabel Torrance, the recently bereaved widow. Margo overheard some people wonder aloud who might have murdered Gerald, but no one seemed eager to suggest a candidate. Sadie Williams, resplendent in a long green skirt and turquoise top with earrings to match, spotted Margo.

"Margo! I almost forgot you were coming!" It was Margo's turn to be air kissed on each cheek. "It's been total madness around here. We're having to redesign the whole show, double quick. It's not going to be anything like as traditional as Gerald wanted. You'll still be able to write your piece, won't you?"

Margo would. In fact, she could describe how a theatre designer sometimes had to change direction at short notice. It gave her an original angle, and that pleased her.

"You've still got the drawings of the old design?" she asked.

"I do. Come and see me after the reading, eh?" And Sadie sailed off to talk to an actor she knew.

"Guess I'm not going to be dyeing any wool for them after all." Roberta pouted, but not for long. "Look, there's Corporal Calloway. And isn't that Izzy McBain?" Roxanne and Izzy were standing at the other side of the room. Roxanne was in earnest discussion with Nell Bronson, the stage manager. They were examining a sheet of paper and Nell was shaking her head.

Margo looked. "She's Sergeant Calloway now. Guess they're both working on the murder case?"

Carla Hansen appeared beside them.

"They're checking the schedule," she explained. "The cops want to talk to Lisa Storm, but she's needed in rehearsal." She nodded towards a small waif of a girl who didn't look any older than sixteen, but of course she must be. She was a trained, experienced actor. "She's playing one of the witches. Here comes Budgie." A door had opened at the far end of the room and Annabel Torrance made her entrance. She was immediately surrounded by members of the cast. They fluttered around her like cooing pigeons.

"Word is that Gerald was having it off with Lisa," Carla muttered in their ears. Lisa looked far too young to be interested in someone Gerald's age. But then, Gerald had been the boss, the one who hired the actors. In this business, he had power. "We don't know if Budgie knows about that. Yet. Gerald was usually more careful. Budgie knew he messed around but he usually kept whoever he was interested in at a distance. Don't know why he cast them both in the same play."

"It was Margo that figured out where Gerald's body was," Roberta whispered back.

Carla looked from one of them to the other. "Really? You're kidding. Are you joining us after the reading? You can tell us all about it. Nell, the stage manager, usually brings her lunch and she knows everything that's going on around here. We can talk!"

Professor Thom Dyck was present. He signalled to Margo. Two portable tables had been pushed against a longer, wooden one and chairs ranged around them to accommodate the large cast and stage management. Scripts were stacked in the centre, alongside jars of sharpened pencils. Other seats were ranged along a wall, for other staff and people who had been invited to listen. Thom indicated that he was saving seats for them.

Tamsin Longstaff marched in, a distinguished-looking man in a grey suit on one side, a dumpy little woman on the other. All the actors and staff stood in a circle. It stretched all the way around the hall. Frank Moran, chair of the board, welcomed them all. He said how sad it was that Gerald was not with them today. The police were working hard to find out who had committed the crime and he hoped they would be able to provide them all with some answers soon. He gestured towards Roxanne and Izzy, who had joined the circle at the opposite end. Meantime, they should do their best. Gerald would have expected it of them. This production would be dedicated to his memory. They all applauded. He especially wanted to thank Annabel for staying on as Lady Macbeth. She was an example of dedication to them all. Budgie held her head up high. The actors on either side of her reached out and took each of her hands.

"We will do Gerald proud," said Budgie. Toby Malleson captured the moment on video. It hit the Internet within seconds.

"I thought we're not allowed to use the name of the play?" Margo whispered to Thom. "Isn't it unlucky?"

"When they're working on it, they have to. There's been dark mutterings among the cast already about how Gerald died just before he was scheduled to direct it. They think this production's cursed."

Tamsin Longstaff introduced Sergeant Calloway of the RCMP and invited her to speak. Roxanne was sorry that the investigation would continue while they rehearsed. The police would try not to intrude too much, but if they did, she hoped they would all cooperate. She thanked them for their help, then left right away. Margo got a tiny nod of recognition from her as she passed. Izzy McBain stayed, watching and listening.

The little, chubby woman turned out to be Jazz Elliot. She surveyed the circle through her big glasses, magenta today. She was wearing a yellow cardigan with pockets over leggings and had homemade knitted slippers on her feet. They were purple, with loose lace around the ankles. Margo saw Roberta take notice.

"Let's introduce ourselves," said Jazz. "And then we can get to work."

So they did, name by name, all the way around the circle. The actors said which character they would be playing, the crew named their jobs: sound, light, scene painters, props builders. Margo had never realized how many people it took to put on a play like this. It wasn't just the stage crew. There were marketing staff, development (the ones who raised money), accountants. PTC's production machine was huge.

When it was his turn, Thom Dyck announced that he was going to head an artistic advisory to choose the next season. A faint rumble rolled around the circle, not entirely approving. Thom seemed quite oblivious, pleased with his new assignment. As soon as the circle broke up, Tamsin Longstaff made a beeline for the door.

"She's interviewing candidates for an admin associate to assist us. We need a person right away," Thom confided to Margo and Roberta as they took their seats. The actors sat in their places and copies of the script were passed around. Each also received a pencil.

"They'll be making cuts to the text," Thom continued in his role of the man who knew. "A lot of the descriptive lines can go. They'll make up for it with visuals. And action."

Margo was happy to have someone who could explain this mysterious theatrical world to her. She saw Izzy McBain take a seat further along the row. She leaned forward and waved to her. Izzy grinned back. Now Jazz Elliot was speaking.

"Usually we'd be able to show you what the set and costumes would look like right now," she said, "but we are making changes to the design for the production and it's too early to have finished drawings or a maquette of the set. I can tell you that this is going to be very exciting. A new interpretation, based on the culture and politics of the nineteen-eighties."

Colm, the set designer, ran a nervous finger around his collar. The lighting and the new sound technician sat up straight, looking important.

"Jaaazz!" Budgie drawled, waving a pencil in Jazz Elliot's direction. "Does that mean I get tailored jackets that fit? And short skirts?"

"Absolutely. Power suits. Heels. And hair." Budgie looked across the table at Danny Foley, the actor playing Macbeth. Her eyes narrowed and she smiled, sexy and devious, getting into character already.

They'd be going through the script, line by line, for the first week of rehearsal, Jazz informed them, so they would know what every one of Shakespeare's words that came out of their mouths meant. And at the end of that week, the designs would be complete. But now, they needed to do a first read-through.

Margo thought they did a great job of lifting Shakespeare's text off the page for the first time. She was enjoying herself. She was looking forward to seeing Sadie Williams' new ideas for the costumes. She also wanted to hear what Sadie and the others had to say about Gerald's death. Roberta seemed to be quite happy listening to the reading. She had taken a ball of wool and pins out of a bag and was rattling up a garment. No one had objected. In fact, Jazz Elliot had looked her way, interested. They took a break halfway through the rehearsal. Izzy made a beeline for Margo.

"Dr. Wishart! How great to see you again!" Izzy had grown up in the Interlake, not far from where Margo lived. Roberta waved a hand in greeting. Jazz Elliot was at her side, interested in the yarn she had been knitting up.

"I've got to go now," said Izzy. "Maybe see you around," and she scooted out the door as they resumed their seats to listen to the next act.

The rehearsal broke for lunch at one. Food was allowed in the wardrobe room, but only in the area around the coffee machine.

"Not past that table, or the chairs over there," Carla pointed. "Did you bring anything to eat?"

Margo hadn't. She and Roberta were planning to visit an old friend after, for a late lunch. Phyllis Johnson, formerly Smedley, had lived near them for a while but had moved back to the city. Roberta was not with Margo. She was still in the rehearsal hall, examining the contents of her knitting bag with Jazz Elliot, talking patterns. Nell Bronson arrived, a plastic container of salad in her hand.

"The cop woman grabbed Lisa Storm soon as we were done," she announced. "She's being questioned in Gerald's old office. I don't think Budgie knows about her and Gerald. So far."

"Gerald was a busy boy," Sadie Williams said slyly to Margo. "But come see my new drawings." The boxes and Styrofoam heads on her work table had been replaced by pencils, brushes, a large drawing board, tubes of watercolour paint. Margo looked at the new drawing on the board. It showed a character in a royal blue suit, the jacket fitted at the waist, the skirt just above the knee. Her hair was fair, fat and lacquered.

"She wears it looser when she's in her night clothes. When Macbeth murders Duncan and in the sleepwalking scene. We'll need two wigs." Sadie placed that design in front of Margo, a lace negligee over a thin-strapped, silk slip of a nightdress.

The door swung open again and Roberta entered.

"Can you come soon?" she asked Margo. "We've got to go over to Budgie's apartment with her. I'm going to take care of her cats until she decides what to do with them."

"Tarquin and Delilah? Is she going to get rid of them? Gerald would have a fit." Nell Bronson was ensconced in her favourite chair. She speared a broccoli floret. "He adored those beasts."

"I hope she's going to pay you for taking care of them." Sadie folded her arms. Roberta looked taken aback. It obviously hadn't occurred to her. "Don't be a mug. Budgie's loaded. So was Gerald, and she'll probably inherit the lot. Tell her. Ten bucks a day per cat, at least. Fifteen." She unfolded her arms and reached for a folder. "Guess you're not going to be staying. Budgie won't want to be kept waiting." She put the old costume drawings in it and handed it to Margo. "You can take those for now. Text me. I'll be further along with the new designs in a couple of days. Can you come back soon?"

Margo was thrilled. She couldn't wait. She taught in the city on Wednesday and Friday mornings this term. She could visit in the afternoon. She joined Roberta at the door and they said their goodbyes. They were both curious to see where the famous Annabel Torrance made her home, and where the murdered Gerald Blaise had lived.

LARRY SMITH DID a good job of maintaining the condo. The wood that lined the hallways was glossy and the mirrored walls of the elevator shone. Budgie was waiting in the apartment, with two plastic cat carriers. They were empty. Margo stood stock still in the middle of the living room.

"Oh, my goodness. Look at all the paintings on your walls! Isn't that an early Wanda Klassen?"

"Guess so," said Budgie. "Gerald collected Canadian art. I don't know much about it." A bright-coloured Indigenous painting hung above a pair of Inuit prints. Margo looked closer.

"Baker Lake," she breathed.

"He's had some of the ones in here for umpteen years," said Budgie casually. "There's more. Can you grab that cat? I don't want to get fur all over me." Roberta scooped up a big furball and stroked him. Tarquin purred deeply. Margo wandered into a dining area. Small sculptures sat on side tables. A large Cape Dorset soapstone carving standing on a sideboard dominated the area.

"There's an interesting mix of work here," said Margo.

"Suppose so. You're from the Interlake, right? Have you seen any of Annie Chan's paintings?"

"I have," said Margo. Roberta had boxed Tarquin and was trying to persuade Delilah to cooperate. She had cornered her on a sofa but the bushy grey tail was swishing back and forth and the cat was starting to growl. She stopped, hearing what Margo was saying.

"What's that about Annie?" she said.

"Well, come see. He has one of hers." Budgie opened a door. "It's supposed to be worth loads of money." She led them into what appeared to have been Gerald's study. It was cluttered. Budgie stopped and stared.

"Oh my God!" she cried, her hand to her mouth. "It's gone!" She was looking at the wall above a sideboard. A framed drawing hung there. "The Chan one should be there, not that thing!" Budgie blurted. "The Chan was way bigger than that. It almost filled that wall. Someone must have taken it!" She turned to face Margo and Roberta. "We have to tell that woman. The Mountie. Whoever killed Gerald must have robbed him too."

9

ROXANNE CALLOWAY SCANNED the walls of Gerald Blaise's study. One was entirely given over to bookshelves but the other three were hung with framed drawings and paintings. The only picture with any wall space around it was the drawing that Annabel Torrance insisted had replaced the Annie Chan.

Budgie couldn't see anything else missing but buying art had been Gerald's thing. She hadn't paid much attention, but she did remember the Chan because it was so big and striking. It had been dark purples and green, with a dash of orange. Could she get back to rehearsal? Right now? She was needed, she insisted, tapping her toes on the hardwood floor. The actors couldn't proceed without her.

"Soon," said Roxanne. If there had been an actual art theft, it changed everything. It gave the murderer a motive. Had Gerald caught a thief and been killed in his apartment? If so, would there be evidence of blood? Perhaps he had tried to sell the painting and the transaction had gone wrong.

Roxanne had just spent a fruitless half hour interviewing Lisa Storm. The young actor had turned out to be tougher and more astute than her delicate, childlike appearance suggested.

"I wasn't fucking Gerald Blaise," she had said. "I flirted with him, sure I did. He liked that kind of attention, we all did it, all the women who worked with him. It was how you got along with Gerald but it didn't mean anything. If that's what people are telling you, they've got it all wrong. Sleep with Gerald? He was old enough to be my grandfather. Yuck." Gerald was sixty, Lisa twenty-four. Roxanne could see her point.

"People talk a lot of garbage in this business," Lisa had said, straight-backed and indignant. "Don't believe a word they tell you, Sergeant."

Margo Wishart and Roberta Axelsson waited on a sofa in the condo's living room. Delilah the cat had permitted Roberta to scratch an ear but was resisting being held or stroked. Margo had called their friend Phyllis. Lunch would have to be postponed to another day. They would be going straight home with their furry cargo.

"Have you any idea how much a painting by Annie Chan is worth?" Roxanne asked Margo. She didn't know.

"Hundreds of thousands," said Budgie. "I have got to get out of here. Nell Bronson has texted me twice."

"Gerald would have kept an inventory of his collection," said Margo. "And he probably had an agent."

"Oh, right." Budgie reluctantly remembered. "Maxwell Fergusson. In Toronto. I've had dinner with him."

"He's a well-known dealer." Margo had heard of him. He had a solid reputation. Roxanne sat on the arm of a chair opposite her. She knew that Margo taught art history at the university and she knew from past experience that she could be relied on.

"If we get our hands on a list of his holdings, could you check it for us? Against what's hanging here? So that we can find out if anything else is missing?"

Margo beamed, pleased to be asked. "Absolutely," she replied. "I have to do research at the theatre for something I'm writing and I teach at the university Wednesdays and Fridays, late morning, so I can stop by after. Was there anywhere else he stored paintings? A safe, maybe?" Budgie was standing at the door, arms folded, still tapping her foot. She shrugged. She didn't know. "But meantime I need to get Roberta and these cats up the road to Cullen Village. Would you like me to speak to Maxwell Fergusson?"

"No! We'll handle that," Roxanne said quickly.

Shortly after, they were in the elevator. Roberta had seized a yowling Delilah and stuffed her into a carrier and Margo carried one containing the more placid Tarquin. A bag of cat litter and another of kibble rested against the wall.

"Roberta charges fifteen dollars a day per cat," Margo said to Budgie, who hadn't offered to carry anything. Roberta looked about to protest.

"Sure," Budgie replied, her phone in her hand, tapping a message. "E-transfer's okay?"

"Yes, it is," Margo said, before Roberta could say anything. They reached the ground floor and walked to the back door of the condo building, down a carpeted, panelled hallway. It opened onto the lane behind the theatre. Budgie headed straight for the door opposite, the one that led to the PTC offices upstairs and to the basement. Roxanne picked up the bag of cat litter, Roberta took a cat in each hand and Margo lugged the cat food to her car.

"If we find an inventory I'll let you know." Roxanne helped loaded up Margo's car and waved goodbye. Budgie had disappeared into PTC. She must have a key to the back door that led off the back lane, too. How many of the theatre staff could access that unmonitored back door? Roxanne walked over to the stage door and buzzed herself in.

"SERGEANT!" TAMSIN LONGSTAFF called out as Roxanne passed her office door. "I've hired a new admin associate. Come along, you should meet her." She trotted off down the hallway, leading the way. A lean, smiling young woman sat at a desk, searching through files on a laptop.

"Marla Caplan," Tamsin introduced her. "We're so lucky, she's able to start right away." The girl's fair hair was pulled back into a fashionably messy bun. She wore a neat shirt, tucked in at a trim waist, skinny jeans, and glasses.

"Hello!" she said.

"Marla's tracking where Gerald had got to setting up next year's season. Your people are supposed to get his laptop back to us real soon." Tamsin turned her attention to her new employee. "Did you get hold of Thom Dyck?"

"I did," Marla replied, smart as a whip. "He'll be here later today to meet with me."

"Good." Tamsin was on the move again, across the hallway. She unlocked the door to Gerald Blaise's old office for Roxanne.

"That was a quick hire." Roxanne peeled off her coat and hung it on the rack that Gerald Blaise had provided for himself and his visitors.

"It was." Tamsin stood in the centre of the doorway, poised to go. "Such luck. She moved to Winnipeg recently. Has all the right training and experience. Used to work for the Toronto Arts Council, so she knows the business. And available right away." She turned on one of her tall heels.

"Wait." Roxanne called her back. "I need to ask you about something." Tamsin's forehead furrowed in frustration. She had work to get to, as always. But she sat. Gerald had lined his office walls with photographs, mainly shots from plays he had directed, but there was a large staff photograph, with himself centre. It was as if he was present, eavesdropping on what they were about to say.

"What do you know about Gerald's art collection?"

Tamsin's eyes narrowed. "You've found something?"

"We don't know yet." That was true. Gerald could have removed the Annie Chan painting himself. It might not have been stolen. "Do you know where Gerald kept his records? Of art sales? Of what he had bought?"

Tamsin permitted herself to relax. She almost laughed. "Good question! Gerald couldn't keep things organized to save himself. Especially paperwork. That's why I need that Marla girl, to help sort through what he's been doing. Alison Beck used to keep everything straight for him but since she's been gone he's got it all into a mess. Gerald had great instinct when it came to people. He was one of the most persuasive people I've ever met, but records? It just wasn't in his genes."

"So how would he have tracked what he owned?"

"Maybe he didn't. Maybe he just hung what he'd bought on his walls and enjoyed them. Tell you though, Gerald did like making lists. So, if he did write anything down about his paintings, I would bet it's in a paper notebook, in a drawer in that study of his. Or his dealer might know. Maxwell. You know about him?"

Roxanne nodded. She did. "How about Alison Beck? Would she know?"

"Oh, her? I suppose."

"And he must have had an accountant?"

"He did. Some woman called Irma something. In Toronto. You'll have to ask Budgie. She'll be on a break in an hour or so. We done here? I really have to go." She rose briskly and strutted off.

Roxanne called Dave Novak at Ident. Had his guys found anything about art sales on Gerald's laptop? There was correspondence with a guy called Maxwell Fergusson, about an art auction coming up in Toronto, he told her A couple of items in it might interest Gerald, Fergusson had said. Photos had been attached. Weird artsy stuff.

"Does he say anything about selling a painting by an artist called Annie Chan?"

He didn't know, but they'd checked Fergusson's website. He dealt with people all over the world. Had a gallery in Toronto. There was a phone number. Roxanne called it. A rich, plummy voice answered.

Maxwell Fergusson had heard about Gerald's death. "Quite appalling!" he commented. "Who would want to kill Gerald? Such a genial chap."

"That's what we're trying to find out, Mr. Fergusson." Roxanne was Googling his name as they spoke. She looked at his photograph on his website. Maxwell Fergusson cultivated the look of an English country gentleman. He wore a tweed jacket and had a large moustache.

"How can I help you, Sergeant Calloway?" Roxanne could hear him settling himself into a chair. Gerald didn't sell much, he told her. He bought. Not often. He was choosy. "And he had to have been running out of space to hang what he had," he said. He didn't believe Gerald stored any of his art. "He bought paintings so he could enjoy them." He clicked his tongue at the mention of the missing painting by Annie Chan.

"He'd had that one of hers for years. Got it for hardly anything, just as her star was starting to rise."

"How much would it fetch?"

"One fetched a quarter million at auction in New York last year," he said.

"Could Gerald have been contacted by someone who wanted to buy it privately?"

"He could." Fergusson drew in a breath, then continued. "I just don't think he would have proceeded without consulting me. He valued my services and he wouldn't have cut me out of a big deal like that. He'd have wanted me to handle it for him." He sounded peeved, as well he might. The commission on a sale of that size would have been substantial. If he heard that the painting had been bought, he'd be sure to let her know, he said. Word usually got around.

He did know Irma Friedrich, Gerald's accountant. Several of his clients used her services. Roxanne wrote down the number he gave her. Did Maxwell Fergusson know about a sculptor in B.C. called Timothy Baldwin?

"Ah. You're onto that," he said knowingly.

"Onto what?"

"Beautiful boy. Gerald met him here, at my gallery. I had a show for Timothy in May. Gerald was very interested."

"In the art or Timothy?" Roxanne asked.

"Both, Sergeant. Gerald was a man of eclectic taste," was the arch reply.

"Didn't he get involved with younger women?"

"Oh, yes. Those too. Like I said, Gerald had varied tastes." He lowered his voice, spoke confidentially. "He was a charming fellow, you know."

"I've been told that. Were any of his affairs serious?"

"Never!" Maxwell Fergusson asserted. "Gerald liked to dabble. He and Annabel had it all worked out. She had her own interests too, although I don't think she plays it both ways like he did. They were each other's insurance, in a way. They told all the people that they got involved with that it was temporary. That they always went home to one another. It was a kind of game with them."

How did he know that, Roxanne wondered? Had Maxwell Fergusson been involved himself with Gerald during their long acquaintance? Or Budgie? Or both?

"Gerald said he wanted to buy a sculpture from Tim Baldwin, a smaller one than I had in stock, but that was just an excuse to go visit him for a weekend, in his studio on Denman Island." He didn't know when, exactly.

"Did you keep track of all the art he had bought?' she asked.

"From me? Of course. I have that all on file, Sergeant, dates, prices, everything. I'll send it to you right away. But he did buy some pieces on his own as well, you know. Directly from the artists, especially the newer ones. I don't have a complete record of his collection."

Budgie Torrance pushed the door to the office open without knocking. "I need to talk to you, now," she announced.

"I have to go. Can I call you again if anything comes up?" Maxwell Fergusson would be delighted to assist any way he could. Meantime Budgie was glaring at Roxanne, arms akimbo.

"You thought Gerald was having it off with Lisa Storm?" she snapped. "How dumb is that? You know she bawled me out in front of the whole cast? How she'd never fancied him and what was I doing spreading rumours about her and making you guys think it was her that cut Gerald's throat?"

"I did not tell her that." Roxanne got to her feet to face Budgie. She did wonder how Lisa had known how Gerald had died. That was not public knowledge. But Tamsin Longstaff certainly knew. Had she told another member of staff? Toby, her talkative marketing director? If so, it was probably common knowledge throughout PTC by now.

"It wasn't Lisa he was fucking this time," Budgie ranted on, "It was some student he met at the university this summer. Skinny. Dark hair. Chloe something or other. Go talk to her."

10

LATER THAT DAY, Roxanne walked through the rooms of Budgie Torrance's condo again, trying to see what she and the Ident team might have missed. Budgie had been warned that someone might have the keys to her apartment. She should sleep elsewhere until the locks could be changed.

Izzy was checking, too, in the kitchen. There were empty takeout containers in the garbage can. Budgie didn't cook. "This looks tidy," she said, "but it's not. Nothing's organized in these cupboards. Look, flour, coffee beans, tomato soup."

Roxanne yanked open a drawer. Inside, it was a shambles, rubber bands tangled with plastic bags and small implements, a garlic press and a potato peeler among them. Spices were ranged neatly in glass jars on a shelf but there was no special order. Gerald must have been an impulsive cook, who threw things back into cupboards and onto shelves without any sense of order. There was a small whiteboard beside the door with a marker on a tiny shelf. Words that were largely indecipherable were scrawled on it. Maybe they said potatoes, salt? Superficially, the kitchen looked clean and tidy but that was probably the work of the cleaner.

The apartment spoke of two people who had a need to present a public face that was beautiful, perfect, but who were quite different in their private lives. In the bedroom that they once had shared, there were clothes scattered on a chair and the bedcovers had been roughly pulled up. They each had a walk-in closet. Their clothes were all hung on hangers. It wouldn't do to go out looking unkempt. A few were covered in plastic, back from the cleaners.

Gerald must have sent his shirts out to be laundered. There were at least a dozen, of different colours.

Izzy went into the bathroom. Face cream and makeup lay scattered on the bathroom counter. Two electric toothbrushes stood, side by side, a reminder of a marriage that was over. It appeared that Budgie hadn't put anything of Gerald's away. A towel had been left on the floor. She opened the medicine cupboard. It held the usual, Tylenol, Band-Aids, cough syrup. No sign of any prescribed medications.

There was a utility room. Beside the washer and dryer there was a treadmill and a rack of weights. And a space where a cat litter box had been.

The photographs on the walls of Budgie's study told the story of a career in theatre. There were ones of a playful young girl. A sexy one, teasing the camera. The *Medea* portrait showed a more mature woman, one who was tough and uncompromising, not one to mess with. Annabel Torrance was a chameleon, able to shift her appearance at will. It wasn't done by applying makeup or changing her clothes. She did it through altering her expression, through how she moved, sounded, looked. So who, Roxanne thought, was Budgie really? Or Gerald for that matter? Theatre was full of illusions, where people pretended to be whoever they wanted you to think they were, where they talked and gossiped and, if Lisa Storm was to be believed, made it all up. How could you grasp at the truth in this make-believe environment? She sank into a wicker chair with a fan back, scarves draped behind her. It smelled of perfume, warm and musky.

There was nothing haphazard in this room. It was busy, but everything was in a place that worked for it. The desk was pretty, but orderly. A wrought iron chair, painted white, with a colourful padded cushion, sat in front of it. The filing cabinet had a paisley scarf draped over it to mask its grey and angular coldness. Roxanne lifted it. In the space between the cabinet and the wall was a small safe.

"Izzy!" she called. "Come see this."

Izzy joined her. "Ident didn't open it?" she asked.

"They were looking for blood, signs that Gerald might have been killed here. They didn't find anything like that. If Budgie has a home safe, why wouldn't Gerald have one too?"

Together, they looked around Gerald's messy study again. Big desk. A swivel chair similar to the one in his office at the theatre. The armchair, set for reading. Gerald had enjoyed his comforts. There was a low wooden cabinet along one wall. An angular metal sculpture sat on it, alongside three small clay figurines. Inside, there were boxes of old CDs, videos of shows, office supplies, all thrown together in no particular order. Nothing was locked. His bookshelves were laden with theatre books and play scripts; there were no surprises. And no sign of a safe.

"Is it behind something?" asked Izzy, peeking behind a painting. They looked behind them all, one by one. Nothing.

"Maybe it's in another room," said Roxanne, going out into the living room. Izzy glanced back into the study before she left.

"Just a minute," she said. One wall had a mid-section that protruded into the room. Perhaps there had once been a fireplace. A wooden panel, painted the same warm mustard yellow as the other three, supported a painting, a street scene in blocky, vivid colours. She walked closer and ran her fingers down the edges of the panel. "This thing's got hinges," she said. It did. They were narrow, embedded in the side, hard to see. She reached out and pulled at the right-hand side. It swung open easily to her touch. And there it was, Gerald Blaise's hidden safe.

Roxanne called Ident once more. She looked out a window while she waited for Dave Novak to pick up. The sun hung in the western sky, making the river glow like gold. To the left she could see parts of the French area of Winnipeg, an old, burned-out cathedral silhouetted against the skyline. The corporal answered. He would send someone to try to open the safe in the morning. Izzy swung the wooden panel closed again.

"Budgie must know about the safe. Why hasn't she said anything about it?" she asked as they left the apartment.

"Good question. I guess we'll need to ask her. And get her to tell us what is in her own." Roxanne needed to get over to PTC. The theatre prof from the university was supposed to be there this afternoon. She wanted to talk to him.

"Can you get an address," she said to Izzy, "for Alison Beck?"

"Is she a suspect?" They stepped out the elevator into the hallway of the condo.

"No, but she was fired from PTC. She might not tell us the same story as everyone else, how Gerald was a great guy. How it's all happy families over there."

"Want me to go find out?"

"Sure," said Roxanne. She watched Izzy bounce off in the direction of the brown sedan, happy to be allowed to tackle an interview on her own.

ROXANNE FOUND THOM Dyck engaged in an animated conversation with Marla Caplan. He was a small, thin man with intense dark eyes. He reluctantly agreed to take a break and meet with Roxanne and followed her down the corridor to Gerald's old office. There, he gazed intently at a photograph on the wall. "*All's Well That Ends Well*," he said. "Good title, eh? Hope that's true for this case you're investigating." He tapped the glass. "We did that one three years ago. I got to assist Gerald. I was on sabbatical."

He remembered the girl called Chloe being at the party that he had given, only because he had noticed that Gerald was paying her a lot of attention.

"I think she's a Fine Arts major," he said. "She looks like it. Dark clothes, eye makeup, funky, it suits her. A pretty thing. I had to warn Gerald off. We can't have instructors making advances to students these days. Used to happen all the time, I know a couple of them who ended up married, but no more. Got to watch out for those things."

"And Gerald was definitely interested?"

"Oh yes. We all knew that Gerald had an eye for a girl. And Budgie was gone a lot, for months at a time. She was around that night, though. She was back from acting at Shaw, middle of August. Gerald was teaching a summer class in Canadian theatre for us. Quite a few of the students showed up that night. And there was Gerald, in the kitchen, chatting up that Chloe girl. I don't think Budgie was bothered, she was holding court with a couple of young guys herself, but I did have to have a word with Gerald, afterwards. 'No sex with the students,' I told him. He just laughed." The course had ended the following week. He didn't remember the girl's last name, but that wasn't a problem. The departmental secretary would have a class list.

"Gerald should have one too," he said. "Haven't you found it?" They hadn't. "Oh shit," said Thom Dyck, consternation written all over his face. "I'll bet he never got his marks in either. And now he's dead."

ALISON BECK'S APARTMENT building was old, red brick, a walk-up, but it looked in good shape. She was home. Izzy saw her waiting on the first-floor landing, the door to her apartment open behind her, short but sturdy, sandy haired, bespectacled, in old jeans and a loose shirt.

"Come on in," she said. "I was just going to make some tea."

The apartment was bright and sunny. They passed an open door. There were posters from the theatre and other arts events on white walls. A bearded man sat at a desk, tapping at a laptop.

"Greg Baxter," said Alison Beck, in the way of an introduction. "My partner. He works from home. Greg writes plays and theatre reviews." He pulled his eyes reluctantly from his screen when he heard his name and stood up. He was very tall and thin.

"Constable Isabel McBain. With the Major Crimes Unit of the RCMP." Izzy still got a thrill, saying that out loud. She didn't like to be called by her full name, but it sure worked when she needed to be taken seriously. "I'm hoping Ms. Beck can help us with our inquiries."

"Are you now?" He looked half interested but he didn't smile. He turned back to his writing table but left the door open, perhaps so he could hear what they said.

The kitchen walls were a sunny yellow, hung with more posters, this time from travels, maybe to Mexico, or Cuba. White painted wooden cupboards filled one wall and the stove and fridge were older models. Izzy could smell something cooking, simmering in a slow cooker on the counter. A rack of fresh muffins was cooling beside it.

Alison filled a kettle and opened a can of tea bags. "Hang your coat behind the door and have a seat." There was a small table, with room for two. It was very cozy. Izzy closed the door and hung her jacket on a peg.

Alison Beck talked while she made the tea. She hadn't found work since she'd been let go but she was hopeful. Most people in the business still respected her, she'd been given a couple of leads. Meantime it was hard, not having work to go to. She'd been happy working at Prairie Theatre Centre. Been there for five years.

"I'm so sorry about what's happened to Gerald." She reached for a tissue and blew her nose. "I loved that guy. He was such fun to work with."

"You loved him?" asked Izzy. Alison Beck wiped teary eyes.

"Oh, that." She attempted a smile. "Not me. I wasn't Gerald's type. Not pretty enough. And that was okay, you know. We were just pals. And I have Greg. Sex wasn't an issue with me and Gerald. We got along just fine." She was round and rather plain but when she smiled she looked more attractive than she gave herself credit for.

"Until you were dismissed."

"Well, yeah. But that wasn't Gerald's doing. That was Tamsin." She put the lid on a teapot and went to the fridge. "She thought

I was after her job." She waved a carton of milk at Izzy. "You want some?"

"Please. And sugar." Izzy McBain burned off everything she ate, unlike Alison Beck. "Were you? After her job?"

"Not really," said Alison. "Not right now. I'm not ready to take on one that big yet. But maybe later. When she finally retires. That would be fun, wouldn't it? If I went back someday and replaced her."

"So how come you lost your job?" Alison Beck halved a couple of muffins and put them on the table. She added a slab of butter.

"Why do you need to know?" she countered. "What has that got to do with why Gerald got killed?" She poured tea into both mugs and pushed one towards Roxanne. "Do you suspect me?"

"No. Is there any reason why I should?"

"No! Not at all! Like I said, I loved the guy. He wasn't just my boss. He was a good friend."

"That didn't stop you from getting fired."

"Don't think he had much choice." Alison tucked one leg up onto the chair as she sat. "Look," she said. "I wasn't given any real reason why I was let go. I was told to go to the boardroom one day and there was the chair, Mr. Moran, and Tamsin and some HR person they'd brought in. Irreconcilable differences, they said. Gerald was away at the time. In Toronto. I asked if he knew what they were doing and they said, oh yes, he was in complete agreement.

"I tried calling Gerald after but he wouldn't answer my phone calls or my messages. He'd probably been warned off by Moran. He's a lawyer. Or the HR woman. They left me with her afterwards. Severance package. Counselling services. They had it all worked out. She asked for my keys and marched me to the door, right through the lobby—James, the house manager, was there with some trainee ushers—and then past the box office. Everyone stood and watched with their mouths hanging open. It was the most humiliating moment of my life.

"I got legal advice. To find out if I had a case for wrongful dismissal. It wasn't very encouraging. So that's that. People in the arts community have been great. Lots of them were outraged, especially because of the way it was done. It was so cold-hearted. Pedro, the production manager, came around with a bottle of wine one night. And I ran into Toby Malleson at a gallery opening the weekend after. He gave me a big hug. But I won't get that job back. Time to move on. Have one of these." She pushed the plate towards Izzy.

"Did you resent the fact that Gerald never got in touch?" Izzy buttered a muffin. Alison Beck sighed.

"Well," she said, "Gerald could never cope with conflict. He liked to go with the flow. Easygoing, you know? Kept his nose clean. That's why I can't figure out why anyone would want to kill him. Gerald didn't make enemies. Could it have been an accident? Was he just in the wrong place at the wrong time?"

"Maybe," said Izzy. "He was interested in other women?"

"And men." Alison Beck untucked her leg and sat forward on her chair. "You know about the latest? The one in B.C.?"

"Timothy Baldwin?"

"Yeah, him. Tim." She wrapped her hands around her mug. "I don't think the murder has anything to do with that, though," she said. "Gerald was always fooling around with someone. It was never all that serious. None of them ever stuck. Something else had to be going on."

Her head tilted to one side as she considered what to say next. "Do you know that Gerald was thinking of quitting? Leaving PTC? He hadn't decided yet. He wasn't sure. He used to ask me over to his place to eat some nights during the week, when he was on his own and Budgie was away. Greg works late a lot. We'd keep each other company, he'd make dinner, he was a great cook. We'd split a bottle of wine. And talk. That's how we got to be such good friends. He confided in me. He trusted me."

Her voice tapered off. In the end, when it came to firing her, Gerald had betrayed that trust. Then she resumed her story.

"He was tired, Constable. Of the paperwork. The politics. Of having to come up with yet another season of plays. He'd been doing it for twenty years, he'd had enough. He thought he'd like to move to B.C. Go to a better climate. You know he inherited a pile of money, about ten years back?"

Izzy nodded.

"He could afford to retire and focus on his art collection. He'd talked about it with Budgie though and she hated the idea. She wanted him to stay on for one more term, five whole years more. She liked being the wife of a successful artistic director. Being married to a retired old guy didn't fit her image — well, that's what I think. Gerald didn't say that.

"You know his contract was coming up for renewal? 'I'll sniff the wind, Alison,' he said to me one night. 'See how it blows. If it looks like they're going to give me the shove, I'll beat them to it and walk on my own. But if they're going to renew, I dunno. Maybe I could manage three more years. Don't know about five. But it would keep the peace at home for a while.' So, I wonder," said Alison, "if he and Budgie got into a row about it. She's got a wicked temper."

"Budgie was in Regina when he died," said Izzy.

"It's not far. An hour by plane." Obviously Alison Beck had thought this through. "And then there's Tamsin," she added.

"He'd told her he was thinking of leaving too?"

"I don't know. But she's smart enough to have figured it out for herself, isn't she? You know that she and Gerald go back? Way back?"

"He had something going with her as well?"

"Oh, long ago. Before she ever became GM. Some people think that's how she got the job." Alison picked up a chunk of muffin and bit into it. She chewed and swallowed. "So, they're close. Way closer than they should be," she said. "Maybe, if she thought he was going to leave PTC, she got worried. She might not get along with a new AD, the way she did with Gerald. Does that give her a motive? Maybe she got mad at him. She did sometimes, you know. Maybe she killed him."

You wish, Izzy thought and polished off the last of her muffin.

11

AT NINE THE following morning, Roxanne and Izzy met with Corporal Dave Kovak at HQ. Izzy rolled in a portable whiteboard. The first photo she stuck up was one of Gerald Blaise, alive and smiling. The second was of his body, huddled in the trunk of his car. They had received the autopsy report.

"He was slashed from the front, by someone who's right-handed, and probably shorter than him," said Dave. "There's a slight upward angle to the cut. He bled out in the trunk of the car, so he was still alive when he was dumped in it."

"How long did he take to die?" Izzy nose crinkled at the thought.

"It was over in seconds. The carotid artery was cut." Dave had sent a member of his unit to the Blaise condo to let a locksmith in and have a look at Gerald and Budgie's safes. He'd got an earful from Budgie Torrance when he had arrived.

"She wasn't supposed to be there," Roxanne said. "She was told to stay at a hotel last night. She can't sleep in that apartment until the door lock has been replaced."

"The locksmith's having to rekey the doors to the building when he's done with us. She opened her own safe for us but didn't know the combo to Gerald's, so he's working on that. We need to get her out of there, though. So we can do a more thorough search. We were looking for signs that the murder happened there before, but now that's all changed.

"Now we think that Blaise was killed right beside the car." Dave Kovak pointed to the photo of the open trunk, the body nestled inside it, pooled in blood. "And his body pushed into the trunk while he was dying. That could have happened anywhere. Maybe it was driven to the theatre parking lot after, where Zeke Sinclair said he had found it, if what the kid says is true. Gerald had a parking spot in the basement of his building. Why would he have left his car outside?"

Roxanne pulled Zeke's photo out of the pile and stuck it up. "He's been released from the Youth Centre. Into the care of his aunt, Tracy Ross. He's got a court appearance in a couple of weeks. This is his brother, Jeremiah." It was a police mug shot. Jem Sinclair stared into the camera with a look of studied indifference. He'd been in trouble with the law since he was eleven. Now he was seventeen, a seasoned criminal and a member of a notorious street gang. "He's known to use knives. The city police are trying to find him for cutting up the school kid who talked about Zeke finding the body in the car. They're going to let us know if they pick him up."

"You think he did it?" the corporal asked. "That he mugged the guy, stuffed him into the trunk of the car, and drove it back to the PTC lot? How would Jem Sinclair know where Gerald Blaise worked?"

"His address would have been on his driving licence."

"So, his killer went up to the apartment, right beside the theatre, after he dropped off the car with the body in it? Had a look around and helped himself to a painting? Why would a kid like Jem Sinclair do that? There was booze in the apartment, right? Jewellery. Wouldn't he have taken that instead?" What Dave was saying made sense.

"And why would Jem bother to put up other pictures in its place, to make it look like it wasn't missing? How would he know that the Annie Chan was worth a lot of money?" said Izzy.

"He could have taken it as a souvenir." Roxanne didn't think it likely but sometimes murderers helped themselves to an item that reminded them of the victim. "Maybe he just liked the look of it and it was sheer luck that he lifted a valuable one." They all sat in dubious silence for a moment.

"Alison Beck thinks Budgie might have killed Gerald because he was going to leave his job at PTC and move to B.C.," said Izzy. They had received a report late the night before from the Vancouver officer who had interviewed Timothy Baldwin. Gerald's latest lover was bereft. He and Gerald were going to live together, he had said. That wife of his must have killed him off. "They should arrest the bitch," he had wailed.

"Alison Beck says Budgie could have flown in from Regina and done the murder, then flown back again," said Izzy.

"Did you check the plane flights?"

"Not yet." A photo of Annabel Torrance went up next to those of her dead husband. It was a professional head shot, sleek and glamorous.

"Alison thought Tamsin Longstaff might be responsible for killing him, too, but that might be just because she's mad at her," Izzy continued. "She thinks it was Tamsin that fired her from her job at PTC."

"What about Alison herself?" Roxanne flipped through an old theatre brochure, looking for a photograph of her. "Could she have wanted to kill him?"

"Suppose so. She liked Gerald a lot and he let her down. But I don't think so." Izzy shrugged. "She sounds like she's got over it."

Roxanne's phone lit up on the table in front of her. Sergeant Cooper Jenkins was calling again. "Give me a minute while I take this," she said, and went out into the hallway.

"Hey," Jenkins' voice drawled in her ear. "You know that Dyck guy that teaches drama at the university?"

"Yes," she said. "Talked to him yesterday."

"Well, he's dead. I'm looking at the body right now. It's in the wood at Riverside Park and he's been stabbed."

RIVERSIDE PARK LAY on a bend in the river, not far from the university. Professor Dyck liked to go there for an early morning run, weather permitting. A road cut through the park, following the riverbank. Police cars blocked access at each end of it. One of them pulled over to let Roxanne through when she showed her ID. She'd brought Izzy along.

A forensic team, summoned by the city police, was already at work. Two white-suited technicians were examining a car in the parking lot. They issued Roxanne and Izzy with protective gear and directed them towards a line of trees. Once they were suited up, they crossed a grassy area, passed a children's playground and entered a wood. Well-groomed trails cut through it. The trees were mainly poplar, their grey branches almost bare of leaves, interspersed with scrubby oaks.

"Nice place," said Izzy. It was, quiet and peaceful when the police activity going on around them was out of eyeshot. The sky was blue, there was hardly any wind. It would have been a good morning to be out for a run.

They followed a path. Ahead was a chain-link fence, marking the boundary of the park. It stretched all the way to the road, where a white van from the provincial medical examiner's office was parked. Another path ran along it and on it lay the body of Thomas Dyck.

"Well, look. It's Foxy Roxy with one of her cubs," said Coop Jenkins as they approached. Izzy McBain almost laughed. Dr. Abdur Farooq stood at Cooper's side. He looked amused too. Roxanne hunkered down beside the body. Best to ignore Coop Jenkins' jibes.

Thom Dyck lay face down on a bed of leaves, pale yellow and gold, studded with shades of brown, some of which were dark bloodstains. He wore black sweatpants, tucked into his socks, and a T-shirt.

"You know he was stabbed, for sure?"

"The blade's still embedded in his chest," said Dr. Farooq. Roxanne walked around to the other side and looked. Dyck's corpse lay slightly towards his right side. She could just glimpse the handle protruding below him on his left.

"It was a right-handed thrust?"

"Same as Blaise," said the doctor. He had performed the autopsy on Gerald Blaise's body. "But a different kind of move. And probably a different kind of knife."

"Who found him?"

A couple had been walking their dog before eight this morning. A policewoman from Jenkins' team was taking down their statements. They were here most mornings, they had said. And Thom Dyck often jogged past them. They didn't know who he was but he always said "good morning." They had been coming here for years. So had he. It was usually quiet that early. They hadn't seen anyone else around. Now they sat at a picnic table in a clearing, their spaniel at their feet. He had been running off leash and had reached the body first. His hairy feet had mopped up some blood. He'd got some on his muzzle too, sniffing at the body. The wife had tried to clean him up. A wad of bloody tissue lay on the table beside her.

Two medics approached with a stretcher. When Dyck was turned over, they got a better look at his face. He had looked surprised when he died. They waited until he was covered up and carried off to the waiting van. Abdur Farooq pulled off his protective gloves. Jenkins had gone to talk to the couple with the spaniel.

"This is going to be a joint case? City and RCMP?" Abdur asked.

"Looks like it," said Roxanne.

"Good luck with that," he said before he followed the stretcher out of the wood. When part of a crime happened in the RCMP's jurisdiction and another inside the city, the two police forces sometimes had to collaborate. That could be tricky. The couple with the dog walked away. Cooper introduced his woman colleague, Detective Constable Meera Singh. He lit up a cigarette as they all walked back through the wood towards the car park.

"I talked to him yesterday," Roxanne said. They reached the playground. Cooper sat down on a rounded metal post. Across the road, the river flowed gently by. Roxanne chose another post, close enough to talk but far enough away that she didn't catch any of his smoke. Izzy found a swing and listened as they talked, lifting her feet so the plastic covers didn't drag on the ground as she swung slowly back and forth. Meera Singh leaned against the iron frame. "He was at PTC. It was late in the afternoon. I wanted to know what happened at a party he gave at his house. One that Gerald Blaise and his wife attended."

"They knew each other?"

"Dyck was on the PTC board, and Blaise taught a class for him at the university in August." She pulled the plastic hood back off her head. Her red hair caught the sunlight. "There was a student at the party that he was interested in. Chloe something or other. I need to get her last name from the university."

"Hey, Meera, find that out, will you?" Meera Singh nodded and pulled out her notepad. "So, Blaise and the professor were friends?"

"Sounds like it," she said.

"We've got the keys to his house," said DC Singh. "And his address." Dyck had also had a billfold containing his driver's licence, a twenty-dollar bill and a debit card in a zipped pocket. He hadn't been robbed.

"Want to go see where he lived?" Jenkins asked. He stood and stomped out his cigarette, picked up the stub and flipped it into a nearby waste bin, not waiting for Roxanne to reply, acting as the man in charge. They walked to their cars and peeled off their plastic coverings.

"Meera will get rid of those," said Cooper Jenkins. Izzy and Roxanne handed over theirs to Jenkins' assistant. Izzy raised an eyebrow in apology and Meera Singh rolled her eyes. The DC wasn't as compliant as she looked. Coop swaggered over to a big Silverado.

Izzy laughed. "Look at him, thinks he's a cowboy," she said.

THOM DYCK HAD lived in a townhouse close by, two bedrooms and a bathroom upstairs and a kitchen, living/dining room and a toilet downstairs. There was an attached garage. The front lawn was mown and weed free, bordered with flowering perennials. Large pots of mixed flowers stood on the front steps.

"Boy, is this ever tidy!" said Izzy. There were vases of fresh flowers in the hallway and living room, carefully arranged. The walls were painted white, hung with framed photographs, theatre shots and posters. Dyck had been a bookish man. One room upstairs was a home office, the walls lined with floor-to-ceiling shelves. The books were all about theatre and the teaching of it. They were arranged by category and alphabetically by author. Downstairs, his books were novels and poetry. He had a large TV, a collection of DVDs, and VHS tapes of old movies going back to the early days of film. There was a powerful music system. He had liked jazz. Roxanne stepped out the back door onto a patio. A table with a furled umbrella and padded chairs sat at its centre.

Half of the fenced garden was given over to vegetables. The professor had dug up some potatoes recently. Tomato vines had been stripped before the frost, but there was squash in abundance, clumps of herbs, a couple of orange pumpkins. Roxanne pulled some rosemary leaves and rubbed them between her fingers. She liked the smell. There was a shed at the back. She peered in the window. Gardening tools hung from hooks; there were folding lawn chairs, stacked pots, a lawn mower, all neat and in order. She walked back to the house. The forensic search would continue here when the Ident guys were done at the park, but, meantime, Izzy was opening and shutting drawers.

"There's not a thing out of place," she said. "He folded his underwear. His socks are in rows, by colour."

Roxanne found Coop Jenkins in the garage. He stood by a garbage can, a blue recycling bag beside it. There were several wine bottles in it and one empty of gin.

"Either our guy's had another party or he enjoys a drink," he said. It was one of the cleanest garages Roxanne had ever seen. Izzy appeared in the door to the house.

"The Ident guy at the Blaise condo just called," she said. "They've got those safes open."

"I'd best get over to the university," said Jenkins. "We're going to have to touch base later. Okay?" He locked the house and pocketed the keys. "So, what do you think? Are we looking for the same perp?"

"Don't know," Roxanne replied. "Guess we'll have to find out."

"You talk to your boss and I'll talk to mine." He got into his big truck and drove off.

"'Course it's the same killer." Izzy sat beside her. "You just don't want to have to work with that Jenkins guy."

Izzy was right. How would it work if she did? Cooper was a sergeant, like her, and he was used to being in charge. She hadn't been able to reach Brian Donohue last night. He'd been busy. She would text him. If she was going to have to work alongside him, she did want to know more about Detective Sergeant Jenkins.

12

THE FORENSIC TEAM had moved the big, angular sculpture off a sideboard in Gerald Blaise's study. In its place were the contents of his hidden safe: three spiral-bound notebooks in differing sizes, two stacks of paper, a cash box. It contained ten thousand dollars, bundled in large notes. There were legal documents, including title papers to the condo, and a copy of his will. There was also an old large brown envelope.

"Everything in her safe is the usual," said an Ident technician, "A will, investments, a jewellery box. They both owned the condo. He left a couple of charitable donations, to an actors' fund and to PTC to fund an award in his name. And some cash to provide for the care of his cats. But all the rest goes to his wife." Budgie Torrance was going to be a rich woman.

Roxanne and Izzy flipped through the notebooks. The largest but thinnest of them itemized the art he had bought. Gerald had been unusually careful, for him, in his record keeping, when it came to his collection. It seemed that each work of art was listed by date, the name of the person or gallery he'd bought it from, and the amount he had paid, but the writing was a large scrawl, almost impossible to decipher. The numbers were clearer. They could see there were a few early purchases but the record began in earnest about ten years ago, when he had inherited his aunt's fortune. The big envelope contained papers relating to that inheritance, including a record of the sale of her house. There was an old faded photograph. It had been a large, gracious pile, standing in its own grounds in a well-to-do Toronto neighbourhood. "Look, he got over a million for it," said Izzy, "Back then." Real estate values had soared in the past decade. It would have made more a few years later.

The second notebook contained scribbled notes. They could see dates at the tops of different pages. Was it a diary?

"Can you read this?" Roxanne passed the book over to Izzy.

"Barely." Izzy peered at the script. Roxanne sighed. They might need a handwriting expert to decipher it, and that would take time. If Gerald had secrets, would they be recorded there?

The third notebook was a small blue address book. It was old, but looked like it was still in use. You could figure out what some of the names were if you knew what you were looking for. Roxanne recognized some of the capital letters. There was a 'T' followed by a 'B' that looked recent. Was that Tim Baldwin's contact information? It looked like it might be. Was this a general address book or was it more particular? Was this where he had listed his various amorous dalliances through the years? If so, Gerald had been an active man.

"It's too bad we don't have a last name for that girl yet, the one he was seen with at Professor Dyck's party. Wonder if she's in it," said Izzy.

Roxanne's phone buzzed. Inspector Schultz. She went outside the apartment into the hallway to take the call. He didn't talk for long. The city police had been in touch with him about this joint investigation. Some guy called Jenkins was in charge at their end.

"I've talked with him," she said.

"Well, make sure he doesn't dump their workload on you," he said. "You're investigating the Blaise murder. His is separate. Isn't it?"

"The two dead men knew each other, sir. The two killings may well be related."

"Right. Okay," he grumbled. "I'll talk to the city and get back to you." And he hung up. The elevator bell rang. The doors slid open and out stepped Margo Wishart.

"Here you are, Sergeant!" Margo was breathless. She had been hurrying. "Sorry I'm late. I heard the news about Thom Dyck. I can't believe it! It's true he was killed? It's the talk of the whole university."

Roxanne remembered that she had arranged for Margo to come and check out the art on Gerald Blaise's walls. "How well did you know him, Dr. Wishart?"

"Thom? He was just another prof. I was on a couple of committees with him. Seemed nice enough. Worked hard." They walked back into the condo, Margo unwrapping a scarf from around her neck, getting her breath back, her eyes already scanning the paintings on the wall.

"Come see. We found a notebook. With a list of what he had bought, we think." Roxanne led Margo into Gerald's study. "It's hard to read. You know Izzy, right?" Margo did, from the old Interlake case and from living in the same area. They'd bumped into each other a couple of times at the local grocery store.

"Hi there," said Izzy. "We haven't had lunch yet. Will I go pick up sandwiches?" Izzy was hungry. It was two in the afternoon already. Margo was still looking at paintings on the walls, fascinated by what she was seeing.

"Look at these! He had good taste." She reluctantly pulled her eyes away. "Where's that book you mentioned?"

Izzy passed Margo the notebook, grabbed her jacket from the back of Gerald's desk chair and went to get food. Margo sank into Gerald's comfortable reading chair. Roxanne flipped through the little address book, trying to decipher it.

"Well," said Margo. "Will you look at this? It's kind of like a diary." Roxanne stared. Izzy had passed Margo the wrong notebook. Margo was holding the middle-sized one, the one they had thought was illegible.

"You can read that?" she asked.

"Sure. It's not that difficult. It's just a bad italic." Margo closed the book. "I've seen worse. I suppose I shouldn't be looking. It's private." She was right, but Roxanne was dying to know what it said, and she knew from past experience that Margo would be discreet.

"That's okay. We can't read it," said Roxanne. "What does it say?"

"It's scribbled notes. He seems to have written in it most days. Goes back about a year. Would you like me to transcribe it for you?" Margo opened the book again. Then she glanced back up at Roxanne over the top of a page, eyes bright with interest. "But you don't want me knowing too much about this case, do you?" Margo's curiosity had led her into serious trouble before, when she had become involved in the Interlake case, last February.

"We need to know," said Roxanne. "We'll pay you for doing the work. Anything you find out has to remain confidential."

"Well, of course, Sergeant." A dimple deepened in each of her cheeks.

"You could call me Roxanne."

"And I'm Margo. Since we're going to be working together again," Margo teased. "Do you know who Tim is?" She had flipped the book open at Gerald's last entry. "It sounds like Gerald was planning to move to B.C., to live with him."

"Read it." Roxanne listened while Margo Wishart read out the latest entries in Gerald's diary.

"It's dated almost three weeks ago," said Margo, "And it's very scrappy. But he's noted a couple of properties for sale in Victoria and another in Vancouver. He gives the prices. The Vancouver one costs a hundred thousand more. There's a row of question marks after one of the Victoria ones. He writes, 'Good wall space. Ocean view.' Then: 'Would Tim want to live here? Use Denman as summer/studio? Vancouver easier by ferry?'" She raised her eyes from the page. "Do you think he was planning to leave Budgie Torrance after all these years and go live in B.C. with this person called Tim?"

"Does he actually say that?"

"Not really. Here's the most recent entry that mentions Budgie. 'On phone with B tonight. Big row about Mb.' I think that's *Macbeth*. 'Wants a rethink, hates her costume. Wishes I wasn't directing. This is the last time I work with her. Ever.' It doesn't sound like he'd told her, though. Oh, here she is again." This entry was another few pages back.

"'Went to Regina. Decent opening. B in good form. Think she's having it off with Sam Geddes. Good for her.'" Izzy reappeared, carrying a couple of paper bags. One contained wrapped sandwiches, the other, bottled juices. Margo continued to read aloud. "'Drove home next day. Three more whole weeks without B. FaceTimed with Tim. Booked ticket for Nov. 3, day after Mb ends. Can't wait.'"

"Sam Geddes, Globe Theatre," Roxanne said to Izzy, who was already unwrapping a ham and cheese bun.

"I'll look. Soon as." Izzy bit into a fat bun. Margo opened a can of orange juice. She nodded towards the diary.

"I don't suppose I can take this home? I could work on it tonight and send you the transcript tomorrow."

Roxanne shook her head. "No, but we can make you a copy. You should really have a look at what art is on the walls after you've eaten. While we're here. You'll probably be able to read his inventory too." She passed Margo that notebook.

Izzy opened the Globe Theatre website on her laptop, chewing while she did. Sam Geddes had been acting in the same play as Budgie. He lived in Saskatchewan, was in his middle years, smiled for the camera.

"He might have a car," she said. "Budgie could have borrowed it and driven to Winnipeg and back. Five, six hours max? She would have been finished work by eleven that Wednesday night and they probably didn't need her back at the theatre until seven on Thursday. Twenty hours, Regina to Winnipeg and back. It's enough time."

It was possible, but it still seemed like a long shot. The murder didn't seem premeditated and driving all that distance to do the killing required forethought. Margo helped herself to a chicken salad sandwich and continued to read the diary while she ate. Izzy closed her laptop and looked though the papers that had been found in the safe. Roxanne sat at Gerald's desk and glanced through the address book again. She wished she could decipher it. She opened it at the B section and passed it to Margo.

"Can you see Alison Beck's name?" she asked.

Margo scanned the page and shook her head. Maybe this really was a listing of his lovers, past and present. She flipped it over to the letter D. "Thom Dyck's name is here," she said.

Budgie Torrance barged in the door, interrupting them.

"Have you got keys for me? The locksmith said he left them here."

"Try the caretaker," Izzy suggested. Budgie didn't leave.

"Tamsin Longstaff is livid," she reported with some satisfaction. "The whole of PTC will have to be rekeyed. Gerald's master key could open up everything." She looked at the open safe, the notebooks and papers scattered around the room.

"You can't keep that stuff," she said. "Without asking. It's mine."

"You and I need to talk. Now," said Roxanne.

"Don't think so."

Margo Wishart tactfully got up to leave the room but she didn't close the door. She stood, examining a painting on the wall just outside, all ears.

"Can't." Budgie's determined little chin jutted out. "I'm on a break. Have to get back."

"We'll let them know you're detained. Shall we use your own study?"

Budgie picked up an unwrapped sandwich from the desk, the one intended for Roxanne. She grabbed a bottle of cranberry juice as well.

"Oh, well. Might as well eat while I'm here."

Roxanne wasn't fooled. She could see Budgie checking out what Gerald's safe had revealed. Didn't she know what was in it already? Izzy had her phone to her ear, letting Tamsin Longstaff know that Budgie was going to be with them for an hour or so. Roxanne signalled to her to follow and opened the door to Budgie's boudoir. Margo Wishart checked off a painting, pencil in hand, and watched them go, over the top of Gerald's inventory book.

Once inside, Budgie walked straight to the large wicker chair. She took her place in it like a queen on a peacock throne. She unscrewed the juice bottle and drank from it. Placed it down on a side table. Roxanne closed the door firmly behind her.

"What's it all about this time?" Budgie said, and unwrapped the sandwich.

"You know that you inherit most of your husband's estate?"

"All of it. He left everything to me, I left everything to him. That was the deal." She bit into corned beef with mustard. Roxanne took the wrought iron chair with the cushioned seat, in front of a mirrored dressing table. It was scattered with used cosmetics, a hairbrush, some costume jewellery. She faced Budgie.

"You're the person who benefits most from Gerald's death."

The door opened and Izzy slipped in. She closed it behind her and stood, listening.

"You're thinking I maybe killed him? Dream on, Sergeant. I was in Regina, remember?"

"You performed in a play on the night of Wednesday, October 4th," said Roxanne. "And again, the following evening. What did you do in between?"

Budgie chewed some more and swallowed, taking her time. "Went out to eat after the show, probably. Like always. With some actors from the cast. Got back to the hotel, slept late. Exercised. Need to keep in shape, you know. Went online." She turned her attention back to her lunch.

"One of the actors was Sam Geddes?"

Budgie looked up at Roxanne. "Sure. Lovely man. A dear friend." She wasn't at all fazed. She appeared amused that they knew about him. "Look, Sergeant, I couldn't have done it. Gerald died during the night, right? Whoever left his body out there in the back of the car didn't do it in daylight. And there's no planes during the night from Regina. I couldn't have made it here."

Izzy had checked the airlines. Budgie was right about that, but she still could have made it to Winnipeg.

"You could have driven." Izzy folded her arms and leaned against the door. "Your play was done by ten. You could have been here by five in the morning, easy. Maybe earlier. Nobody on the road and it was a clear night. You could have driven fast. Left here by seven. It would still have been dark. You'd have got back to Regina by noon. Enough time to catch up on some shut-eye before you had to be back at the theatre in the evening."

Roxanne watched Budgie's face become an impassive mask.

"I don't have a car."

"But Sam Geddes probably has."

"Ask him," Budgie Torrance stated flatly.

"Gerald was thinking about quitting his job."

"No, he wasn't!" Budgie retorted. "Who is telling you all this garbage? That's just a rumour. He was going to stay on for five more years. Retire on his twenty-fifth anniversary."

"He wanted to move to B.C."

"Sure. Maybe. But not right now. When he was sixty-five." Did Budgie believe that or was she pretending again? She was good at that.

"He was seeing a young sculptor called Timothy Baldwin."

"That right?"

"Was he planning to leave Winnipeg? And you? Go to live with Tim Baldwin in B.C.?"

Budgie sat forward and grasped each arm of her big chair. Suddenly, she looked like a bird about to take flight.

"No way. I told you. He did his thing, I did mine. We always came home to one another. I was his rock, Sergeant. The only person he could really trust."

Alison Beck had said something similar. How many people had Gerald convinced of that?

"What relationship did Gerald have with Professor Thom Dyck?"

"Thom Dyck? What's this got to do with him?"

That question had caught Budgie off guard. The news of his death couldn't have reached her yet.

"Thom and Gerald had a fling, but that was about three years back, when we were doing *All's Well That Ends Well.* Thom was assistant directing. Not much good at it, but it suited Gerald to have him onside. Got him onto the board of the theatre right after. Helps to have friends in high places." She drank some juice. "I've got to eat. We won't get another break until six. That Jazz Elliot is a total slave driver." She lifted her bun again and smiled. She could change her manner in an instant. When Budgie wanted to she could be just as engaging as her charming husband. She lifted the sandwich to her mouth again.

"I have bad news," said Roxanne. "Professor Dyck's body was discovered this morning."

Budgie paused mid-bite. "He's dead?" Her eyebrows arched in surprise.

"Stabbed." Roxanne watched Budgie flinch. "Where were you today before the police and the locksmith arrived here?"

Budgie Torrance thought for a moment, then rose to her feet. She put down what was left of the sandwich and smoothed her skirt. It was short, worn over her usual black tights. "I don't think you are allowed to ask me questions like that without a lawyer present, Sergeant." She spoke the words as if she was delivering lines from a play. "I need to call someone."

"Don't go anywhere without informing us," Roxanne said to her retreating back. Izzy stood aside to let her pass. She saw Budgie raise her phone to her ear as she left.

Margo Wishart was sitting at the dining room table, the large Inuit carving behind her, Gerald's inventory notebook open in front of her.

"I've discovered something," she said once the door had swung shut. "I think two more pieces are missing. Both by local artists, both paintings. Worth several thousand. One by Bruce Foot, quite large. Another by Ivan Waters. I can't see them anywhere."

"The Annie Chan was big too," said Roxanne. "Whoever took them must have been able to transport them away from here. They'd have needed a vehicle."

"Some of the collection is new, bought within the last few years." Margo continued. "Most of it Canadian. He liked figurative work and abstracts with some emotional clout. Dramatic pieces. But then there's that." She indicated the large green soapstone carving behind her. "It's a Cape Dorset carving. That one is museum quality. And he has some other Indigenous work. There's a nice Morrisseau. Two Baker Lake prints. An Odjig. They're older. They're awfully good. He has a nice Kurelek as well." She pointed at a winter prairie landscape, a child skating.

"Worth a lot?"

"Shall I find out for you?"

"That might be useful. Thanks."

Roxanne looked out the window. It faced onto the alley. She watched Budgie Torrance strut across the back lane towards the theatre, then her phone buzzed. "I need to get this." She stepped out into the condo hallway. It was the worker from the Youth Centre.

Tracy Ross had said she was taking Zeke home, he told her. She'd taken him up north. He mentioned a reserve community in the northern Interlake. He did have a cellphone number for her. She called it.

"This is Tracy. I'm in the bush. Can't talk. Back in a week or so," said a recorded message. Roxanne found Izzy and Margo back in Gerald's study, searching through papers.

"He had to have this collection insured," said Margo. "There are over fifty pieces. It's got to be worth a small fortune."

"His accountant will know." Izzy waved a financial document.

It was after four-thirty. Rush hour had started. They began to clean up. Roxanne needed to go look after her son and his cousins. Her sister had a meeting to go to. She'd promised.

"I need to get up the road, too," said Margo Wishart. "Send me the copy of that notebook soon, will you?" she said to Izzy as she left. "I'll get going on it right away."

ROXANNE MANAGED TO connect with Inspector Brian Donohue later that night, after Finn had gone to bed.

"Heard that there's another body," he said. She told him how Professor Dyck had been found that morning, lying dead in a city park and therefore out of RCMP territory. But obviously, the cases were linked.

"I'm going to have to work alongside a city DS called Cooper Jenkins," she complained. "Do you know him?"

Brian laughed. "Coop Jenkins? He's still around? I was on a committee with him years ago. One of those guys that needs to be out there, working cases in person. Not happy at a desk. He's still a sergeant, eh?"

Roxanne liked working out in the field herself. She wasn't ready to sit behind a desk yet, either. But this was her first year as sergeant. She had a few years to play investigator before she tried to move up a rank.

"He calls me Foxy Roxy," she said.

"Could be worse," Brian said. "Surprised nobody's thought of it sooner, with the hair. Hey, are we going to be able get together soon?"

She felt a twinge of guilt. It had been a couple of weeks now. "You know how it is," she stalled. "A case like this. And I have to find time for Finn. I haven't been at the gym for days. I'll never make next year's marathon if I don't get back to it soon." Roxanne liked to run. She was getting out of shape. "But maybe on the weekend?"

"Dunno," he said. "I've got stuff happening. We should talk."

"Okay." She was distracted by a text coming in. Coop Jenkins. "Maybe early next week?"

Cooper Jenkins had written MEET TOMORROW? MY OFFICE? 9?

SURE, she texted back as soon as she'd hung up.

13

THURSDAY MORNING BROUGHT a drop in the temperature and grey skies. Rain turned to sleet, the city's bridges iced up and a major accident snarled traffic heading into downtown Winnipeg. By the time she reached the large, sprawling building that housed the local police service, Roxanne was running late and the parkade was full. She found a space in an open lot two blocks away and hurried back to the entrance, dodging puddles, ice pellets stinging her face, cold and wet. When she asked for directions to the Homicide Unit at the front desk, Cooper Jenkins came to fetch her. He must have just arrived himself. He still wore his bomber jacket.

"Hey, Foxy," he greeted her. "You look like a half-drowned coyote." She lifted her head from shaking frozen raindrops off her coat. "Guess we should get coffee," he said and headed towards the door.

There was a basement café in the next block. Windows ran high along one wall, drizzled with icy rivulets. Lights on each table illuminated the gloom. She went to the washroom and dried off her face and hair as best she could. Ran hot water over her cold hands. Cooper had gone to the counter to get their drinks. She had seen him nod as he passed a couple of occupied tables. The police obviously frequented this spot. When she got back he was standing beside an officer, a patrol sergeant, by the look of his uniform. The guy looked in her direction, turned back to Jenkins and laughed. She found a table by a heating vent and hung her wet coat on a chair to dry. Jenkins passed her a mug, pulled out the chair opposite her and sat. He dumped the contents of a packet of sugar in his coffee, screwed up the wrapper and dropped it onto a tray.

"Whaddaya think, then?" he said, lifting a speculative eyebrow. "Are we both looking for the same guy?"

Warm air rose from the heat vent at her wet feet. She smelled damp wool rising from her coat. "Like I said before, maybe," she replied, the mug in her hands warming her cold fingers.

"Oh, come on," he protested. "Both the guys that got killed are in the same kind of business. Both knifed. 'Course we are."

"Unless yours is a copycat killer." She sat back and sipped her coffee. "Someone wanted the professor dead and wants you to think it's the same. As a distraction." The patrol sergeant Jenkins had been talking to stopped at their table on his way outside, a carry-out coffee in his hand.

"Hi," he grinned. "Hear you're a Gravel Road Cop. Here to work with Coop on a real murder." Roxanne had heard that comment before. In French, the RCMP was the Gendarmerie Royale du Canada. When she was in uniform, the initials GRC were emblazoned on her shoulder. The officer didn't wait to talk. He punched Jenkins' arm as he swaggered off. "Good luck, mate." Jenkins shrugged.

Roxanne didn't bother to comment. Best to get back to business. "There are differences, right?" she reasoned. "Like Abdur said, Thom Dyck was stabbed. Gerald Blaise was slashed. The killer left the knife with Dyck. Didn't with Blaise. Dyck's body wasn't hidden. Blaise's was."

"Oh, come on, Foxy. You gotta be kidding. They were pals, right? Hung out together sometimes. You said yourself that my victim was at the theatre yesterday. They have to be connected. Wanna bet?"

"And stop calling me that," she said.

"What. Foxy? How come? Suits you." He pointed at her red hair.

"My friends call me Roxanne."

"What do your enemies call you?" He smirked, pulling one ankle up across the other knee. Who were Roxanne's enemies? She had them, most career cops did, and not just felons they had once put behind bars. Jenkins would have his too. He grinned, lopsided, not expecting an answer. "My pals call me Coop." She permitted herself a smile of acknowledgment. If she was going to be stuck with working alongside him she might as well try to get along. He carried on talking:

"So how well did they know each other, really? Blaise and Dyck? Some folks say they got real cozy now and then."

"That was long over and it didn't last long. Gerald Blaise slept with lots of people, men as well as women. And he stayed on good terms with lots of them, like Professor Dyck. I don't think they were all that close, but they were friendly enough. Socialized. You've been talking to people at the university. What do people there say about him?"

"He was a loner. Was married once, but that was years ago and it didn't last long. His ex lives in Halifax. He's been out of the closet all the time he's been here. That's ten years. Isn't seeing anyone special as far as people know. Workaholic. They all expected him to be there forever. His students called him Harry, you know, Thom, Dyck and... They thought he was okay. That's all I've got so far. Your turn. Who's your main suspect?"

"Gerald Blaise's wife." And she told him about Budgie Torrance, how Gerald might have been planning to leave her and how much Budgie stood to benefit financially from him dying right now.

"Where was she yesterday morning?"

"In her apartment. The Ident guys got there at nine. She'd just stepped out of the shower. She doesn't have a car of her own and we still have Gerald's Audi. I don't know how she could have got to Riverside Park unless she took a cab. That could be traced."

"Have you thought that she might be working with someone else?"

"Someone who's doing the killing for her?"

"Well, you said she likes other guys too, right?" Budgie did. Was it possible that she was as tired of Gerald as he appeared to be of her? That she had taken another lover and together they had planned to murder her husband so she would be free of him and inherit all his wealth?

"And that person was someone Thom Dyck knew as well?" It was entirely possible.

"I guess that would let the Sinclairs off the hook," he said. The city police were still keeping an eye open for Jem Sinclair for assaulting the kid at the school who had told everyone about Zeke stealing a car with the dead body in the trunk. "Unless she hired Jem."

"How would she know him?" Roxanne asked. "And none of this explains why someone has stolen Gerald Blaise's artwork. I'm not completely done with the Sinclairs, though. I need to know if Zeke lied about throwing away the keys. Maybe the murderer took Blaise's house keys but left the car keys in the car. Zeke's been released from the Youth Centre on a promise to appear in court in a couple of weeks. Into the care of his aunt. She's taken him up north meantime, but he'll be back. Maybe I should talk to Jem."

"Don't you go looking for Jem yourself." Cooper Jenkins' fingers tapped on the side of his mug. "He's an evil little bastard."

She stared at him. "You've told me that already. I can take care of myself."

"Sure, you can," he said, "but I'm telling you, Jem Sinclair is mean. And tough."

"So am I." She tried not to sound riled. "And I can run real fast. Thom Dyck still had his keys on him?"

"Yup." He stretched back and ran a hand through his hair. "A debit card and his driver's licence too. Looks like whoever killed him didn't take a thing. Blaise's wallet was emptied, right?"

"Zeke could have lied about that. He could have stolen whatever was in it. Maybe he didn't find the cash to buy hot dogs in the glove box."

The woman constable who had been at the site of Thom Dyck's murder appeared in the door of the cafeteria. She signalled to Jenkins.

"There's Meera. Guess I'm wanted." He rose to his feet. Roxanne reached for her coat. It wasn't quite dry. Meantime, they agreed that they would check in with each other. Pass on information. Cooperate, if they had to. As she walked out the building, she thought about the idea that Budgie could have persuaded someone to do her killing for her, someone with whom she was in a relationship. Someone in Winnipeg. That person could have killed Gerald as well. If it were true, Budgie herself wouldn't be forthcoming but no doubt someone at Prairie Theatre Centre would be happy to tell.

OUTSIDE, THE SLEET had turned to rain. Eighty kilometres north, Margo Wishart sloshed through the downpour. She'd grown up in Scotland. She knew how to dress for weather like this. She wore a hooded oiled linen raincoat and rubber boots that reached her knees. Bob, her black dog, ran through the puddles. He didn't mind the rain either, and his morning walk was late. Margo had slept in. It had been almost three in the morning when she'd finished working on Gerald Blaise's notebook and got to bed, and after ten when she had wakened. She wasn't planning to walk far. Sasha Rosenberg's house lay not far ahead, with the promise of a blazing fire in the woodstove and brunch.

Soon Bob had been towelled off and lay by the warm hearth alongside his pal, Lenny. Margo sat at a small table in Sasha's tiny living room, opposite Roberta Axelsson. Roberta had brought eggs, fresh laid by her own hens.

"So," Sasha said, bringing omelettes to the table. "What's this job you're working on?"

"I'm not allowed to tell you. It's police business." Margo spread butter on her toast.

"She's checking out all the artwork in Gerald Blaise's apartment. You know, the guy from Prairie Theatre Centre that got murdered. Sergeant Calloway asked her to." Roberta scooped up a forkful of egg. "To find out what's been stolen as well as Annie Chan's painting."

Sasha turned to Margo. "You're working for them? The RCMP?"

"I am. Just advising." Margo tried to think of a way to change the subject.

"But more stuff's disappeared, right? A painting by a guy called Bruce something or other…" said Roberta.

Margo put down a forkful of egg. "Who told you that?" she asked.

"Budgie Torrance told the whole cast of *Macbeth* and Jazz Elliot told me," Roberta waved her own fork, cheerfully complacent. "Jazz says it's a real pain. The RCMP keep wrecking her rehearsal schedule and they get Budgie all worked up."

"You've been talking to Jazz?"

"Sure, I have. She phoned last night. About knitting. She checked out my site on Ravelry. Wants to come out here and see my dyed wool. It's Thanksgiving weekend coming up and she has Monday off so I told her to drive out and I'll stuff a chicken. Early dinner or a late lunch. She said she'd rent a car. Can you both come?"

Margo had forgotten about Canadian Thanksgiving. She hadn't grown up with that feast and now her kids lived elsewhere. But if Roberta was cooking and Jazz Elliot was going to be in attendance, she'd make a pumpkin pie and be there.

"You couldn't have just been working on Gerald Blaise's art collection until three in the morning." Sasha refilled their coffee mugs, pottery ones, fired in her kiln. "What else are you doing that's so important?"

Margo sighed. Both her friends looked at her expectantly. She put down her fork.

"I told you. I can't tell you," she said. "Not for now. It's confidential police business." She looked at them regretfully, her two best friends, her confidantes. "Let's just eat our eggs."

"Ha," said Roberta. "Bet Jazz will know. We'll find out on Monday."

ROXANNE SAT IN her cold car in the downtown parking lot watching rain stream down her windshield while the engine ran. The temperature had risen above zero, just. She was wet again, and cold. She turned the heat up high and checked her phone. Margo Wishart had sent the transcribed copy of Gerald Blaise's diary. That had been quick. There was a message from Frank Moran asking her to call him. Right away.

The secretary patched her through to Moran's office. He did not sound pleased. He had heard from Annabel Torrance, he said. It seemed the police were harassing her. Didn't she, as a woman officer, understand the strain Ms. Torrance was under? How difficult it was for Annabel to tackle the role of Lady Macbeth when she was so recently bereaved? Especially given how Gerald had died, and how recently? It was important that she succeed. The theatre company was depending on it. Pressure from the RCMP was not helpful at this time. Roxanne listened to the lecture, watching the wipers sweep the glass in front of her clean, again and again.

"Confidentially, sir, Annabel Torrance is a suspect," she stated. She looked down the street towards the tall building that housed Frank Moran's large, warm office. She could just make it out through the misty haze. "She inherits a great deal of money from Gerald Blaise's death. She has the motive and the means."

"She was in Regina," Frank Moran snapped back, as if that ended the matter. Budgie could have driven to Winnipeg and back overnight, she told him. "I have to talk to her again," she continued. "There has been a second suspicious death."

"Thom Dyck, right?" He knew about that already. "Go easy on her," he insisted. "You don't really imagine she killed Gerald, do you?" He made the suggestion sound ridiculous. "Those two got along perfectly well. And the professor? She barely knew him."

"We believe that Gerald Blaise was planning to leave her, sir," said Roxanne Calloway. "And move to B.C. to live with someone else."

"He was? Really?" She had actually managed to surprise him. "He was going to bail out on the theatre and do a runner on us?"

"It looks like it, sir."

"Well, well. Don't make that public knowledge without letting me know first, Sergeant. And like I said, try not to get our leading lady too upset. We need her up on that stage three weeks from now. How close are you to making an arrest?"

"I can't say," she said.

"You need to get this case wrapped up quickly," said Moran. He didn't speculate as to what would happen if it was Annabel Torrance that ended up in custody, but she had no doubt he was considering the possibility.

"We are doing our best, sir." She was glad to hang up and drive away.

14

ROXANNE SAT IN her office at HQ and closed her computer. She had finished reading the transcription of Gerald Blaise's diary that Margo Wishart had sent her. It went back to April, when the previous season had concluded at Prairie Theatre Centre. The theatre season ran from October to the spring. It had been an okay year. They'd made enough on sales to break even, but Gerald had been aware of some discontent among his audience and his critics. He played it safe, they said. Same old, same old. Was he getting stale? There was no mention in his notebook of leaving Budgie, or his job, back then. He did worry that he might have to leave PTC sooner than later.

"I'm maybe played out," he had written, April 25th. "I do what I can. I'm not going to change now. Probably lucky I've lasted this long." He thought it possible that his contract might not be renewed. He might only have one year left at Prairie Theatre Centre. And if that was going to happen, he preferred to walk away from the job on his own two feet.

He'd met Tim Baldwin at his art exhibition in May, at Maxwell Fergusson's gallery in Toronto. The attraction was instant. Gerald was thrilled that this beautiful young man seemed to return his interest.

"Couldn't do much about it last night," he had written. "Had Budgie in tow. And I'm off to New York with her for four days. But I'll maybe arrange a trip out to the West Coast when I get back."

And he had. Later that month, he was staying in Tim Baldwin's studio on Denman Island, and he was in love. "I haven't felt this alive in years," he wrote. He wasn't sure if Tim was as smitten as he was. Not then. But once he got back to Winnipeg they had FaceTimed, regularly and soon Budgie had taken off to go work at the Shaw Festival in Ontario.

"The coast is clear," he had crowed. "I'm going to Denman for the weekend!" That had been June. In July, he had taken Tim to the U.K. for ten days to catch some plays, see some art. Then their jaunts together had had to cease for a while. He had already agreed to teach a course for three weeks at the university in August, and Budgie would be back middle of the month.

He and Thom Dyck had been close friends, in the easy, intimate way of old lovers. They sometimes had dinner together. He had told Thom about his new passion.

"Great to have Thom to talk to," he had scribbled on August 15th.

> He thinks I should go for it. Start a new life with Tim, get away from all the pressure of running PTC, I could relax and concentrate on collecting art. Stop having to pretend with Budgie. I can afford it, after all. Why not? Just have to get through this year first. My contract with PTC is airtight. Earliest I can leave is end of July next year.

Then, a few days later:

> Cute girl in class. Had fun chatting her up at a party. Got a lecture from Thom. *Hands off the students.* He doesn't get it that I like women too. It's not happening with Budgie, though. Can't act like I'm interested when I'm not. She pretends she doesn't care, but maybe she does. That Chloe girl would have been a bit of fun. Don't think I can ever be monogamous. Tim wouldn't expect that, would he?

He described how he and Thom Dyck had had lunch at the university's faculty club a few days later. Thom had said to him:

> You'll never settle down with one person, will you?
> Look what happened the minute you set eyes on that
> Delaney girl. Old impulses don't die.

And Gerald had thought he might be right. But, Roxanne considered, could Gerald stand it if he thought that Tim Baldwin was doing the same, screwing someone else? Would he, perhaps, be jealous? Tim was almost thirty years younger than he. And handsome. Might Gerald wonder how long Tim would want to stay with him, a much older man? She soon found an answer. He had discussed it with Thom Dyck:

> Thom says I shouldn't worry. That I'm a man of means
> and Tim's a starving artist. Maybe he's right and the
> boy's only interested in me because I'm rich and I know
> people in the arts. I hope not. His birthday's coming
> up. I should get him a nice present.

He still had to direct *Macbeth* before he could go to B.C. again. Budgie would be off to Toronto after that. She was scheduled to start rehearsing a play for the Tarragon Theatre. She'd be gone for six whole weeks, right through Christmas. He could invite his young man to spend a few days with him in Europe. Florence? Spend Christmas together in Paris? He was sure that Tim had never been there.

Roxanne closed the file. So, Gerald Blaise really had thought about leaving his wife and his job in less than a year, but there was no suggestion that Budgie knew that. It was possible that she knew that their marriage had cooled, but that was different from knowing that they were finally over. They had had difficult times before and had always come back together. Why would she suspect it would be otherwise this time?

The diary revealed that Gerald and the professor had been far closer friends than the police had realized. Perhaps Thom Dyck had known something about Gerald and that had led to his death? She needed to let Cooper Jenkins know about that.

And she could tell him that she had a last name for the girl that Gerald had been interested in at that party in August. Izzy had tracked it down. Chloe Delaney. Izzy would go talk to her, once she knew where to find her. They didn't need to consult with the city police before she did that.

JAZZ ELLIOTT SAT in Tamsin Longstaff's office. "Budgie is not doing well," she said. It was Jazz's lunch break. Neither of them felt like eating. Jazz burrowed into her voluminous sweater while the rain thumped on the roof overhead. "She's a mess. Thinks she's doing fine but she's not. Can't really blame her, can you? Gerald's death has hit her hard. She's trying to hold it together but the situation keeps getting worse. Did you know that the police think maybe she killed him?"

"Really? Why?" Tamsin clicked a sentence into her computer. Her nails and lips were crimson today, to match her suit. "She can't have. She was in Regina."

"Ah, but they've figured out that she could have driven to Winnipeg and back again overnight."

"Geez." Tamsin stopped typing. She folded her arms as she thought it through. Five, six hours either way, two hours to have a fight with Gerald, kill him and stow his body in the trunk of his car. Fourteen hours max. "I suppose she could. But why would she want to kill Gerald? They always managed to get along just fine."

"Not any longer," said Jazz, happily spitting out the bad news, curled into the chair. "He was planning to leave her. But you knew that, didn't you?"

Tamsin shifted on her seat. "Well," she admitted, "he did kind of hint, once. Cooked up a boeuf bourguignon and invited me over one Friday night. Opened some French burgundy to go with it. Chocolate pavlova with raspberries for dessert. We were into a second bottle when he told me. But it was still just an idea. That's how Gerald worked, he liked to talk stuff through before he made up his mind. He'd been arguing with Budgie on the phone. About the Scottish play. She never wanted him to direct it, you know. She hated how he wanted it to look. And she told him so. Hurt his feelings. But that's happened before. He'd have got over it. They'd have made up. They always did."

"He had a new guy in his life. In B.C. Some people say he was going to quit his job here and go live with him." They listened to the drumbeat of the rain outside the window as they gazed into opposite corners of the room.

"He'd told Budgie that?"

"If he didn't, someone else sure has. Did Gerald say anything to you about it?"

Tamsin unfolded her arms and leaned in confidentially. She lowered her voice. "His name is Tim Baldwin. Sculptor. Very good-looking. Gerald showed me a photo. And he really liked him, you could tell, the way he talked. But I wasn't worried. These things never lasted with Gerald. He was flirting with some student at a party not long after he told me. A girl. And would that guy have wanted to go and live with Gerald forever? He can't be much over thirty. That's half Gerald's age."

"But he would inherit all that money if he played along."

"Gerald would have changed his will and cut Budgie out? You think?" They looked intently at one another, considering the fact that Gerald Blaise's wife, the lead character in the play they were producing, had a very good reason to want rid of him.

"Shit," said Jazz Elliot. "What if she gets arrested?" She unravelled herself from her cocoon and sat forward onto the edge of her chair. "We've got to replace her anyway, Tamsin. That's what I came in here to tell you. I'm trying to pull this show together and Budgie isn't up to the job. Not in the state she's in right now."

Tamsin looked down at her from her slightly higher perch. "She's got a contract," she declared. "I offered to cancel. Before you went into rehearsal. She insisted she could do it. What do I say to her? I'm firing you because we think the police are going to arrest you for murder? We don't know that, do we? She'd go legal if we did it and she'd probably win. And the arts community in this town would act like it was character assassination. Social media would eat us alive. They'd hate us for it."

"They'd hate you, Tamsin, not me." Jazz's lips stretched in a sly smile. "Look, I can hold things together at my end. I've got this cast on my side. Most of the actors are imports, they don't have the loyalty thing to Gerald and Budgie that the locals have. I make sure that when we go into that rehearsal hall, the baggage gets dropped at the door. You know how it is. We create our own little world in there." She was getting into her usual stride, waxing eloquent.

"Problem is that the real world is getting far too close. Death and murder in the play, and here it is, going on for real all around us. I think Budgie's on the verge of losing it, and how can she act Lady M going mad if she's on the edge herself? She's wound up tight. We're all trying to get her to relax but Danny, our Macbeth, says it's like acting opposite a zombie. This play isn't good for her right now, and she's useless, the state that she's in. The cast all know it. They bitch to Nell Bronson about it all the time. They're sorry for Budgie, we all are, but she's going to blow it."

"It's that bad?"

"It is. Not surprising, really. Think of what she's got on her plate. The funeral to plan. The lawyers to deal with. The accountant's been bugging her to make decisions. She hasn't had time to grieve. She's burning out on us fast. If she's going to have to go, Tamsin, it has to happen now. You know that. We need somebody good to take over that role, and we need her right away. Maggie Soames. That's who we need."

Tamsin knew that Jazz Elliot was right. The actors who were as good as Budgie were few. Maggie Soames was probably the best of them but Maggie was in London, England, and Maggie would come at a steep price. She also knew that the fallout from firing Budgie might bring down single-ticket sales. Budgie had a loyal following among the Winnipeg theatre-going public. Maybe even Maggie Soames couldn't save them from a loss. There was a rap at the door. Jazz stretched out a hand and turned the handle. Sergeant Roxanne Calloway appeared in the doorway.

"Okay, Jazz. Give me a day to work on this. I'll get back to you."

Jazz lowered her feet to the floor and hauled herself out of the chair. Roxanne reached out a hand to stop her from leaving. "Maybe you should stay," she said. "You might be able to help." Jazz sank back into her chair and pulled her sleeves around her. Roxanne found the one remaining chair.

"I need to ask you about Annabel Torrance," she said. A look of alarm flashed between the other two women.

"You don't really think she did it?" Tamsin said, weariness and dread in every syllable.

"We're considering several options." Roxanne smiled a tight smile in response. She wished she could believe that.

"That's stupid." Jazz peered out from inside her big collar, a bug in a rug, her big glasses, green ones, sticking out the top. "She was in Saskatchewan. How do you think she managed it? Hired a thug with a knife to kill him?"

"No!" Roxanne started in spite of herself. How had they figured that out as a possibility? "Never even thought that! What made you think that?"

"Didn't. The guys in the shop did. You and another cop were seen snooping around with some kid from the North End in the back of a car."

The theatre grapevine was efficient, and sometimes fairly accurate. Everything that happened around here was noticed. Except for the killing of Gerald Blaise. No one had witnessed that.

"I need to know if Budgie is in a romantic relationship with anyone in Winnipeg right now," she said.

Tamsin sucked in her cheeks. It made her look gaunt and older. "Don't think so," she said. "She hasn't been around much this summer. She gets along with Danny Foley. He's playing Macbeth. But Danny's a happily married man. She'd be more likely to have been messing around with someone in Regina. Or at Shaw."

"We've been told about someone called Sam Geddes," said Roxanne.

"Oh, him?" Jazz pivoted her head, owl-like. "Makes sense. Sam's always good for a quick fuck."

"Jazz…" said Tamsin.

"Well, it's true. He's got to have shagged his way through most of Regina by now. Couldn't be him, though. He's a lazy kinda tomcat. Couldn't muster the energy to kill anyone if he wanted to. If that's what you're thinking." She'd got the RCMP's thinking dead right again.

"I can't think of anyone here right now." Tamsin sighed in frustration. She had enough to think about without this.

"Tell you what." Jazz hoisted herself out of her chair. "I think you've got it all wrong. Budgie acts tough but she's not. She really cared about Gerald. She misses him like hell." But then another thought occurred to her. "Although, if she did have something to do with his murder, maybe that's another reason she's having trouble playing Lady Mac. Maybe she's consumed with guilt. I've really got to go. There's a whole cast downstairs waiting for me."

"Don't you say a word to anyone about any of this," Tamsin called after her as she disappeared out the door.

"Who, me?" asked Jazz Elliott without looking back.

15

CHLOE DELANEY SHARED space with a couple of other students in an apartment in a red brick walk-up, not unlike the one that Alison Beck lived in. It was in the same area of the city but was not near the river and was decidedly shabbier. Chloe was not at home, a roommate told Izzy McBain, eyeing her suspiciously around the door. "She's in class. I think."

Izzy drove to the university and found her way across campus from the parkade, past students bustling to class and others lounging in hallways. She knew her way around campus. She'd done a degree in criminology, straight out of high school. The place hadn't changed all that much. She cut through a building, down a long corridor, past closed doors, voices droning inside, then followed a path that passed between grassy lawns and trees. Raindrops dripped down. The few students outside had their shoulders hunched. The rain had stopped but a wind had got up. Izzy pulled up the collar of her jacket and tucked her ponytail in so it wouldn't blow into her face.

The Fine Arts building was newish, grey and glassy outside but inside it seemed grubby. So did its students, most of them dressed in shabby clothes, dark coloured, many spattered with paint. They carried large boards under their arms or lugged heavy backpacks. One of them showed her the way to the office. He pointed with ink-stained fingers.

A middle-aged woman frowned up at her from behind a computer. Izzy announced who she was and held up her ID. The woman hauled herself to her feet and reluctantly approached the front desk. Two other clerks, similarly engaged behind their computer screens, took notice but stayed where they were. Izzy realized that they had thought she was just another student. She should have braided her hair and fastened it up, like she did when she was in uniform. She explained that she needed to find Chloe Delaney. The woman sniffed.

"We don't give out private information," she informed her. Izzy tipped her head to one side.

"I need to speak to her," she insisted. The woman did not budge. Another, older, called to her.

"Martha," she said. "She's police. You can make an exception." Martha obliged, but took her time looking up the day's class records. Eventually she placed a printout in front of Izzy. It showed that Chloe Delaney should be in a pottery class right now. There was a room number.

"Where do I find it?" asked Izzy. The woman indicated double doors to her right.

"Down there. To the end. Then turn left." She watched Izzy go, watchful and wary as a guard dog.

In the hallways of this building, most doors had a window. Izzy glanced into some as she passed. In one, students stood at large easels, painting. In another, they sat astride small wooden benches, their drawings propped in front of them. In a third, cut-out photographs were being picked through and discussed. Izzy had never seen anywhere quite like it. The hallways were mostly empty.

She turned the corner and found the studio number that she needed at the end of another corridor. She opened the door. All the occupants wore loose cotton shirts or large aprons to protect their clothes. Some sat at pottery wheels, spinning round shapes. Others stood at tables, pounding lumps of clay, some red, some pale grey. One was rolling a sheet of it out flat. She spotted Chloe Delaney instantly, recognized her from her photo. Chloe had cropped dark hair, revealing a perfect oval skull and even, symmetrical features, a small, neat nose, a wide mouth and startlingly large eyes, rimmed in black liner. Her eyebrows were finely drawn, the fingers with which she handled the clay were slim and long, and, right now, caked in terracotta. The shirt she wore over torn jeans was spattered with reddish brown dirt and there was some smudged on her face.

"What do you want?" A man, apparently the instructor, stood behind one of the potters. He wore the same gear as his students and had a layer of stubbly beard.

"I need to speak to Chloe Delaney," said Izzy.

"She's busy. You'll have to wait." The man turned his attention back to his student's work in progress.

"Constable Isabel McBain, RCMP," said Izzy. She hadn't wanted to state her credentials in front of the whole class but sometimes you had no option, especially when you looked as young as they did. She'd spoken loudly. The slapping of clay stopped. The wheels ceased spinning. One pot collapsed in on itself. "Oh, shit," said the student.

"Clo," said the instructor. "Get her out of here."

Chloe Delaney reached for a sheet of plastic. "Just give me a minute to wrap this and clean up," she said across the room. She held up a mud-stained hand, apologetic. Even dressed as she was, smeared with dirt, she looked pretty.

Five minutes later, she shook Izzy's hand. Her own was warm and damp, traces of red clay stuck around short nails. She still wore the work shirt, obviously expecting to return to class. "We can go to the lounge." She led the way back along the corridor and opened a side door.

It led to a sitting area, provided with sofas and chairs. One wall looked out onto a courtyard. It was grassed, with some ornamental trees. Pride of place was given to large sculptures, in stone and metal. One was constructed from sheets of coloured plastic. Wooden benches were conveniently placed to sit and contemplate each creation, but for now they were wet and deserted. A group of students was seated in earnest discussion in one corner of the room. They barely glanced as Chloe led the way to a couple of armchairs beside the window. No one was near. It wasn't a bad place to talk.

Chloe Delaney tucked one leg up under her as she sat, loose limbed, graceful in spite of her grubbiness.

"Is this about Gerald Blaise and Professor Dyck?" she asked in a soft, low voice. "They're both dead, right?"

"You were in a class this summer…" Izzy began, pulling a pen and notebook out of her pocket, ready to make notes.

"That's right. Contemporary Canadian Theatre. I did it as an elective. Thought it might be interesting."

"And was it?"

"Not really." Chloe Delaney had a generous smile, perfect teeth. "Well, it was entertaining enough. He told us lots of stories about people he knew, fun, really. I knew a couple of the theatre students. They loved it. They knew who he was talking about. I thought he'd teach us more about the plays, but he didn't." She wasn't reluctant to talk. She seemed eager to help.

"And Professor Dyck?"

"Harry? I hardly knew him. That's the only theatre course I've ever taken."

"But you went to a party at his house."

"Oh, that." Her nose squished as if she had smelled something bad. "The whole class was invited. It was kind of expected that we'd all show up. And there was a guy I liked that was going. Turned out he was taken." She shrugged like it didn't matter. It probably didn't. A girl who looked like Chloe Delaney probably didn't lack admirers.

"We were told that Gerald Blaise really liked you."

"Can you believe it?" Chloe unwrapped her leg from under her and turned her large, dark eyes on Izzy. "Some of those old men just don't know when to quit, do they?" she said. "He wouldn't leave me alone. All smiles and a bit touchy, you know?" Her mouth puckered in distaste. "And his wife was there. She's famous. I saw her watching through the kitchen door. It wasn't like I was encouraging him. I had to signal to a friend to come rescue me. Went home not long after."

"So, was that the end of it?"

"No, it was not!" She leaned forward. Their heads were close. They could have been two girlfriends, confiding in one another. "He texted, later that night. Something about getting together after class for coffee. I wasn't sure what to do. I mean, he was my prof, right? If I said no, would he give me a bad grade? I told one of my roommates. She said, go tell Harry. So I checked Professor Dyck's office hours, he keeps them pasted on his door, and I stopped by on the Monday. Meantime, I got another text from Gerald. Had I received the first, was I okay? Just ignore him, my friend said, so I did."

"You called him Gerald?"

"Sure. He told us to. In the arts, we call most of our instructors by their first names."

"And Professor Dyck? What did he say when you told him?"

"He was just great!" Her wide smile brightened her face again. It made her look even younger than she was. She couldn't be much over twenty, if that, a third of Gerald Blaise's age. She could have been Izzy's kid sister. "I showed him the texts. He said not to worry, he'd talk to Gerald and if I heard from him again I should tell him right away. My marks were okay so far, so he said that shouldn't be a problem either. Told me to keep copies of my assignments and if it became an issue he would deal with it. But you know, it never was. Gerald stopped texting. He didn't pay any more attention to me than he did to anyone else after that, and my marks were good. I got an A. That's all I can tell you. Can I get back to class now?"

"Do you still have those texts?" Izzy asked. Of course she didn't. It had happened a couple of months ago. The class had ended a week after. Chloe Delaney had got on with her life.

"And you didn't see Professor Dyck again?"

"No. It's so sad, isn't it? What's happened to him. All the theatre students are just devastated."

"They liked him?"

"The ones that I know did. They don't think much of the woman that's taking over from him."

"Who's that?" Izzy asked, trying to pretend she wasn't interested.

"Madeleine something. She'll be in charge until they find a new department head and that could take forever. Look, I really should get back." She stood up, shook hands again and walked away. One of the other students said, "Hi, Clo, how're you doing?" as she passed them. They showed no interest at all in Izzy McBain.

Izzy splashed along a path, through the puddles. It was cold and damp outside, not much above zero, but the wind was at her back. Matt Stavros, her partner, was in class too, right now, in the Law building. He'd be done soon. She texted him. Meantime, she walked towards the college that housed the theatre department, her collar up. She could find out more about this Madeleine person while she was here. She passed students hurrying between classes. They paid her no attention.

The entrance to the theatre was at ground level, the door set back in a recess, stuffed with bunches of flowers, protected from the wind. There were photographs taped to the door itself, of Thom Dyck with his students, written notes, cards. A sign promoted a show to be presented in his honour. *We're Just Wild About Harry* it was called. It seemed he had directed a student production and set it in the nineteen twenties. Shots from that show decorated the poster. Kids doing the Charleston, grinning. Thom Dyck looking happy. The students had ignored the police tape that blocked access to the doorway so they could lay their tributes. So did she. She ducked under it.

"Hey, you!" a voice hollered. She turned. "Oh, it's you. Foxy Roxy's sidekick," said Cooper Jenkins. "Whatya doin' here?"

She told him. She'd learned nothing much from Chloe Delaney and now she wanted to find out about a prof called Madeleine.

"Bissett," he said. "She's a bitch. I'd tell you but I've got a date coming up with your boss. I'll fill her in." And off he strode. Matt was walking towards her from the opposite direction. She waved, glad to see his friendly face.

"Let's go grab a pizza," she said, and tucked an arm through his.

JEM SINCLAIR HAD been taken into custody. He sat, looking mean and cool, in the chair that his younger brother had occupied on Sunday morning, a worker at his side, an older and tougher one than the one who had accompanied Zeke. Jem focused on a spot on the far wall, equidistant between Roxanne and Cooper Jenkins' heads, not acknowledging their presence. He didn't look much like his brother. Jem was slim, serious, his symmetrical features impassive, his lips and eyes arranged in narrow, horizontal lines. He was good-looking. Girls probably found him attractive. He'd been in trouble with the law since he was eleven and he understood the system well. He knew when he could keep silent and when he needed to reply. That wasn't often.

He didn't respond to questions about Gerald Blaise's red Audi and how it had been driven to The Locks by his brother Zeke, or to the suggestion that, since he was good with knives, he might have carried out the murder himself. His eyes didn't flicker when asked if he had taken Gerald's condo keys from his key ring and helped himself to some items from his apartment. He sat, one foot placed casually across a knee, hands in his lap, apparently at ease, as though he was waiting for their questions to end. He reacted only once.

"You beat up on that pal of Zeke's," Coop said. "Cut him up while you were at it. Why was it so important to get him to shut up?"

"Nobody messes with my brother." Jeremiah Sinclair turned a cold stare on him.

"Then tell us what you know about the Audi and its keys," Roxanne said. "Do that, then we won't have to talk to him again."

Jem Sinclair's black eyes turned to meet hers. "You heard me, bitch." The threat was spoken quietly, intense with loathing. Roxanne almost flinched.

"Respect, Jeremiah," Coop interjected. Jem Sinclair went back to studying the wall behind them. Roxanne had been threatened before. It came with the job and you didn't back off in the face of it.

"Did you know the guy who owned the car?" she demanded. Jem said not a word. Roxanne gave up. Pursuing this line of questioning was getting them nowhere. They watched as Zeke's handsome but dangerous brother was led out of the room, still ignoring them.

"I'm not going to find out about those missing keys," she said to Coop. It was grey and wet outside, rain dripping off trees.

"Got time for a quick coffee?" He had reached into his pocket for a pack of cigarettes. He lit one, his hand cupped around the flame. "You can tell me what you've been up to and I'll tell you all about Madeleine Bissett, the prof that had it in for Professor Dyck. The one that the university folks think might have wanted to get him out the way."

It was almost time to pick up her son from her sister's house, but she could text a message. Finn would be okay, he'd be happy playing with his cousin and their puppy and she knew her sister was home for the evening.

There was a coffee shop nearby. Cooper loaded his coffee with cream and sugar, as usual. She poured some tea. It came in a pretty ceramic pot, orange, to cheer up this wet day, said the server.

"Ladies first," he said. She wasn't going to argue. Budgie Torrance was still her main suspect, she told him. Budgie had the motive and she might have the means, especially if someone had collaborated with her.

"Not strong enough, is it?" Cooper Jenkins looked skeptical. "Why would anyone want to carry out a murder for her?"

"Money." Rain had begun to drizzle down outside again.

"Maybe." He wasn't convinced. "There's two murders. Why would she want the professor dead? He had nothing to do with Blaise wanting to leave her for another guy and take all his money with him."

"Unless Professor Dyck knew something. Gerald Blaise liked to confide in him." She lifted her cup. "Or maybe the two cases aren't linked at all. Maybe it's just a coincidence."

"Not a chance." Coop Jenkins reached into his pocket and pulled out some nicotine gum sticks. He unwrapped one and popped it in his mouth. "I don't believe in those."

"You just put out a cigarette," she said.

"So? I like a smoke with my coffee."

She drank some tea. If he wanted to kill himself with too much nicotine it wasn't her problem.

"What about the missing art?" she asked. "Did Thomas Dyck collect paintings? Has anything been stolen from him?"

Cooper Jenkins slid his mug aside. He put his forearms on the table and leaned forward. He smelled of smoke.

"Nope," he said. "Madeleine Bissett's the one we need to check out. She's a prof in the theatre department, was working there before Dyck, wanted the job that he got but she was too young back then, got passed over. And," he paused for effect, "she hated Dyck's guts. She'd been trying to get rid of him for years."

"Says who?"

"Everybody. Staff. Other profs. Older students. They all knew. See, there was this smear campaign, about three years back. Someone said he'd been 'consorting with boys.' Younger students. Not young enough for it to be pedophilia, she couldn't get him for that, but 'unprofessional conduct.'" He drew quotation marks with his fingers. "There was an inquiry. Found nothing wrong. The students said so, the other profs. Dyck liked to hang out with the kids after rehearsals, stuff like that, that was all. Nothing to it, they said. Your guy stood up for him."

"Gerald Blaise?"

"Yeah, him. Character witness. So there you have it. A connection." He sat back again, pleased at having proved his point.

"How do you know it was her who started it? The smear campaign?"

"Because people said so."

"And you've talked to her?"

"You bet." He tucked the wad of gum into one cheek. It made his face even more lopsided. "Ambitious, you can tell. Dresses artsy but expensive. Lots of black. Shiny Doc Martens. Hair shaved on one side, you know the type. Has her buddies, ones that back her up, women like her. Feminists." He watched her to see if she would react. Seemed to think it was funny when she didn't. "They encourage her. Say she should have had the job all along. Publishes more, works harder, is smarter than poor old Dyck."

"Where was she when the murders took place?"

"Home with her partner. Music prof. A guy. She's not a lezzie." He didn't bother to see if Roxanne would respond this time. "She was with him the night that Blaise is supposed to have died. Tuesday morning, she had a meeting at eleven. Says she was in her office before, but not long. So, nothing great in the way of alibis."

"Would she be capable of using a knife to kill someone?"

"Got a killer instinct," Coop Jenkins drawled. "You can tell. And she's fit. Works out. She swims. What do you know about Tamsin Longstaff?"

"Tamsin?" Roxanne lifted her cup. "Why are you asking?"

"This Bissett woman says that's who we should be talking to. Says she had it in for both of them, Blaise and Dyck. She works at PTC, right?"

"She does," said Roxanne Calloway. "Did Madeleine Bissett tell you why she thinks that?"

"She says Tamsin Longstaff was having it off with Gerald Blaise for years, then he got involved with Dyck a few years ago and broke it off with her, so she spread all these bad rumours about Dyck. Says she was the one who tried to get him fired, back then."

"And now?"

"Well." He spat the gum into its wrapper, folded it and dropped it into his coffee mug. "She says Longstaff's the one who makes everything happen at the theatre. Blaise let her get on with it, he was dead lazy, so she was in charge and the board knew it. The place is all she really cares about these days, Madeleine says." He pronounced her name syllable by syllable.

"How would she know that?"

"Oh, they're good buddies. Go for drinks, girlie stuff, you know. So, she thinks, Bissett does, that Tamsin Longstaff found out that Blaise was going to quit on her and she lost it with him. Got mad enough at him to kill him. She's pretty burned out, Bissett says. Works way too hard. Must have just cracked. But then," Coop continued, "the board chose Thomas Dyck to be in charge of some committee or other after Blaise was gone. That pissed her off, so she got rid of him too."

"Wow," said Roxanne. "Good story. Conjecture, every bit of it."

"Yeah. I need to check it out. At PTC. On your turf." He grinned. "But that's okay, right?" He wasn't asking. He was telling.

"Let's talk to her together," she said. "I'll see if she's available tomorrow."

"You do that." Coop Jenkins stood. "But if we find out it's her that did it, I get the credit, okay?"

Roxanne reached for her jacket. "And I need to talk to Madeleine Bissett too."

"Be my guest," he said. He waved goodbye as they reached the door. It was raining again. Roxanne pulled up her collar and hurried to her car.

16

FRIDAY MORNING FOUND the city encased in ice. The sun shone bright, making buildings and frosted grass sparkle; the air was crisp and cold and the roads were lethal. Crews were out doing their valiant best with sand and salt but cars kept sliding off highways and landing in ditches and radio stations advised which streets it was best to avoid due to collisions. Roxanne Calloway crawled her car to her sister's driveway and dropped off her son. She watched him slide his way up the path to the house. A tow truck drove by, dragging an SUV with the front fender bashed in.

The clock on her dashboard said it was just after 8:30 and her appointment with Dr. Madeleine Bissett was not until ten, but she began to edge her way to the university. Normally, she would have driven there in fifteen minutes but on this morning it took over an hour of stop and go in an endless traffic queue spewing exhaust fumes. Then she had to drive all the way to the top level of the university parkade to find a vacant spot. Fortunately, the paths that criss-crossed campus had been sanded to allow for safe walking at a reasonable pace. She was almost on time when she spotted Izzy McBain, sitting on a picnic table near the front door of the theatre building, wearing a winter parka, hood up, thumbing at her phone with fingerless mitts.

"Relax," said Izzy. "Bissett's running late. I got here early. Dropped Matt off. He had a class." Roxanne dropped onto the bench beside her. Izzy told her about Chloe Delaney, squinting into the sun. "I don't think she knows much, but that Blaise guy sure fancied himself. She's cute. And really young."

"Let's get inside," said Roxanne. She wasn't dressed as warmly as Izzy and she was cold. Inside, heat blasted down corridors as students scurried to class. The theatre department's secretary had not quite recovered from the shock of Professor Dyck's sudden death. She had a box of tissues to hand in case a memory caused tears to well up.

"Lovely man," she said. "Respectful. Kind. Wonderful to work with and the students loved him." She was more circumspect with regard to Dr. Bissett.

"I'm not surprised she's late for your meeting," she said. "Happens all the time, not just when the roads are bad." Meantime, she unlocked Thom Dyck's door for them. "The police, the other ones, have been through it all," she said, obviously curious as to why the RCMP were now snooping around.

"We just need a quick look." Roxanne had no intention of telling her anything.

Ident had removed any computer equipment that had been on Dyck's desk. Two walls were stacked, floor to ceiling, with bookshelves, filled with neatly arranged books, binders, papers. A window ran the length of another, facing north, away from the sun's glare.

"There's Dr. Bissett coming now." The secretary pointed at a figure in black approaching along a path, wearing a large hooded black cape, a long leather skirt and boots to match.

"Looks like a bat," said Izzy McBain.

Before long, they were escorted to another office. The professor hung the cape up on a hanger behind the door and indicated two upright chairs that faced her desk. She didn't smile. She was too cool for that. Now she took her seat, laced her fingers in front of her and sighed.

"Such a busy time," she said. "So much to do in the wake of Dr. Dyck's unfortunate demise." And here she was having her precious time eaten up yet again by the police, she implied. She had a faint British accent, evident in precise enunciation and a lengthening of the vowel sounds. She had studied for her PhD in the U.K., she answered, preening at being asked. She spoke as if she inhabited a Victorian novel. "It is unfortunate, so unfortunate." She herself had a full schedule and now there was a department to run, plus the student council had decided to present this benefit show in honour of poor Thomas. "One could not say no."

"The city police are investigating," she continued. "And you are RCMP? May I ask why you are involved?" She pronounced the word like an upper-class Englishwoman, with a diphthong.

"We are investigating the death of Gerald Blaise," Roxanne explained.

"And?"

"You knew him?"

"I did. Of course. You think the two deaths are connected?" Like Frank Moran before her, Madeleine Bissett apparently preferred to ask the questions herself.

"Tamsin Longstaff is a friend of yours?" Roxanne asked back.

"Indeed, she is. Why do you wish to know about Tamsin?"

Izzy was looking from one to the other as the questions bounced back and forth, like watching a tennis game.

"She may have told you about how things were run at the theatre. About her relationship with Gerald Blaise," Roxanne hinted. The professor unlaced her fingers and swivelled her chair so she could gaze out the window.

"I see," she said, as she considered how she might reply. Roxanne and Izzy waited.

"Tamsin is a very dear friend," she said, having made her decision. "Has been for many years. She does wonderful work at PTC, she is an absolute treasure. She is the person who keeps the place running, has done for years. Gerald Blaise was a bit of a loose cannon, if you ask me, but Tamsin was able to keep him under control. Ensure he didn't make any rash decisions, didn't blow the budget."

"She was once romantically involved with Gerald. Wasn't she?"

The lips pursed. Gimlet eyes turned on Roxanne. "I see. You've discovered quite a bit already, haven't you?" she queried, not expecting an answer. Then she sighed again, as though having to tell this was a great burden.

"Tamsin adored Gerald," she remarked. "His death has been very hard on her. You must be kind to her, officer."

Roxanne remembered the tight-lipped, constrained expression on Tamsin Longstaff's face when she had seen the dead body at the morgue. "He was married to Annabel Torrance and he had a lot of affairs. The one with Tamsin was long over," she felt compelled to point out.

"Indeed. But she was still close to him."

"How close?"

"Oh, nothing like that. You're right, it was years ago. But their relationship had evolved." There was that old pronunciation again. "She became his right arm. He depended on her. Theirs was a true and lasting partnership of a different kind."

"And if Gerald Blaise was going to leave PTC, it was about to end."

"But was he? If Tamsin thought that she never told me," Madeleine Bissett cut in, too quickly. Roxanne didn't believe her.

"She confided in you. Over a drink or two."

"She did. Still does. And I hope she will continue to do so," declared Dr. Bissett. "Of course, Tamsin is older than me. By quite a few years. She's getting close to retirement age, over sixty, although she doesn't look it. A change of leadership at the theatre is unfortunate at this point in her career. She expected Gerald to be there for another five years. By then she might have been ready to retire herself. She would have helped the board find a new artistic director, made sure the theatre was in good financial shape, and then bowed out, graciously. She had it all planned. She told me, more than once. Killing Gerald right now wouldn't make any sense at all, so if that is what you are imagining, I suggest you put that idea aside. And Tamsin has quite enough on her plate trying to keep things going in the wake of that dreadful murder without you casting blame in her direction."

Roxanne could see Izzy McBain supressing a smile as Dr. Bissett continued to talk down to them in her affected accent. Madeleine Bissett might think of herself as knowledgeable and very smart but she didn't seem to realize that she had just incriminated her friend, lent credence to the theory that Tamsin could have reacted badly on hearing that Gerald Blaise did intend to leave his job, wrecking her own plan for the final few years of her career.

"Is she for real?" asked Izzy as they walked back across campus afterwards. Where the sun hit the ground, the ice had melted. Where it hadn't, the grass was still crusted with frost. "What a drama queen. Who does she think she is? Helen Mirren? Did you see those pictures she had on her wall?" There had been a large abstract painting hanging behind Madeleine Bissett's head. It was not the only one. Roxanne had counted three others. They were smaller but also darkly dramatic. "One of them looks a bit like one of Annie Chan's." Roxanne had forgotten that Izzy had visited Annie's house in the Interlake and had seen some of her work.

"You're right," said Roxanne. "And if she buys paintings, she had something in common with Gerald Blaise. But right now, I'm more interested in what she knows about Tamsin Longstaff."

"So how come we're going to talk to Margo Wishart again?"

They were walking towards the Fine Arts building. Margo had said she'd be free after class, and there had been no message to say that the icy highway had deterred her from driving into Winnipeg that morning.

"Because we're here, and she's been checking stuff out. About all that art Gerald had." Roxanne's phone buzzed. Tracy Ross. "I need to take this. I'll catch up to you." She watched Izzy stride away, her ponytail bobbing behind her. She stepped off the path to allow a clutch of students to pass but stayed in a patch of sunlight.

"You wanna talk to me?" The voice at the other end of the phone was loud, with a trace of an Anishinaabe accent.

"I do," said Roxanne. "Is Zeke still with you?"

"Yep. You talked to him already." The answer was wary.

"I have. I just have a question…"

"Just one?" Zeke's aunt interrupted her.

"I think so."

"You can ask it on the phone? I don't need to bring him in to see you?"

"Can I talk to him now?" Roxanne asked.

"Hey, Zeke," she heard Tracy Ross call, "that woman from the RCMP wants to ask you something." Then she was back on the line. "Just one question. Okay? That's all."

"That should be it."

"Better be. I'll be listening." Tracy Ross, Mama Bear, wasn't at all scared of some woman sergeant from the RCMP.

"Hi." Zeke sounded reluctant to talk.

"You remember the keys you said you found in the red Audi?"

"Yeah."

"The ones you said you threw in the river?"

"Right." He sounded less wary, now that he had some idea of why she was calling. "I got rid of them, told ya already."

"Was there just the car key on the ring?" she asked. "Or were there house keys as well?"

There was silence at the other end. She could picture Zeke Sinclair screwing up his face, trying to figure out why she wanted to know.

"Don't think so," he finally said.

"So there was just a car key?"

"It was one of those fancy ones." She could hear the shrug in his voice. Telling her this didn't matter much to him. "A big one, the kind that has buttons you push and the key pops out. There was a little key as well. A yellow one."

"The kind you'd open a padlock with?" she prompted. "Or a mailbox?"

"Yeah, sure, like that. And a leather tag, for that Volkswagen place in St. James."

"Nothing else? You're sure?"

"Maybe another key, but not for a house," said Zeke Sinclair. "We done?"

"You sure?"

"I said so, didn't I?" She could hear an edge creeping into his voice.

"Go eat your Cheerios," she heard Tracy say. Zeke must be having a late breakfast. "You got what you wanted?" snapped the aunt's voice again.

"He's been very helpful," said Roxanne. "Tell him thanks from me."

"The cop says thanks," she heard Tracy say loudly. "You want to talk to him again, you call me first. Right?" And she hung up.

Roxanne walked along the path, pocketing her phone. Zeke was probably telling the truth. The car keys were gone. A padlock key could be for many things. A storage locker, a box, a door, anywhere. And had Gerald kept the missing house keys on the same ring? It wouldn't be difficult to find out. Budgie Torrance would know. So would Tamsin Longstaff. If they were gone, the killer probably had taken them.

Roxanne received a warmer reception than Izzy had done the previous day at the front desk of the Fine Arts building. Perhaps it was because she looked less like a student, was older, appeared more professional in her tailored black wool coat, with her cap of neatly trimmed red hair. She displayed her ID and was greeted with a thin smile. Dr. Wishart was summoned and soon led her upstairs. Her office was tiny.

"I'm a mere sessional," she said. "I share it. Mine is the tidy side." One half of the desk was littered with papers, books. On the other was a MacBook, a paper notebook, some written notes and a telephone. A fabric hanging was suspended behind Margo's side, a nude drawing in black ink on the other. There were two bookshelves, one Margo's, the other her colleague's. On top of the neat one there was an espresso maker, cups and a carton of milk. Izzy sat in the only visitor chair, drinking a latte.

"I made one for you. Margo showed me how." She pointed at a cup.

"Aren't those machines great? Shall I get you one as a wedding present?" Margo stopped on her way into the hallway to fetch another chair.

"We're not getting married," said Izzy. "What's my mom been saying now?"

"She talks to Roberta," Margo laughed. "She's telling people it'll maybe be this summer."

"She wishes." Izzy drank her coffee. "The house is going up fast," she called after Margo's disappearing back. "She expects we'll move in."

"You won't?" Roxanne had expected that Izzy and Matt would stay in town while he worked on his degree, but the new house in the Interlake was only an hour's commute away.

"Haven't decided yet." Izzy shrugged.

Margo's desk lay along one wall. She returned and passed Roxanne a chair, then sat on the same side as her guests. They formed a cozy trio as they sipped their lattes, but Roxanne hadn't come here to listen to neighbourhood gossip. She pointed to the notes on Margo's side of the desk.

"What have you found?" she asked.

Margo was happy to tell. She had had an interesting evening, the night before, talking to Maxwell Fergusson in Toronto while the lake outside her window roared and surged and the rain that battered her windows turned to sleet, then froze.

"He says the collection that Gerald's aunt and uncle amassed was worth millions. They were buying art back in the fifties and sixties, for quite reasonable prices. Their house was full of it when Mrs. Balfour died. It had all accumulated in value. They donated most of it to the Art Gallery of Ontario."

"They gave it away?" Izzy looked incredulous.

"Mrs. Balfour's estate would have got a tax break for the donation," Margo explained. "But yes. They believed it belonged to the nation. They were arts philanthropists. Other people have done the same. Gerald got to choose six pieces for himself, the AGO took the bulk of it and the rest, the pieces neither of them wanted, were sold. Gerald got the money." She smiled. "Guess what else Maxwell told me."

She wrapped the scarf she wore around her neck a little closer and crossed one leg over the other, as if she was hugging the secret to herself. Then she announced, "The Balfours had a daughter. Emilia. Their only child. Ran away, back in the sixties. Maxwell was only a child at the time but his father told him all about it. How Mr. Balfour followed his daughter and tried to get her to come home but she wouldn't. She was living in some kind of commune in B.C. Wouldn't leave. After a while, the Balfours wrote her off. They were proud, Maxwell says. Presbyterian. Upright citizens. They disinherited her. And Gerald became their heir instead. They paid for him to go to a good school, supported him when he wanted to go to theatre school. Introduced him to all the right people. They were wealthy art patrons so they knew everybody."

"Did the daughter ever come back?"

"She did. After the old lady died. Maxwell says he saw her at the funeral, in Toronto. She was thin and frail. Must have been about sixty but looked much older."

"She didn't challenge the will?"

"He says he doesn't think so. It might not have been worth it. She wouldn't have stood a chance. The whole Toronto establishment would have ganged up against her. They didn't want to lose that collection for the AGO. And Gerald's lawyers were the best. She disappeared off where she came from and was never heard of again. The gallery got its collection. Maxwell Fergusson says he made some money off the art that was sold and now he's hoping Budgie will want to offload some of what Gerald owned. He thinks he could get three hundred thousand for the Kurelek alone." Margo smiled, remembering it. "It's a beauty. He says those six older pieces, the ones Gerald inherited, are probably worth a million between them. And the newer ones, the ones he bought himself, are good for a few hundred thousand more."

"Gerald was even richer than we thought," said Roxanne.

"Oh, yes. Maxwell says that the old house, the one the Balfours lived in, was full of antiques. They were all the rage ten years ago. They fetched a good price too. And Budgie got all of Mrs. Balfour's jewellery. He said she had a lot of nice pieces."

Roxanne and Izzy exchanged a look. They might be in the jewellery box in Budgie's safe. Izzy had put down her mug and was making notes.

"What I don't understand," said Margo, "is why the person who stole the Chan and the other two paintings chose those ones, when they could have taken one that was worth four or five times as much."

"How valuable were they?"

"The Chan was worth lots but the other two? About five thousand each."

Roxanne checked the time. She needed to go. It was past one already and Tamsin Longstaff had said she could talk with her and Cooper Jenkins at two. It was one of those days, meeting after meeting, but she didn't want to be late for that one.

"Talk to that accountant that Gerald Blaise used," she said to Izzy as they hurried towards their cars. "Find out how much he was really worth. Then see if you can find out what happened to Emilia Balfour. Maybe she had kids of her own and Gerald Blaise has some cousins out there."

17

COOPER JENKINS WAS waiting for Roxanne in the lobby of Prairie Theatre Centre, examining a display of photographs from past productions.

"See?" He poked a finger at one. "I saw that. When I was married to Mel. She liked going to this kind of stuff."

"Did you like it?"

"Was okay."

"And you're not married to Mel anymore?"

"Hell, no. She was a long time ago. Looks kinda dead in here with the lights off."

Cooper obviously didn't intend to talk about his personal life, or his lack of one. Roxanne glanced around the empty lobby. He was right. It was drab and dull, lacking the bright glow of the chandeliers and track lighting that shone when it was thronged with theatregoers. It was silent, too. Without the chatter, the buzz of anticipation, it felt lifeless.

Tamsin Longstaff held the door that led upstairs open for them. She wore her customary high heels, a fitted scarlet suit with a short skirt, a cream silk blouse with a loose bow at the neck. Every hair on her head was in place and her fingernails, as usual, matched her ensemble. She was lean and trim, looking ten years younger than her actual age.

Jenkins leaned over and whispered in Roxanne's ear as they approached the door. "My interview." Then he raised his voice as he reached Tamsin. "Nice place," he said.

"It is," she replied. "We do our best to keep it that way." When you got closer, dark circles under her eyes were evident. For a second, Tamsin Longstaff looked exhausted, then she assumed her usual smiling, professional look. She escorted them to her office.

"Why have you come here together?" she asked as they took their seats. "Is there something new? Has there been a breakthrough?"

There hadn't. Instead of answering, Jenkins went straight on the offensive. "You and Gerald Blaise were real pally," he barked. Tamsin Longstaff's eyes widened, surprised at the hint of accusation in his voice. So was Roxanne. She'd thought he might be assertive, but not right off the top.

"That's no secret," Tamsin said. "Sergeant Calloway has already asked me about that. Gerald and I had worked together for fifteen years and we got along very well." She looked towards Roxanne for confirmation. Jenkins fired another question before she could respond.

"So, what happens to your job now he's gone?"

"Nothing," Tamsin remarked smoothly. "I carry on as usual." She maintained her poise. Confrontation was nothing new to Tamsin. Working where she did, it happened often. She eyed this city cop like he was some kind of interesting specimen, nothing more. Her big swivel chair brought her up to his height, her scarlet fingernails rested on each arm.

"But nothing's usual." Cooper's mouth took on its lopsided look, more of a sneer than a smile. "Not now. Everything's changed, right? Gonna have a new guy in Blaise's seat, he'll have new ideas, want to do things differently. Things might not go your way any longer."

"I've always welcomed change." Tamsin said, as though she found his questions tiresome. "You don't survive in this business unless you do."

"You've acted like the boss around here." Cooper poked again, looking for a weak spot. "You get to make all the important decisions because that guy you worked with, the one that's dead, was kinda lazy and he let you."

"You've been listening to gossip, bad gossip," Tamsin said, crisp and dismissive. Her hands had shifted onto the desktop in front of her, folded together. "I am here because I am good at my job," she explained, sounding mildly exasperated. "I worked well with Gerald Blaise because I knew his strengths and his weaknesses. Gerald had great instinct. Emotional intelligence. He was great with people but not good at business management. I am. So we complemented each other. I will get to know his successor and—"

Cooper Jenkins cut her off. "Bet you will," he drawled. "But it's going to be different. Real different. New guy's going to be years younger than you for a start." The insult was deliberately provocative. Roxanne wished he'd back off.

"What makes you assume it will be a man?" Roxanne watched Tamsin and Jenkins lock eyes. She seized the chance to intervene.

"Tamsin," she asked, "how many years are left on your current contract?"

"Three." It didn't work. The answer was automatic. Tamsin's attention was entirely focused on the adversarial cop sitting opposite her.

"A woman might be worse," Cooper fired back. "She'll want to make her mark. Might be just as bossy as you."

Tamsin turned icy. "What on earth has this got to do with Thom Dyck's murder, Sergeant?" she inquired, her chin high. "Isn't that the murder that you are supposed to be investigating?"

"And I am." Cooper grinned, pleased to have finally provoked her. "A little bird tells me that you had it in for him. Tried to get him fired a few years back, didn't you?"

Roxanne reached for her phone, turned on the audio and laid it flat on the desktop. "I am recording this interview," she said. She should have insisted on that to begin with. She wished they had taken Tamsin in for questioning. If Cooper was going to be so tough it would have been better to make it official, conduct it in an interview room equipped with a recorder. Both Tamsin and her interrogator continued to ignore her.

"I did no such thing," said Tamsin Longstaff.

"You tried to damage his reputation," Cooper continued. "Spread rumours about him. Said he was fucking his students."

"I did not!" Tamsin took a very deep breath and sat back. Her fingers returned to the arms of her chair and tapped for a second. "I know nothing about how Thom Dyck behaved around his students. I only ever saw him here, at the theatre. He worked with Gerald sometimes as an assistant director. He attended board meetings." She leaned forward. "Someone at the university would know how he related to the students. Someone who worked there and had good reason to want him gone. And that wasn't me. I think you are targeting the wrong person, officer."

They both knew whom she meant. Dr. Madeleine Bissett. Tamsin sat back again, satisfied that she had made her point. Jenkins smiled, like a wolf about to bite.

"Well," he said. "Y'know what I think? I think you're in cahoots with that actress Gerald Blaise was married to. I think you both wanted rid of him. Because he was going to quit the job here and wreck what you both have going on…"

"Just what are you talking about?" Tamsin's voice was low, puzzled. Roxanne was curious too. She had heard nothing of this previously.

"Known her as long as you've known Blaise, haven't you? It wasn't him you were really looking out for, was it? It was her. You made sure he chose the plays she wanted to act in. You made sure he was happy so nothing went wrong on the work front as well as the home one, because he was the one with the money. Were you a threesome? Or was it just her and you?"

Tamsin had gone pale. Her mouth hung open.

"Was she going to give you a cut of the money once Blaise was dead and buried? Or were the two of you going to take off somewhere? Set up house together, just the pair of you?"

"Get out!"Tamsin sprang to her feet, her composure gone. "You filthy, evil-minded bastard! Liar!" she spat at him. Roxanne rose also. So did Jenkins. He reached out and grabbed Tamsin's arm.

"I'm taking you in, lady," he said.

Tamsin twisted away from him. He hung on, pulled back, hard. She resisted, grabbed a statuette from a shelf behind her with her other hand, one awarded annually to a local arts administrator. It was made of glass, on a brass plinth. She seized it around the head. "Get off me!" she shouted as she swung. The heavy base caught Coop Jenkins above the ear. He tipped over and fell, slowly, towards Roxanne. The other side of his head caught the edge of the desk. He slid to the floor, his eyes rolling up into his head.

"The bitch got me," he gasped.

Tamsin was screaming, and she still wielded the statue. "You," she yelled at Roxanne. "You're just as bad. All you've brought here is trouble." She swept a pile of papers off the desk with her free hand. They cascaded over Cooper Jenkins. Roxanne ducked down behind the desk for cover.

"Keep still, Coop," she said. She grabbed her phone and punched a number. The office door burst open. Toby Malleson stood there.

"Jeez, Tamsin," he said.

"Get out!"The statuette flew straight for his head. He jumped aside. It hit a large framed poster on the wall opposite. The glass shattered. Toby disappeared down the hallway.

Tamsin picked up her laptop and threw it, too. It hit a metal filing cabinet. More papers followed. Roxanne asked for backup and an ambulance. Cooper needed medical help and Tamsin was out of control. She should have seen this coming. The woman was burned out, exhausted, and Cooper had just pushed her over the edge. She wished she'd intervened. Now Tamsin had turned and was throwing binders off the bookshelves behind her. Budgie Torrance appeared in the doorway. She wore a long silk gown with a lace negligee. Lady Macbeth's nightgown. She had been in the wardrobe for a fitting when Toby burst in with the news that Tamsin had gone berserk.

"Oh, Tamsin!" She held out both arms. Tamsin turned to look at her and burst into tears. "Don't cry!" said Budgie, and hurried around the desk to get to her, stepping over Jenkins' prone legs. She paid no attention to him, or to Roxanne, huddled by his head, talking on the phone. Cooper was awake but bleeding copiously from a head wound. There had been only a couple of tissues in her pocket. She needed more.

Tamsin fell into Budgie's arms and sobbed. Budgie stroked her back.

"Please don't cry," she said.

Was Cooper right? Were they lovers? Tamsin and Budgie Torrance?

Sadie Williams and Carol Hansen appeared in the doorway and gaped when they saw the scene. Then they sprang into action. Sadie grabbed a box of Kleenex from a counter and dropped to her knees beside Roxanne.

"He's coming to," said Roxanne. "Ambulance is on its way."

"I'll go get ice," said Carol.

"Don't lift your head," Sadie instructed Cooper, and pressed a wad of tissue onto the gash.

Roxanne left him in Sadie's care and walked slowly around the back of the desk to where Budgie and Tamsin stood. Budgie had her arms wrapped tightly around Tamsin, who still wept on her shoulder. Roxanne reached out to try to move her aside. Budgie's head turned.

"Don't touch me," she hissed. "And leave her alone."

"Let go of her," said Roxanne. "Now." Carol Hansen had returned. She passed an ice pack to Sadie and came to Budgie's other side.

"Come on, Budgie," she said. "Let go of Tamsin." Together, she and Roxanne prised Tamsin out of Budgie's grasp.

"Look at this mess," said Carol. There was a red lipstick stain on the lacy shoulder of the costume and dark blotches where Tamsin's mascara had run. She touched the marks with a finger, vexed at the stains. "We need to get you out of this, Budgie. Come with me." Jenkins was struggling to get to his feet again.

"Stay where you are, mister." Sadie Wilson placed a large hand on his chest and stopped him. It was no contest. She was as big as he was and he was a pallid shade of grey.

Roxanne charged Tamsin with assaulting a police officer. Tamsin looked at her with teary eyes, smudged black, her lipstick smeared, snot running from her nose. She sank into her chair, helpless now that all her fiery energy was spent.

"I can't leave Tamsin," Budgie said stubbornly. Sadie had found a waste bucket. It was filling up with bloody tissue. Cooper's head wouldn't stop bleeding. Toby Malleson reappeared.

"Ambulance just pulled up," he said. He looked at the chaos around him and went to Carol's aid.

"Come on, Budgie," he said. "You can't stay here." Together, he and Carol edged Budgie out the door. Roxanne stood watch over Tamsin.

"Don't you dare lay another finger on her," Budgie snarled over her shoulder as she disappeared. Roxanne looked at the dishevelled mess that was now Tamsin Longstaff. Had Coop Jenkins actually got it right? The implication that she loved Budgie had sparked the breakdown. Had the story about an old relationship between Tamsin and Gerald Blaise been a smokescreen? Had it hidden the fact that the actual lovers were Tamsin and Budgie? Had they conspired to kill Gerald, and had Tamsin carried out the act of murdering him? She had the opportunity. She worked late at the theatre all the time and knew how to enter and leave the building without being seen on any camera. And now it was apparent that she was capable of violence.

The paramedics arrived and took Sadie's place at Cooper's side. They ignored his muttered protests that he was going to be fine.

They said they were taking him to the hospital. That skull needed to be X-rayed and he must be concussed.

A couple of RCMP constables arrived, cuffed Tamsin and took her off to a waiting car.

Sadie Williams wiped blood off her fingers and looked at the shambles that had been Tamsin Longstaff's tidy office.

"What's going to happen here?" she asked. "Who's in charge now?"

Roxanne didn't tell her that it was about to become worse. More police were arriving. She walked towards the wardrobe room, a uniformed constable at her heels. She was taking Budgie Torrance in for questioning.

IZZY MCBAIN CALLED Irma Friedrich, the accountant, in Toronto. She had liked Gerald, she said. Had done his accounts for almost twenty years. Gerald had appointed her as his executor, and if it would help the RCMP find his killer, she would do all she could to help.

"Why don't we Skype?" she said. "I like to see who I'm talking to."

Izzy agreed. Ms. Friedrich was pale, fair hair turning discreetly grey, even featured. Her files on Gerald went back years. She also managed Ms. Torrance's account.

"I work for a lot of people in the arts," she said. "Most of them are self-employed. Maxwell Fergusson sends a lot of clients my way." She estimated Gerald's worth at over seven million. "It's well invested," she said. "He's done well since he inherited his aunt's money."

"So he didn't need to work?" asked Izzy.

"Ah, but he loved it," said Irma Friedrich. "I can't imagine Gerald without having one foot in the theatre. It's such a social art form and Gerald thrived on company. He needed to be around people." There was a safety deposit box, at his bank, in Winnipeg. "The papers for his investments will be in it." She didn't know why the deeds to the condo and his will were in his home safe. The contents of the condo, including the art that it contained, was certainly insured. "He used to complain how much it cost to cover those old items, the ones he inherited," she said. "They have increased so much in value the past few years."

And Budgie? She hadn't kept all the jewellery she had inherited when Mrs. Balfour died.

"She sold most of it. Kept a few pieces. Got them remounted into something more contemporary. She has a beautiful ring, with a single diamond. She wears it quite often. And a pair of emerald earrings."

Budgie had realized almost a hundred thousand from the sale. It was invested also. And she made a profit each year from what she earned. She was nowhere like as rich as Gerald had been but she had built up a nice little portfolio.

"And Gerald was always generous. She had everything she wanted. Now, I suppose, she is going to be very wealthy. She's been in touch. She needs to spring some cash to buy a car. She doesn't have one of her own and the Audi belonged to Gerald. It's part of his estate. I'm chasing up Autopac to find out if it's a write-off. We're also figuring out a budget for the celebration of Gerald's life. He's being cremated next week, but there will be a big event at the theatre the following Monday."

Izzy's phone buzzed. There was a text from Roxanne. Call her, right away. She excused herself as soon as she could and listened as Roxanne told her, briefly, what had happened. She needed her at HQ right now to be with her as she interviewed Budgie Torrance.

18

CAROL HANSEN, SADIE Williams and Toby Malleson watched Budgie Torrance being led away by a uniformed Mountie, followed by Sergeant Roxanne Calloway.

"I'd better call the rehearsal hall," said Carol. Toby disappeared along the corridor. He started to pick his way across the broken glass in the hallway outside Tamsin's office, then he stopped and went inside. Tamsin kept a list of board members pinned to a bulletin board. He left a message for Frank Moran, then started cleaning up the mess.

"Might as well pack it in for the day," Jazz Elliott said to her stage manager, Nell Bronson, soon after. The actors stood in clusters around the room, discussing the news. "I knew we should have replaced Budgie."

Pedro Diaz, director of production, walked in from the shop, a tool belt strapped around his hips. Pedro's job was largely administrative, but he liked to get hands-on when he could, especially when there was an interesting set build happening, and this one was fun.

"What ya reckon, Jazz? Are we ever going to get this show up and running? Does anyone know if Tamsin authorized the payroll before she cracked?" The staff and cast at PTC were paid biweekly. This was payday.

"Don't ask me. We keep losing Budgie and everyone wants Wednesday afternoon off next week as well, so they can go see Gerald get cremated." Jazz reached for her knitting bag. "This

Scottish play is doomed, I tell you. How am I supposed to get it up on its feet when I can't rehearse it? I'm going to go think."

"I'll go find Toby Malleson," said Nell. "We'll need to get a board member to come in and make sure everyone gets paid."

Jazz looked at the anxious faces of her cast. "Tell them to go home. Be here ready for a fresh start tomorrow at ten," she growled to Nell, then she stomped off towards the door that went upstairs.

"Tamsin lost it?" Pedro shook his head in disbelief. "Can't imagine. What pushed her over the edge?"

Nell stuck her hands deep into her pockets. "Dunno. She's always so in control. Wonder who'll be in charge now?"

MARLA CAPLAN ARRIVED at the stage door, padlocked her bike to a rack and hurried upstairs. The cast members who were leaving filled her in on their versions of the day's big event. She found Toby Malleson stacking papers on Tamsin's desk.

"Oh good, you're here." Toby was too busy to lift his head and look at her. He pointed in the direction of the wastebasket full of bloody tissue. "Can you do something about that?"

"Should you be cleaning this up, Toby? Isn't it a crime scene?"

"She didn't kill the guy, did she?" Toby muttered, gathering up more paper. "And it's not as if the police don't know what happened. They were here. They caused all this, if you ask me. The executive's called an emergency meeting." He raised his head and looked hopefully at Marla. "You couldn't take minutes, could you?" Marla held the wastebasket gingerly in one hand.

"I suppose so." Marla turned and looked at the broken glass in the hallway. The statuette still lay on the floor, propped against the wall.

"She almost got me with that thing!" Toby blurted out. He plopped down into Tamsin's swivel chair. "It came flying at me, straight for my head. I thought I was going to die." His voice wavered. Marla put down the basket.

"Come on, Toby," she said, and walked to his side. She took the rustling papers from his hand. "You're pretty shaken. Let's go see if Carol's got the kettle on. Then I'll come back here and see how much I can get tidied up."

BUDGIE TORRANCE HAD demanded that she get to make a phone call. She had put it to good use. Her lawyer was young, smart and a rising star in the firm of Moran, Stevenson and Baillie. They took their places opposite Roxanne and a sergeant named Dawes sent by the city police to deputize for the injured Detective Sergeant Jenkins.

Budgie had assumed the role of ice queen. She condescended to answer a question if it suited her. Most times she pivoted her little head on its long neck in the direction of her lawyer and raised her eyebrows. Should she answer or not? When he nodded, she did so, in a clear, cool voice, devoid of emotion. Other times, the lawyer deflected the question with one of his own.

"Why are you pursuing this line of questioning? My client is blameless," he asserted. "She was in Regina when her husband was murdered. She has told you already that she and Tamsin Longstaff were acquainted. They worked together and socialized occasionally, when required by the fact that Gerald Blaise and Ms. Longstaff were colleagues. That was all."

Budgie grew even colder when confronted with the suggestion that she and Tamsin had been lovers.

"That," she said, "is too ridiculous. Ask around. Anyone will tell you. I don't do girls. Never have, never wanted to. I like men, Sergeant. And do not lack good male friends."

Sergeant Dawes from the city police was a stolid kind of guy, not happy to be called into service on this case, late Friday afternoon before Thanksgiving weekend. He had kids. He wanted to be home, not here being patronized by this prima donna and her expensive lawyer. He folded his arms and let Sergeant Calloway take the brunt of it.

"You know all about Sam Geddes in Regina, don't you? 'Course you do. You've been snooping around there, asking questions, haven't you? Lovely man, Sam. Always available when I needed him, and he knew the score. Fun while it lasted." Budgie sighed deeply. "There's no one that I fancy much in the cast for the Scottish play, but I'm not in the mood anyway. Gerald was the real love of my life and now he's gone. Do you always harass grieving widows?" Each syllable was a sarcastic, crystalline stalactite. "You police do have disgusting minds, don't you?"

She took time to eyeball both of them. Budgie knew how to work her audience. "I suppose it comes with the job. Tell you what. Why don't you get your minions to call all the theatres I've worked for over the years and ask them if they have ever heard tell of me making a move on any member of my own sex. And I'll tell you what you'll find. They will all tell you that the idea is ludicrous."

"I think you have your answer, Sergeant," said the smooth young lawyer, capping his fountain pen.

"No." Budgie stretched out an elegant hand and touched his arm. "I insist. You police don't believe a word I say. You think I'm acting all the time. So you need corroboration, don't you?" The look that she fixed on Roxanne was contemptuous. "Maybe you can tell me one thing, Sergeant. Was it you or that thug you brought with you that destroyed Tamsin Longstaff with your threats and accusations?"

"Enough." Her lawyer rose to his feet, eager to quit while they were ahead. But Budgie wasn't quite finished.

"I didn't especially like Tamsin," she said, rising to her feet. "But she was good at her job. She was a great GM and she worked her butt off for that theatre. I took pity on her when I saw the state you people had reduced her to, as any decent human being would do." She spoke directly to Roxanne again before she exited. "You should be ashamed of yourself."

The lawyer looked satisfied as he said goodbye and followed her.

A GLOOMY CIRCLE huddled around the coffee table in the wardrobe room at PTC. Toby Malleson was wrapped around a mug of hot tea. Jazz Elliott's knitting needles clicked.

"She snapped. Too much pressure. And she's been working way too hard." Sadie sprawled in one of the armchairs. "Who'll run things now?"

They shrugged. No one knew. Carla Hansen had Budgie's stained lace negligee in her hand. It was ruined. She'd have to replace it. If Budgie was arrested, she'd have to rebuild all Lady Macbeth's costumes to fit a different actor. Nell Bronson walked in, followed by Pedro Diaz.

"Toby," she said, "you look like shit. Go home."

"Marla Caplan's called the board treasurer," Pedro said. "She's coming in a meeting. She'll sign off on the payroll while she's at it." He puffed out his chest. He had more important news. "Budgie's been released and she's taking a taxi home."

"Good," said Sadie. "We'll all get paid and our lead actor's back in business."

Toby put down his cup and pulled himself up onto his feet.

"I wish someone could get Tamsin out of this mess," he said. "But I guess that isn't going to happen. I should go make sure Marla's okay."

"She'll be fine." Carla tossed the damaged negligee into a garbage can. "Nell's right. You should go home. We should all go home. This has been a godawful day. I'm going to come in tomorrow, start fresh."

"Good idea." Jazz stuffed the knitting pins into her usual bag. She tapped Toby's arm. "Give me a lift, eh? Back to the hotel."

"Me too." Sadie peeled herself out of the chair.

"Someone should check up on Budgie. Make sure she's okay." Nell watched as they piled on jackets, pulled on boots.

"You're right!" Toby stopped, halfway to the door. "I should go do that."

"No way." Jazz pushed his back lightly. "You're driving me, remember."

"Budgie'll be okay. I'm staying. Got some welding to do." And Pedro strode off down the corridor towards his shop. He started to whistle. Stopped.

"Fuck's sake, Pedro." They all glared at him.

"Sorry!" Pedro spread his hands, apologetic. Whistling in the theatre brought bad luck.

"As if things aren't bad enough already," Sadie growled as she led them off in the opposite direction.

"WELL." SERGEANT DAWES put his phone back in his pocket. "Looks like I'm stuck with this job for now. Jenkins is still in hospital, with a concussion. He's supposed to take it easy. He won't be back on the job for a couple of weeks. Are we about done for the day? It's Thanksgiving weekend, dammit."

"I've still got to talk to Tamsin Longstaff."

The RCMP had had a doctor check Tamsin out. He'd said she was fit for questioning.

Izzy walked in the door, in time to hear Roxanne. "Too late. She got bail. Ten minutes ago."

Roxanne was stunned. "How come? She injured a police sergeant!"

"Dunno."

The corporal who manned the front desk told the story. Another sleek lawyer from Moran, Stevenson and Baillie had shown up and demanded to see his client, Ms. Longstaff. He'd emerged from the room and bawled them all out. Wanted to know why the lady was still locked up, in her condition. How well qualified was the doctor who had said she was fine? She obviously was not. He was going to get a second opinion.

"She was all right, wasn't she?" Tamsin had been docile the last time Roxanne had seen her, being led from the office she had just destroyed.

"Guys said she just sat in the corner of the cell, shivering. Wasn't making a fuss. Total mental breakdown, says her lawyer. He's taking her straight to the hospital."

"She attacked Coop Jenkins. She smashed a statue into his head. I saw it. I charged her with assault." Roxanne shook her head in disbelief.

"Lawyer says it was self-defence. That he assaulted her first. Got bail."

Roxanne replayed the scene in her head. Tamsin had yelled but she'd made no physical threat before Coop grabbed her. And he'd hung on. Then she had reacted, violently. He had restrained her, but had he needed to? Could that be construed as a physical attack?

"I have to go write a report," Roxanne said. She needed to write down exactly what had happened while it was fresh in her head.

"Guess I'm done for the day!" Sergeant Dawes took the opportunity to make a beeline for the door.

"You can go, Izzy," Roxanne said. There would be no interview today.

"You sure?" But Izzy looked relieved. She had mentioned that she and Matt were planning to go out to the new house near Cullen Village this weekend. It was going up fast. They needed to get the kitchen measured out. Roxanne texted her sister. She'd need another hour before she could pick up Finn.

She listened to what she had recorded of the scene between Coop Jenkins and Tamsin. Coop was aggressive, no doubt, but Tamsin had held her own until he brought up the suggestion of that possible sexual relationship between her and Budgie Torrance. That was when she had lost control.

There was no doubt that Cooper had made the first physical move. Tamsin's voice, yelling, "Get off me!" could be heard, loud and clear, before a thump as the base of the statue made contact with Cooper's head. You could hear another noise as his head made contact with the desk. But Tamsin had told him to let go before she had hit him. Her lawyer would make good use of that timing.

Roxanne wrote up her report and sent it to Inspector Schultz, along with a copy of the audio. She could do no more. It was late, dark outside. Time to go home.

She didn't notice that her car looked like it had shrunk until she reached for the handle. She looked down at the front tire. Flat. Then the back one. Also flat. Slowly she walked to the other side. Same thing. All four tires were flat. She hunkered down, turned on the flashlight on her phone to look closer. The wall of each tire had been deliberately punctured, stabbed with a sharp instrument. It looked like the work of Jem Sinclair. He might have been released. If he was on the loose, this could be a warning, in retaliation for having spoken to his brother. The car would have to be towed. It was the long weekend. Four new tires were going to cost her. Or she'd need to make an insurance claim.

The desk corporal rolled his eyes when she told him about the car, but he was helpful. He'd get a tow truck to haul her RAV4 to the garage. And he'd find out if anything was available in the carpool. Meantime she called the Youth Centre. Jem Sinclair had been released on a promise to appear in court. There was a contact number. It was disconnected, no surprise.

"There's a Ford Focus you can have," said the corporal. "It's blue." That was good. There were lots of them around. It was fairly anonymous. She drove it home. That night, once Finn was sound asleep, she poured a glass of wine and connected with Brian Donohue online.

"It's been a rough day." She sighed as she told him about how Tamsin had fallen apart, and why.

"Budgie denies she's ever been interested in women, far less Tamsin. And that might be true. But Tamsin's a loner. I don't think she's ever married. She's supposed to have been in a relationship with Gerald Blaise years ago but there doesn't seem to be anyone close to her right now. Maybe she was actually carrying a torch for Budgie." Roxanne swallowed a mouthful of cab sav.

"You've got no proof."

"I know, but it explains why she flipped."

"Coop Jenkins has a reputation for crossing the line." Brian had asked around on her behalf. She saw him frown on the screen. "That's why he's still a sergeant. He gets results but he doesn't always follow the rules. Why didn't you insist on taking her in? Make it a formal interview?"

"Didn't think that he would be so aggressive." Roxanne swallowed another mouthful, annoyed with herself. "Schultz insists that I make sure the city carries its share of the workload. So I did. It was Coop's interview."

"Was she a threat?" asked Brian. "Why did he go for her?"

"He grabbed hold of her. He didn't hit her or anything."

"But he made the first move? Well, sounds like Moran's rallied his best troops in her defence. They're going to eat him alive if they get a chance. And you too, if you're not careful."

"Thanks, Brian. I really needed to know that. Enjoy your weekend." She ended the call as politely as she could. She was too tired to argue.

She had a message from Inspector Schultz. MY OFFICE TOMORROW 10.

"Oh, great," she thought and poured herself another glass of wine.

19

INSPECTOR SCHULTZ LOOKED casual out of uniform. Less authoritative. More approachable. He was dressed for golf. He had a game booked for later this morning, he told Roxanne as he hung his jacket on a hook behind his closet door. He didn't want to miss it. Last outing of the season. He was probably right about that. The sun was shining this Saturday morning and promised to do so all weekend, but snow was on its way, coming Wednesday, a Colorado low bringing ten to twenty centimetres of the white stuff, the weather reports said. An early snowstorm, maybe a blizzard. But not today.

"This won't take more than an hour," he said briskly, pointing to the chair at the opposite side of his desk. He wasn't being hopeful. He meant it. He wasn't going to miss his game. He had read her report and listened to the recording, what there was of it.

"Why wasn't she brought in for questioning?" He pulled in his chair, getting straight to the point.

"That was Detective Sergeant Jenkins' call." Roxanne didn't intend to take the blame for Coop Jenkins' actions. She needed to make that clear. "It was his interview. He was following up on a report that Tamsin Longstaff had tried to force Professor Dyck out of his job at the university several years earlier. And after Gerald Blaise died, Dyck had been in a position to make important decisions at the theatre that affected how Longstaff did her job. She resented that, according to his witness."

"That's not the line of questioning he pursued." Schultz pursed his lips. His shiny bald head and slightly bulbous eyes made him look like a bullfrog.

"No, sir. I didn't know he was going to accuse her of colluding with Budgie Torrance."

"Who?" asked Inspector Schultz.

"That's what people in the theatre call the actor Annabel Torrance."

"Silly name," her boss said dismissively. "Why didn't you stop him?"

Roxanne had known he would ask that. "I was surprised at how she reacted," she explained. "He'd been assertive to that point, but she'd coped well, so I saw no reason to intervene. She changed when he mentioned a possible sexual relationship between her and Ms. Torrance, so much so that I wondered if there was some truth to the suggestion. Then it all went wrong…"

"Sure did." Schultz's eyes wandered to the window. Outside, the birds chirped and the links beckoned. "He grabbed her first?"

"He restrained her."

"Why? Was she a threat?" The big round eyes became suspicious slits, the lips compressed.

"No," she admitted. "I don't think so. She was upset…"

"You can hear her yelling 'Get off me' on the recording. What's that about?"

"He seized her arm, sir. She resisted, he pulled at her. And then she swung that statue at him."

"To get him to let go?"

"Maybe." It certainly had looked like that. "But she hit his head hard. It was a complete surprise. And it happened fast. There was no way to have stopped her."

"Okay." Schultz sat back. "There's been a complaint lodged. Her lawyers are talking about force being used against her."

"Mr. Moran, QC?" she asked. He raised eyebrows, inviting an explanation. "The lawyers who are representing Annabel Torrance are both from his firm. And he's exerting pressure, right?"

"Well, then." He looked her squarely in the eye. "He knows the rules. He knows better than to meddle."

"But he's also the chair of PTC's board. He's going to act in their interest."

"The city police might have to investigate. Jenkins is going to be off for a week or two with that concussion. Who's replacing him?" asked Inspector Schultz.

She told him. Sergeant Dawes.

"Good," he said. "I've met him. Sound man, Dawes. When can you talk to the Longstaff woman?"

She couldn't, for now. She had called the hospital first thing that morning. Tamsin had been admitted for psychiatric treatment as a voluntary patient. They had done an initial assessment but they were waiting for a full psychiatric examination after the weekend. Tuesday at the earliest.

"Jenkins played a hunch," she said. "And he might be right. She could have carried out the murder. She often works late at the theatre and she knows which door has no surveillance camera. She could have accessed the Blaise condo and the parking lot where the Audi was found without anyone seeing her. And she owns a car. Riverside Park is only a twenty-minute drive from where she lives. I need to check when she arrived at work the day that Thomas Dyck was killed. And I need to find out if Sergeant Jenkins had any solid grounds for thinking that the two women were sexual partners."

"Okay." Schultz got to his feet. "Sounds like a possible lead but tread carefully. Don't know how you're going to talk to Jenkins, though. He's toast for now. Maybe Dawes will know something." He was reaching for his jacket already. She followed him to the elevator and watched as he strode off to his car.

Her son was at hockey practice. She should go to the rink and watch, but she wanted to see what she could find in the office that Tamsin Longstaff had trashed the previous day. She watched Schultz drive off with his golf clubs in the back of his hatchback and headed for downtown.

Tamsin's office was no longer messy. It was neat and tidy. Behind the desk sat a young woman, not tall, big boned and sturdy, reading financial pages through round tortoiseshell-framed glasses.

"Hello!" she welcomed Roxanne, hand outstretched. "I am Alison Beck. I've met one of your colleagues, Constable McBain. Do sit down. I've been asked to fill in here until the theatre knows what's happening with Tamsin. Would you like a coffee?"

There was a carafe on top of the cabinet behind her, where a glass statuette had stood less than twenty-four hours ago. Matching pottery mugs, glazed green and blue; a cream jug and sugar bowl to match were arranged beside it.

"Didn't you work here before? Weren't you let go?"

"I was." Alison smiled as she poured. "But they need someone right away who knows the ropes, and I do." She passed the jug and a mug of coffee across the desk. "And I'm available. It's short term. They're pretty sure the charges against Tamsin won't hold but it looks like she'll be on sick leave for a while. So I am filling in."

"Didn't the board fire you?"

"That was Tamsin's doing." Alison Beck sat in an ergonomically designed chair, not the one that Tamsin had used. Some pictures on the walls had changed too. A couple of them featuring Tamsin, including the one of her with Gerald Blaise, had been replaced with production shots. "Mr. Moran was there when they showed me the door. Now he's being nice. But it was Tamsin who got rid of me. I threatened her."

She hadn't stopped smiling. She could be right, if PTC was willing to hire her back so quickly. The job might be temporary but it would clear her reputation of any taint left by the firing.

Alison leaned in. "You know that Frank and Tamsin had a thing going on?"

"Really?" Roxanne asked cautiously. This young woman had good reason to dislike both Tamsin Longstaff and Frank Moran. And, perhaps, to malign them. Was what she was saying true, and if so, was Cooper Jenkins' assumption that Tamsin was a lesbian wrong? "Why do you think that?"

"Because I know. I have evidence." Alison Beck reached down and opened a desk drawer. She took out a paper file and passed it to Roxanne. It contained printouts of emails between Tamsin and Frank Moran. They went back several years. There were also pages from Tamsin's calendar.

"How did you get all this?" asked Roxanne.

"I looked."

"When?"

"I'd been keeping track for a while. Just in case Tamsin decided to get rid of me. I never got a chance to collect my things before I was marched off the premises. They put some personal stuff in a box and let me know I could pick it up at the loading dock the next day. My old files were put away in a box in a storage closet. Back there." She nodded towards the corridor. "They stashed them away until someone had time to go through them. And shred them. But, of course, no one ever did. Everyone's always too busy around here. So I went and dug them out, after they rehired me. Last night, after everyone went home. I was concerned that someone would have found them but no one had even looked. So there you have it. Tamsin and Frank have been seeing each other since not long after he joined the board, seven years ago. He visits her in her apartment regularly."

"He's married?"

"Sure. Has been forever. Doesn't seem to matter."

"And what does this have to do with my investigation?"

Alison swung her chair smoothly from side to side. "Well," she said. "Our theatre grapevine says that you think she was having it off with Budgie." Her face lit up with amusement. "Did you really? Why would you think that? Budgie's only interested in guys, isn't it obvious? She didn't even like Tamsin very much, if you ask me. Not that I have any proof of that." She stopped swinging the chair and came to a full stop directly across the desk from Roxanne. "She's saying that you think she and Tamsin planned to kill Gerald and live off all his money afterwards. You've got it all wrong, Sergeant. Can you please back off on Budgie? Until we can get this production up and running?"

There was a knock at the door. It opened a crack and Marla Caplan poked her head in. "Oh, you're busy." She looked curiously at Sergeant Calloway. "Can I just give you this?" She handed a set of keys and an envelope to Alison. "The keys to Budgie's new car. And the papers. I told her I'd leave them with you. She said she wanted to take it for a spin on her lunch break. I've got the rest of the day off. Tell her I'll be back at six. We're going out for dinner."

"Marla's been reassigned," Alison told Roxanne. "Board decision. She's Budgie's new personal assistant. Budgie needs to have company when she's not at work and some help sorting out her affairs. The guys have found a bed in storage and set it up in Gerald's old study so she can sleep over, because we think that's a good idea, so don't think start thinking anything funny's going on there."

Alison and Marla looked like they both found that hilarious.

"Not a chance." Marla laughed, then she turned serious. She folded her arms. "Budgie's got a lot on her mind, Sergeant." She frowned down at Roxanne, her head tipped to one side. "You people have no idea, do you? You think because she has a funny name and playacts for a living that it's all fun and games, don't you? You have no idea how hard someone like Budgie Torrance works."

"It's true." Alison Beck backed her up. "We need her to be able to focus on the production."

"Plus there's a funeral to plan. And the accountant wants to talk to her about all that money she's inheriting. She wants to sell up and move, soon as this play is done."

"Where to?" asked Roxanne.

"Stratford, Ontario. She's got the word out that she's looking to buy there." It made sense. Budgie worked regularly at the Stratford Festival and there was a community of actors that she knew. "She wants to be gone before December. She hates Winnipeg winters. And she's planning to sell most of the artwork."

"Oh," said Alison. "Gerald had a couple of paintings Greg and I wouldn't mind buying."

"You'd better talk to her. She's going to ship them off to Toronto for auction, soon as." Roxanne expected that Maxwell Fergusson would be handling that sale. That would make him happy.

"Do you have keys to the condo?" Roxanne asked. Marla nodded. "Is there a small key? One that would unlock a padlock?"

Marla fished around in a pocket and held up a bunch of keys. Among them was a small yellow one. "This one? I think it's for the storage unit, in the basement, beside the garage." No one had mentioned storage before, or searched it. Roxanne scooped up the papers Alison Beck had given her.

"Can you unlock that unit for me?" she asked Marla.

"'Course!"

Roxanne followed Marla out the building via the back door of the condo. Larry the caretaker was still working on the damaged doorway in the lobby. He nodded as they went into the stairwell that led down to the underground parkade. A storage room lined with wire cages was off the garage. The small key unlocked one of them.

"Budgie told me Gerald was keeping a lot of stuff in case he ever wanted to write a memoir." Marla was right. There were boxes of posters, programs, cast lists and director's notebooks for all the productions that Gerald had worked on, ever since he had left theatre school. They found photographs and newspaper clippings. Binders full of reviews. It all seemed to relate to his professional life, though.

"What about Budgie?" Roxanne asked. "Was she planning to write a memoir too?"

"Don't think so," said Marla, opening a box. She had time, she said, to help. "Budgie lives in the present. I don't think it would occur to her. She saves costume bits and photographs. Well, you've seen her room upstairs. All her stuff's probably up there."

There were some larger boxes at the back. Roxanne uncovered some old silver, a tea service, well wrapped in flannel to prevent it from tarnishing. "This must be from the old aunt's house," she said. There was more. China dishes, vases, all antiques.

"Budgie hated that old woman." Marla had found some photos, still framed, each one wrapped in paper. She was looking at one of a man and woman, elegantly dressed in fifties clothing. "She said she was an evil, judgemental old witch. Oh." She had found another. "There they are with their daughter, the one they abandoned." She held it gently between her hands. The couple stood on either side of a girl in school uniform, her hair pinned back with a barrette.

"You know about that?" asked Roxanne.

"Budgie told me. We talked for ages last night." Marla put the photo back in its wrapper and placed it back in its box.

"She said she thought they were cruel. They cared more about their reputation than their own child. She didn't want anything that belonged to that old lady. She was glad that Gerald got rid of most of the paintings that she left to him and started buying his own. And she sold most of the jewellery that was left to her. She got some of it melted down and made into new pieces. More contemporary ones. They're fantastic."

"If they hadn't disowned the daughter, Gerald wouldn't have inherited their fortune." Roxanne had opened one of several suitcases. They were all empty, ready for travelling.

"And Budgie thinks he might have still been alive if he hadn't."

"She said that?"

Marla raised her head from another box. She held some of Gerald's binders in her hands. "She did. Budgie misses him, Sergeant. That's why it's not good for her to be alone in that apartment right now. She gets too sad when she's up there by herself. There's no way she's responsible for what happened to him."

"You don't mind having to take care of her?"

"Being her PA?" Marla put the binders back in the box and closed it. "It's okay. Alison doesn't need me doing her old job. She knows it backwards. I'm just glad to still be paid and working for PTC."

They closed up and emerged into sunshine. Marla Caplan unlocked her bike and rode off. Roxanne phoned Coop Jenkins' number. It was turned off. She left a message. The phone buzzed in her hand. Tracy Ross.

"Hey, Sarge," she said. "You were looking for some keys?"

"I was," said Roxanne. "Have you found them?"

"Turns out Zeke had them all along. He needs to give them back to you. Want to meet us at Freda's down on Pembina? In half an hour?"

Should she go? Roxanne was pretty sure now that the Sinclairs had nothing to do with the murders but she did want those keys, and meeting Zeke would send a clear message to his brother that she was not to be intimidated.

"Sure," she said.

20

FREDA'S RESTAURANT WAS popular on Saturdays. It had started as a bakery and made soups and sandwiches but Zeke Sinclair held a burger in both hands and had a chocolate milkshake at his elbow. He looked up as Roxanne approached and avoided eye contact. His Aunt Tracy didn't smile either.

"You're the cop?" she asked as Roxanne pulled out a chair.

"Sergeant Roxanne Calloway, RCMP." Roxanne didn't order anything to eat. She was hungry, but hopefully this wouldn't take long. "You've got something for me, Zeke?"

Zeke placed his burger on the table and reached into the pocket of his jeans. He slid a bundle of keys across to Roxanne. Then he lifted the shake and sucked on the straw, this time fixing an unblinking stare on her.

The black car fob bore the Audi logo and was exactly as he had described, studded with silver buttons. Press one and the key popped out. There were five door keys, three of which looked similar. One of them could be the master key to Prairie Theatre Centre, the one that had required the whole building to be rekeyed when it went missing. The fourth and fifth probably unlocked the apartment where Gerald Blaise had lived. There were two small keys, one yellow, one silver. One probably unlocked the padlock to the cage that housed Gerald's stash of memorabilia, the other, a mailbox. Then there was a long, thin key, the kind that opened a safety deposit box. They weren't the set that he had described to her, as if the house keys were missing, but at least she now had them.

"What ya gotta say, Zeke?" said his aunt. She had already demolished a sandwich and was halfway through a mug of coffee. A heap of half-eaten french fries, doused in ketchup, lay between them.

"Sorry," mumbled Zeke. He didn't look at all sorry.

"You said you threw them in the river." Roxanne fingered the keys. "Why did you lie?"

"Just did," he shrugged.

Roxanne didn't need to know why. It was obvious. He'd found a body in the trunk of the car. He'd wanted to avoid more trouble. "The house keys are here. Did you go into the house?" He continued to look straight at her and bit his burger. His aunt nudged him.

"No, ma'am," he said.

"You found them?" Roxanne asked Tracy Ross.

"He left his jeans lying on the floor and I picked them up to throw them in the wash," said Tracy. "They fell out of his pocket." She had given them back to Zeke so he could hand them to Roxanne himself. And say that he was sorry. Tracy Ross was doing her best to keep her youngest nephew out of trouble. She had her hands full. Roxanne rose to go.

"Tell Jeremiah that I don't appreciate getting my tires slashed," she said.

"Jem's none of my business," said his aunt. "You wanna tell him, tell him yourself."

Roxanne walked outside into bright sunshine. The town was busy this Saturday morning. Everyone who could take time off was doing so, enjoying being outside before the snow hit. Finn would be done on the ice at the rink by now. She should go pick him up. Get lunch. Her phone rang as she reached the car. Coop Jenkins.

"Got your message," he grunted.

"So, you're off for a while?"

"Well, yeah. Them's the breaks." Coop sounded nonchalant.

"How're you doing?"

"Fine," he lied. "Want to go grab a coffee?"

Should she? The smell of the food in Freda's had reminded her how hungry she was. And she did want to know why he had thought Tamsin was in a sexual relationship with Budgie Torrance. Finn was with his cousins. He'd be fine.

"How about lunch?"

"The Forks again? See you in twenty."

As she drove out of the parking lot, she passed the window where Zeke Sinclair sat with his aunt, finishing off the last of the fries, watching. He didn't take his eyes off her until she disappeared from view.

ROXANNE WAS FAR from being the only person still at work this long weekend. Business had resumed at Prairie Theatre Centre. Theatregoers still attended. Rehearsals continued. Jazz Elliot and her stage manager, Nell Bronson, watched Budgie Torrance and Danny Foley finish rehearsing the scene where the Macbeths murder King Duncan.

"*A little water clears us of this deed*," she said, holding out her hands as if they really dripped blood.

"She's doing better now that Marla's taking care of things for her," said Nell.

"Yep." Jazz nodded in agreement. "Hiring Marla was a great idea. That Alison Beck's real smart."

"Sure is. She made sure she got Marla out of that office fast as she could. Marla's as clever as she is. Alison doesn't want any competition on the job."

"She won't be there for long. Tamsin will be back, right?"

Neither of them knew whether or not that was true. Tamsin was shut away in the psych ward for the weekend, out of sight but not out of mind. Alison Beck's appointment as her temporary replacement was not finding favour everywhere at PTC.

In the sewing room, Carol Hansen stood at an ironing board touching up the lace on Budgie's new negligee. She looked up, the iron steaming in her hand, as Sadie Williams kicked the door closed behind her and slapped an envelope down on the nearest flat surface.

"That Beck bitch has just canned the new designs for *A Christmas Carol*," she announced.

In another week, the play being presented right now, the one that matinee audiences were just arriving to see, would close. Jazz and her cast and crew would move onto the big stage and rehearsals would begin for another new production in the rehearsal hall. *A Christmas Carol* was a perennial favourite at PTC. Audiences loved it. Going to see it had become a winter holiday tradition that many Winnipeg families looked forward to with eager anticipation. Gerald had produced it in his first year as artistic director twenty years ago, and there had been a couple of attempts to replace it, but nothing else was as popular, nothing else sold as well.

So each year, the set was dragged out and refurbished, some of the same actors showed up, including the ones who always played Scrooge and the Fezziwigs. It was like an annual reunion for them. However, the costumes were long past their best. This had been the year that Gerald had ordered new ones. Sadie had been asked to stay on after *Macbeth* to design and supervise the rebuild. Now that wasn't going to happen. Alison Beck had cancelled the contract. Things were too precarious right now, she had told Sadie, to incur that expense. And a new AD might not want to keep presenting that old chestnut of a play. It wasn't worth investing in all those new, expensive costumes.

"You're allowed to make that decision?" Sadie had asked.

"Oh, yes." Alison had smiled and stretched her spine like a well-fed cat. "The executive is in complete agreement."

"Wish we could get Tamsin back." Sadie lowered her large frame into one of the low armchairs. "She would never have agreed to this. Guess I'll be gone once *Macbeth* is up on its feet.

I turned down a couple of good gigs too, so I could do those big costumes for *Christmas Carol*." Theatre artists worked contract to contract. She'd be paid something to compensate her for the time she had already put in on the designs but it wouldn't make up for the loss of income.

Carol switched off the iron and plugged in the kettle. "Maybe they'll find out Tamsin didn't kill anybody and we will get her back," she said. "Alison's just doing this to suck up to the board. She always was good at that."

"Wouldn't count on it. There's only a couple of weeks until I was supposed to start in on the *Christmas Carol* designs," Sadie grumbled from the depths of her chair. Carol perched on the arm of the other.

"It's too bad," she said. "It would have been fun to have you around for a few weeks more. And those old costumes are in bad shape. Some of them are falling apart. It's going to be almost as much work to fix them up as it would have been to make new ones."

"Go tell that to the board." Sadie hauled herself upright. "Maybe I'll talk to Jazz. They might listen to her since she's famous. We're going to drive up to Cullen Village in Budgie's new car on Monday. Go see Roberta Axelsson's hand-dyed wool. Jazz wants to buy some. And eat a Thanksgiving lunch. Probably won't work but it's worth a try."

COOP JENKINS WORE a ball cap to cover the shaved, taped-up patch on his skull, and a purpling lump protruded above his left eyebrow. They went inside, bought food and found a table beside a window, one that looked out across the plaza to the river. It was thronged with shoppers and people strolling, talking, children running around. Roxanne had chosen Chinese vegetables and rice. Coop picked at a sandwich but he didn't look hungry.

"You look like you should still be in the hospital," she said. "How come they let you out?"

"Glad to see me go." Coop looked around him, checking everyone out, force of habit.

"Aren't you supposed to be lying down? Don't you have a concussion?"

"Don't know that for sure. I'll be fine." He didn't look fine. His skin was sallow. "Guess I got it wrong about the Longstaff woman and Budgie Torrance."

"You sure did. What made you think that they were a couple?" Roxanne speared a floret of broccoli and bit into it.

"Dunno. A hunch, I guess." He stared out the window at people relaxing, hanging out, having fun. "It's got to be one of them, right?"

"Not your case right now, Detective Sergeant."

"Well, Dumbo Dawes isn't going to help you solve it." He pushed the uneaten food aside. "We're just talking, right? Keeping up to speed." The right side of his mouth lifted in a crooked smile, almost. "Tamsin Longstaff was the only one of them who had a reason for wanting rid of the drama prof. That's why I went after her like I did. Bet she's your murderer." Coop drank some Coke from a large paper cup using his one good hand. "Did you see how mad she got at me? And violent with it. Bad temper. What if she got pissed off like that at Gerald Blaise? She's strong too. She sure clocked me one." He put down the cup and fingered the lump on his forehead. "And then what if Prof. Dyck figured it out? He must have known she didn't like having him hanging around at the theatre. Knew she didn't like him. Bet he didn't like her neither. He's a smart guy, right? Maybe he figured it out and that's why she did him in."

"Do you always make up stories like this?" asked Roxanne.

"Sometimes I get it right," said Coop Jenkins. There was that attempt at a smile again.

"And sometimes you don't," she replied. "Neither Budgie Torrance or Tamsin Longstaff has ever shown the least interest in having sex with other women."

"Win some, lose some." Coop looked away from the window and looked back at her. "How d'ya know that?"

"Budgie has a reputation with guys." Roxanne put down her fork. "And Tamsin has had a thing going on with Frank Moran for the past few years."

"That right?" Coop snorted. "Figures. He's a jerk. So, if they didn't do it, who did?"

"Don't know, Cooper." She had cleaned her plate. Coop's still sat off to one side, virtually untouched. "One thing's for sure. If Tamsin actually was involved, nobody's going to get killed this weekend. She's safely tucked away in the psych ward. You got any other good stories that might explain what happened?" She reached for a plastic tray and put her empty plate and cup on it.

"Nope." There was silence.

"We done then? You finished with that?" She added his uneaten food to the pile, walked to a waste container and tipped the lot inside.

"How did you get here?" she asked as they walked towards double glass doors.

"Got a daughter," he said. "She dropped me off."

A couple of children were playing on a low stone wall as they exited the building. One of them reminded her of Finn. She felt a momentary twinge of guilt. She really should go spend some time with her son. She'd better offer to drive Coop Jenkins home first though. He looked old and tired. It wouldn't take her long.

She led the way to a three-storey open parkade. The Forks was a popular spot on holiday weekends. The ramps were lined with cars. She could hear a band warming up at a sound stage in the distance. The blue Focus was parked halfway up the second floor.

"You're driving that?" said Coop. "What happened to your Toyota?" Then he stopped and peered at it. "Someone's been at it with a knife." They walked around the car. Its paintwork had been scratched deliberately, all the way along each side. The letters F U COP BITCH were carved onto the hood.

"Well," said Roxanne, reaching for her phone to photograph the damage. "At least it's driveable this time."

She told Coop how her tires had been slashed the previous day, right outside the RCMP HQ, as they drove west towards his apartment building. "It's maybe a message from Jem Sinclair. To tell me to stay away from his little brother."

Coop remembered Jem's threat, back when they had talked to him in the Youth Centre. "How would he know you were driving this car now?" he asked.

"Because I met Zeke again, just before you called me. Zeke watched me leave in this car."

"But how would Jem know you were going to the Forks?"

"Maybe he was watching." She glanced involuntarily behind her. "Maybe he's following me."

"Jem's a bad bastard," said Coop Jenkins. "Is he still a suspect? For the murders?"

"Don't think so. If he had done it he wouldn't be drawing my attention to him like this."

"Well," said Coop, "you can't drive around in this all weekend."

She might have to. It might not be easy to get another replacement today from the carpool. The RCMP liked to patrol the highways in unmarked cars on long weekends, watching out for speeders. Or drunk drivers, heading back to the city after a boozy evening out of town.

"My truck's not going anywhere. I'll trade you."

She turned her head towards him, astonished. "Your Silverado? Are you kidding?"

"Can't drive it, can I? And it's only for the weekend." The last thing she had expected was an offer like that from Cooper Jenkins.

"Anyway," he drawled, "you'll have to bring it back, right?"

She got it. This was Coop's way of staying in touch with the case. And he was right. She couldn't take this vandalized car home where small boys might notice the message carved onto it. Finn was learning to read and catching on fast. There would be awkward questions.

She drove around the block where Coop lived twice, slowly, both of them watching to see if anyone was following her. It looked like whoever had caused the damage was long gone. Coop's truck was parked behind his apartment building. Eight floors up, he told her, and pointed to a balcony. They swapped keys. She backed the big green Silverado truck out, and he drove the blue Ford into the vacant spot. She waited until he sloped off towards the back door of his apartment block. She lowered the window and called out, "Thanks, Coop."

"You're welcome." He touched a finger to his forehead and was gone.

She drove south, towards home and her sister's house. She remembered the kid playing on the wall at the Forks, out in the sunshine, having a good time. Her son and his cousin would love this big truck. She'd go pick them up and drive to the park. Maybe take the puppy along. She'd stop at the bakery on the way. Buy a couple of pies. One pumpkin, one apple. And a tub of ice cream. Her contribution to Thanksgiving dinner, tomorrow, at her sister's house. Baking was not Roxanne Calloway's thing.

21

MARGO WISHART HAD made a pumpkin pie for Thanksgiving from scratch. She and Sasha Rosenberg had driven to a farmer's market out on a farm road north of Cullen Village on Saturday to stock up on fresh fall produce before they closed for the season. After this weekend, the stalls would all be boarded up, and if the weather forecast was right, buried in snow by the middle of the week. Margo had found a round, dark orange sugar pumpkin, just right for making pie, and so she had baked on Sunday. Now it was Monday and time for Thanksgiving lunch at Roberta's house.

"The guests of honour are here already," she said as she pulled up alongside a shiny light-blue Prius, its glossy surface dusted with dirt. Budgie Torrance had trusted her GPS to lead her to Roberta's house. She had gone astray only once, found herself cruising down a gravel road, but Sadie Williams was a decent navigator. She had consulted an on-line map and got them back on track, no trouble at all.

Margo raised the hatch on her Honda. She lifted out a box containing the pie and a container of whipped cream. Sasha picked up a large pan wrapped in towels to keep the contents warm. They opened Roberta's front door and walked in, smelling roasted chicken and sage.

Budgie Torrance was standing in Roberta's porch, looking out across a grassy field to a stand of spruce. A few brown hens pecked in the dirt.

"You kill them yourself?" she said.

"Sure do." Roberta was hauling boxes of dyed yarn out of a closet. "Don't like it, but how else are we going to eat them?"

Sasha paused en route to the kitchen. "I've brought vegetables," she said to Budgie. "You can fill up on those if you'd rather." The pan contained root vegetables, beets, carrots, parsnips mixed with chunks of squash and dotted with garlic cloves, corn kernels, thyme and rosemary, roasted in oil and butter. Sasha didn't cook often, but for this traditional feast she had made an effort.

"That's okay," said Budgie. "Smells good." She had dressed for a day in the country, her style. Designer jeans, a fitted silk shirt, a leather belt with an ornate metal buckle and brown leather shoes with heels that were not too high. Golden hoops swung at her ears. A large diamond set in sculptured gold was on her finger. She was polished and shiny, incongruous in Roberta's shabby little house.

Jazz and Sadie were delving into heaps of yarn while Roberta explained how she created colour using local plants, like goldenrod or birchbark. Sadie had opted to wear tweeds, a skirt and tailored jacket. She had even found a pair of brogues that fit. Jazz wore her usual bright sweater, a mohair effort in fuchsia, green and purple this time. Roberta held up a dark brown skein.

"Dyed with black walnut," she said. "My neighbour has five trees growing in his yard. And the wool's alpaca."

Jazz reached out and took it from her hand. "I want," she said. "How many of those have you got?"

"Is that my cat out there?" Budgie pointed to a clump of rhubarb leaves. A large furry plume waved above them. Roberta glanced over, more interested in talking about her yarn.

"That's Tarquin," she said. "He's hopeless. Keeps trying to catch a bird but he's too fat and slow. Delilah's great though. She's a good mouser."

Budgie placed a hand on each hip. The diamond on her finger caught the light. "Those cats are pedigree Persians. They're supposed to be kept indoors. Have you any idea what they're worth?"

"Yeah," said Roberta, "but they're still cats." She was rooting around in the closet again, searching for bags. "He's happy out there."

Sadie sauntered over and watched the tail switch back and forth. "Bet he thinks he's gone to heaven after being shut in an apartment most of his life," she said. "You should let them stay, Budgie."

"Didn't your husband leave money for them to be cared for?" Margo stood in the door to the kitchen, a tea towel tied around her waist.

"How do you know that?" Two blue eyes, sharp as lasers, swept around to focus on her.

"Margo works for the RCMP sometimes as a consultant," Roberta remarked casually. She started to tally up how much wool Jazz had bought. Math wasn't her strong point. Two full bags added up to a tidy sum.

"Geez, Budgie," said Jazz. "Give the woman the cats. You can afford it."

"You need to pay her for taking them off your hands," Margo insisted. "There'll be costs. Grooming. Vet bills. Cat food."

"Okay, okay." Budgie turned her back to the window. "I'll get the accountant onto it. Aren't you going to put these in water?"

She had brought a bunch of fall flowers, big chrysanthemums, Shasta daisies, dahlias, shopped for her by her PA, Marla Caplan. They still sat in their wrapper on a sideboard. Soon they stood, resplendent, in a vase.

They all took their places at Roberta's long kitchen table and watched her cut up the chickens. She had roasted two of them, to be sure there was plenty and to compensate for the fact that this wasn't the traditional turkey. Budgie had also brought three bottles of wine. "They should be good," she said. "Gerald was picky about the wine that he bought."

"Those came from Gerald's wine rack?" asked Margo, passing a gravy boat.

"Someone's got to drink the stuff," said Budgie. "I'm not shipping all those bottles back to Ontario."

"You're definitely moving?"

"To Stratford." Budgie helped herself to a chicken thigh. "There's an old guy living there, was a set designer, retired years ago. His house is great and it's getting to be way too much for him. He needs to move into a care home."

"Is he going to oblige?" Jazz was sitting beside Sadie. She knew who Budgie was talking about.

"If he doesn't, it'll be okay. I can park the stuff in storage for a while. Once *Macbeth* closes I'm going to be in Toronto at the Tarragon."

"You do work a lot!" said Roberta with her mouth full. She liked her own leisurely life out in the country. "How do you cope with it and everything else that needs to be done?"

"She's got a PA," said Sadie.

"A minder." Jazz grinned. "Great stuffing." She waved her fork at Roberta.

"If I can get the condo sold I could get it all packed up while I've got Marla to help me. But first there's the cremation on Wednesday. And the funeral next Monday," Budgie reminded them. They chewed, not sure what to say about that. None of them wanted to talk about Gerald's death at what was supposed to be a celebratory meal. "You know, I'm not sure I want that girl sleeping in my apartment."

"Thought you didn't like being alone?" said Jazz.

"Yeah, but she does want to talk all the time," said Budgie. "And I've got good pills now to make me sleep. Maybe I'll tell her just to work days. She needs to get that art collection shipped to Toronto."

"So it's true you're going to sell all of it?" asked Margo.

"I am. Do you know if the RCMP still have that book where he wrote down the names of all the paintings he had? I need to get it back. Did you figure out how much it's all worth?" Budgie inquired. Margo lifted her glass and sipped. It was an excellent French Bordeaux.

"Maxwell Fergusson will price it for you, won't he?" she said.

"Oh, Maxwell." Budgie sighed theatrically. "Have you any idea how much that guy charges?"

"I can imagine," said Sasha. She occasionally sold sculptures in a Toronto gallery. "He's going to make a killing." Several eyebrows shot up at her use of the word. "Hey!" She was unapologetic, and the thought triggered an idea. "Maybe he did it! Killed off Gerald so he could sell off all that art."

"He lives in Toronto," said Margo.

"There's planes." Budgie's head tipped to one side as she thought about that. "The RCMP had this crazy idea I'd driven all the way from Regina overnight so I could murder Gerald myself." They all stopped eating. She looked around the table, knowing she had their full attention. "It's not so far-fetched, is it? Maxwell could have flown in, booked himself into a hotel, met up with Gerald, murdered him and shipped out back to Toronto." She reached for the nearest wine bottle and topped up her glass.

"You've got a great imagination, Budgie." Sadie pointed as the glass filled. "Aren't you driving?"

"Last one." Budgie put down the bottle, raised the glass and swallowed a defiant mouthful. "It's not a bad idea, though, is it?"

"Maybe not." Margo began to collect the plates. "How would he have known that you would sell all that art once you inherited it?"

"Because I told him so." Budgie smirked, triumphant. "Eons ago." She watched Roberta bring the pie to the table. "I can't eat that. I don't do dessert. Where's the cheese?" Sadie and Jazz had splurged on cheese and crackers at a deli near the theatre. "Someone should talk to that RCMP sergeant and tell her. You know her, right?" she asked Margo, who had deposited the used dishes and returned with a cake knife in her hand.

"They think they've got the killer. That Tamsin did it. Stupid idea." Jazz glared around the table, defying anyone to contradict her.

"Wonder what the hospital serves up for Thanksgiving?" Sadie watched the pie being cut.

"You could take her some of this," Roberta said. "There's plenty left over. And you'll be back in the city before visiting hours are done." They were eating lunch rather than dinner so that the guests could leave to drive back to the city in daylight.

"Can't." Budgie cut herself a wedge of ripe Gorgonzola. "She's locked up in the psych ward."

"We could try!" Sadie accepted a wedge of pie and dolloped cream on top.

"We could," Jazz agreed. "I wish we could have Tamsin back. That Alison Beck is cutting costs like mad. I got a warning against overspending yesterday, like I'm blowing the budget, which I'm not. She's trying to save money so she can impress the board."

"She really wants to be GM. All the techies say that's why Tamsin got rid of her."

"Won't happen," said Budgie. "I told her so yesterday. Frank Moran, the board chair, is a lawyer. He'll make sure that Tamsin comes back soon. And he'll get the police off her back, double quick." She lifted a cracker and cast a significant look across the table to where Jazz and Sadie sat. "Do you know that Alison's been talking to Maggie Soames in the U.K. about replacing me? Maggie emailed me, wanted to know what was going on. I'm going to have to have a word with her."

"Is this pie homemade?" asked Sadie. Margo smiled, pleased that she had noticed. "Yum," said Sadie.

They headed off before four. The sun hung, pale gold, in the west and the sky was already turning orange and pink.

"That Budgie's a case," said Sasha as she watched them drive off.

"Yes. But talented." Margo waved as the taillights turned onto the road.

"Gets away with blue murder," said Sasha. "Let's go help Roberta clean up, then we need to go home and let the dogs out."

BUDGIE WAS PERSUADED to stop at the hospital. She, Jazz and Sadie trooped into the reception area carrying a container of chicken, vegetables, potatoes and gravy, and another of pie and cream. Roberta had insisted they bring some of the flowers, too. They found their way to the correct floor, but there they were stopped.

"Ms. Longstaff is doing well," a polite but firm nurse informed them. "She'll be seeing the doctor tomorrow. Perhaps she'll be allowed visitors after that." She took the flowers. "I'll make sure she gets them," but rejected the offering of food. "Our patients have already eaten."

"Poor Tamsin," said Sadie as they walked away. "What will we do with it?"

"Give it to Marla," said Jazz. Marla Caplan had the evening off but would be back to sleep in Budgie's apartment. She'd said she was meeting friends at a restaurant. Italian. She wouldn't have had a real Thanksgiving dinner. They all piled back into the blue Prius and Budgie dropped Sadie and Jazz off in front of the grand old hotel where Jazz was still staying.

"I'll walk." Since Sadie had been supposed to stay in Winnipeg for three months, the theatre had found her a suite with a kitchen in a cheaper hotel a couple of streets over.

Budgie drove her car towards the condo. She cut down the lane between it and the theatre. At the far end, near the loading dock, was a BFI bin. She stopped, got out and dumped the food containers into it. Then she unlocked the door to the underground garage and drove her new car inside.

ROXANNE CALLOWAY SAT at her kitchen table while her son slept and wrote down the names of all the people who had a reason to want Gerald Blaise dead on a large sheet of paper. She drew three columns: motive, means and opportunity, that old mantra known to investigative police worldwide.

Budgie Torrance had the strongest motive. She would have saved herself the embarrassment caused by being left by her husband of thirty years and dumped in favour of a handsome young man. She'd have pocketed his substantial fortune. Opportunity was possible, but weak, and where was the means? Could she have used a kitchen knife, taken from the apartment? Or one brought from Regina, in a car? And why would she have killed Gerald in the parking lot? Had she connived with someone to do the killings for her? She could be charming and persuasive. And she would have the money to pay well, if that was necessary. She had no apparent reason to kill Thomas Dyck, though. Gerald's old friend might have known something that he shouldn't, but if he had they had yet to find out what.

Tamsin Longstaff was a more promising candidate. Her motive was less obvious, but Gerald's plan to leave could have alarmed her. She did have plenty of opportunity and there was no lack of sharp knives at the theatre. She was volatile, as Coop Jenkins had discovered to his cost. And she had reason to dislike Thom Dyck. Was it strong enough to kill him? Roxanne drew a red star beside the name. It was too bad Tamsin was in the hospital, out of reach, but that would not last. Soon she could talk to her again.

Jem Sinclair was trouble, but his only reason to kill Gerald would have been to rob him. That death wouldn't have been premeditated, but Thomas Dyck's certainly had been. Someone had waited for Thom at the park, had known that he ran there most mornings, had taken along a sharp blade. Could Jem have been hired to do the job? By Budgie? She shook her head. She didn't think so. Jem aspired to lead his gang, was cultivating his own pack of hounds, he wouldn't want to act on someone else's bidding. Unless he'd been paid very well. She ran a red arrow up to Budgie's name and marked it with a question mark.

Maxwell Fergusson stood to profit from Gerald's death, if Budgie sold the art collection, as rumour said she would. But how would he have known that would happen? He had as little opportunity and means as Budgie. There was a plane that flew into Winnipeg from Toronto late at night and another flew out in the morning, just after nine. It would be easy to check the flight lists. But did Maxwell Fergusson even know that Thom Dyck existed?

Alison Beck had benefitted from Tamsin's sudden absence at the theatre, but no one could have predicted that that would happen. Alison had known both Gerald and Thom Dyck, but so did all the administrative staff at PTC and the members of the board, including Frank Moran.

Madeleine Bissett, the theatre prof, had despised Thomas Dyck and wanted him gone. Her ambition gave her a motive, but why would she have wanted to get rid of Gerald? Apart from her, the only link they had found between the two dead men was the girl Chloe Delaney. But Gerald had only been a temporary inconvenience for her and she had barely known Professor Dyck.

Then there was the question of the missing daughter, the one who would have inherited the Balfour fortune if she had stayed home. What had happened to her?

Roxanne sighed and stretched. There were so many leads, going nowhere. It was getting late. She had arranged to drive over to Coop Jenkins' place first thing tomorrow, after she dropped Finn at her sister's, as she usually did. The truck had been a big hit with the boys. She had had to tell her sister why she was driving it.

"Finn's lost one parent already," Susan had said. "You shouldn't be putting yourself at risk. Why are you in the Major Crimes Unit? Can't you get yourself a safer job?"

"This is what I do," she had retorted. "I'm careful." It wasn't the first time Susan had mentioned that. Roxanne didn't like to be reminded. She'd messaged the carpool. She could swap the Focus for another car. They'd have several to choose from Tuesday morning after the long weekend. Her own car was still in the shop, waiting for delivery of the new tires.

Brian Donohue had left a message. When could they get together? They needed to talk. She had no idea when that could happen. She'd reply to him tomorrow. It was after midnight. Time for bed.

She woke, hearing her phone. 2:12 am, the screen said.

"Dawes here," boomed a loud voice. "Got called to that condo where your victim lived. Girl that lives there said his wife was missing."

"Budgie Torrance?" She was suddenly wide awake.

"Yeah, her. We found her. At the theatre. You need to get down here and see this."

22

ROXANNE PEEPED IN at her son, sound asleep, his mouth slightly open. Her sister Susan would be sleeping as well, in her own house.

"I can't make it right now," she told Dawes by speaker phone, biting her lip in frustration. "Send me photos?" She printed them as they came in. They showed a body lying on the floor of PTC's rehearsal hall, the mouth slightly agape, blue eyes open wide. Budgie Torrance wore jeans, a buckled belt, polished shoes, a silk shirt stained with blood. The black handle of a knife protruded just below her left breast, towards the centre, aimed straight for her heart. Her hands were wrapped around the handle.

Her script for *Macbeth* lay open at her feet. Some lines were highlighted in yellow.

> *Life's but a walking shadow, a poor player*
> *That struts and frets his hour upon the stage,*
> *And then is heard no more.*

Roxanne remembered them vaguely from high school.

"There's a bunch of highlighters," Dawes told her by phone. "In a box on a table. Her keys, her phone and her wallet are in her pockets. Isn't she your main suspect?"

"She was. One of two. The other one is the woman who attacked Coop Jenkins and she's still in the hospital."

"Looks like this one's done herself in," said Dawes. "That book's the one from some play she's acting in. The woman who unlocked this place for us knew all about it. Says the bits that are highlighted are about a woman who killed herself. She says this woman was on sleeping pills. Was depressed, but she didn't show it much. Actor type, right?"

"There's nothing else? She didn't write a letter?"

"No. But it has to be suicide."

"Don't know about that, Detective Sergeant." Roxanne peered at a close-up of the body. "It's another stabbing. We've had two other deaths involving knives. And since she died in Winnipeg it's going to be your case."

"Yeah," he reluctantly agreed. "But it's got to be linked to your first victim. She was married to him, wasn't she?"

"How did you find her?" asked Roxanne.

Marla Caplan had been dropped off by some friends at the front door of the condo, just before eleven. She'd let herself in. Had her own keys. She'd thought the Torrance woman had gone to bed already but opened the door to make sure she was all right. The bed was empty. Looked like it hadn't been slept in. She knew that Ms. Torrance was going to drive out to Cullen Village for a Thanksgiving lunch earlier with some people from the theatre, so she'd called one of them, who said Ms. Torrance had dropped her off downtown after 6:30, and she was in good spirits. Marla had gone down to the basement to see if the car was there and it was. There had been those other murders already. So she had phoned the police.

They'd decided to search the theatre. Marla had told them to call some woman called Beck. She came down right away and let them in. Lights had been left on in the rehearsal hall. And there they had found Budgie Torrance.

"Solves both our cases if she did it herself," said Dawes, still hopeful. "She bumped off her husband and the theatre prof, then had a guilty conscience. Or thought she'd be found out. Buckled under the strain. Ms. Beck says they had to pay the woman who reported her missing to help look after her, she was so stressed out. High-strung lot, these theatre folks, aren't they?"

"It looks so staged," Roxanne said, looking at the photographs spread out on her kitchen counter. "Maybe that's what we're supposed to think."

"Yeah, but she still could have done it herself," he insisted.

The Ident Unit was measuring and photographing. They knew already that there was only one set of fingerprints on the hilt of the knife, Dawes said. Dr. Farooq from the medical examiner's office was on his way. Rigor hadn't progressed much. Budgie couldn't have been dead more than four or five hours. With a bit of luck, the body would still be in place when Roxanne finally got there.

The sheet of paper Roxanne had worked on earlier was tacked to the side of her fridge with a couple of magnets. She looked at it again. Was Dawes right? Was Budgie responsible for both of the deaths? Had she decided enough was enough and chosen to end it all, like Lady Macbeth in the play they were rehearsing? Had she walked over to the theatre, taking a knife with her, opened her script at her chosen place and highlighted the quotation, arranged herself on the floor, then thrust the sharp blade into her heart, making herself look like another Shakespearean heroine she had probably acted several times when she was younger? She did look like Juliet lying in her tomb.

Or had someone lured her over there, killed her and laid out the body to make it look like suicide? Chosen that quotation to make it appear that she was depressed enough to kill herself? That she'd had enough of life? Used highlighter to disguise the fact that it was not Budgie making those marks? Budgie's writing was distinctive and samples of it were throughout her script.

Roxanne ran her eyes over the list again. Tamsin Longstaff was tucked away in a hospital bed. She couldn't be responsible for this. Jem Sinclair was unlikely. He wasn't a theatre person, and if anyone had killed Budgie, they had access to the theatre and knew Shakespeare's play. Maxwell Fergusson was a possible suspect. He knew theatre. He'd be familiar with the plays. And he could have met Budgie at the apartment. Used her keys after. That theory assumed Maxwell had managed to get to Winnipeg, which didn't seem likely but was easily checked. She texted Dawes. Someone should find out if anyone resembling the gallery owner had booked a seat on a plane to Toronto. That left Alison Beck and Madeleine Bissett, and there was little case against either.

She sent two texts, one to her sister saying she'd be dropping Finn off early and the other to Coop Jenkins. She'd have no time to take his truck to his place in the morning and go swap it for the damaged Focus, then go to the carpool and exchange it. That would have to wait. She set her alarm and lay down on her bed, pulled up the duvet and tried to sleep, but tossed and turned instead, running possible scenarios in her head. She was up and showered by 6:00 am. It was still dark when she strapped her sleepy boy, still in his pyjamas, into the cab of the Silverado and drove off. Her sister met her at the door and took Finn into her arms, shaking her head as she did so, and Roxanne headed back to work.

Prairie Theatre Centre was surrounded by police vehicles and tape. The scene in the rehearsal hall was theatrical, but this time the drama was for real. The body lay in the middle of the taped-out floor, brightly lit. Budgie's open eyes made her look startled—at the sudden pain as the knife entered her body or appalled that someone was killing her? She had not used highlighter anywhere else in her script. The words marked in yellow were clearly meant to be noticed.

Corporal Dave Kovak was over at the apartment. She called him. Marla Caplan had been sent home. Her fingerprints were all over the place. So were Budgie's. They had found others. One set belonged to the caretaker. Larry had been asked to fix the bathroom door, which kept sticking, on Friday. The cleaner had come that day too, but Larry had still been around after she had gone. Roxanne thought about the paintings on the walls. Gerald's killer had taken artwork, maybe as souvenirs. If the same person had stabbed Budgie, would another piece be missing?

"It was Alison Beck who opened up the theatre for you?" she asked Detective Sergeant Dawes.

Alison had. She had stayed right through, was still up there in her office. Right now, she was talking to a tall, bony woman and another little fat one who said they both worked here.

Roxanne guessed why Jazz Elliott and Sadie Smith would be ensconced with the acting GM this early. This death would cause huge problems for PTC. Their lead actor was dead, their rehearsal hall a crime scene. She remembered being told that Marla Caplan had placed a call to someone who had driven out to Cullen Village with Budgie the previous day. It was past seven. Margo Wishart might know something about that and she might be awake.

Margo said she was just making some coffee. "What's up?" She listened while Roxanne told her where she was and how Budgie had died.

"That is awful!" Roxanne could hear her pull out a chair so she could sit. "It looks like suicide?"

"It could be."

"Strange," Margo mused. "She was perfectly fine when she left here. She had plans. To sell up and go live in Stratford. Go do a new play at the Tarragon after *Macbeth*. She'd bought a new car. A Prius. She was going to drive it to Ontario herself, was looking forward to it. Jazz Elliot and Sadie Williams were with her when they left here. It was just after four. They'd be able to tell you if anything happened after they left."

"You have photos of all of Gerald's art collection in place on the walls of his apartment?" Margo did. She would send them to Roxanne and Izzy right away, so they could check to see if anything new had been taken.

Jazz and Sadie were still in Alison Beck's office. Roxanne could hear raised voices as she entered the corridor.

"Think about it, Alison. You'll have to get Maggie Soames to replace her, if this play isn't going to tank." Roxanne had heard of the famous Maggie Soames. She was impressed. The door opened and out stomped Jazz Elliot. She stopped when she saw Roxanne walking towards her.

"Good. It's you." She poked a finger straight at Roxanne's chin. "We need to talk." Sadie Williams loomed behind her. She waved a key card.

"The sewing room," she said. Roxanne let her walk by and lead the way. Alison Beck came to her door and watched.

"I need to talk to you after," said Roxanne.

"I'm not going anywhere." Alison went back into the office and closed the door behind her.

"That's who you should be arresting," Jazz muttered as she looked back along the corridor. "For murder. She's rooting for some local actor to take Budgie's place. Bet she got rid of her. She's power mad."

"The play's going to go on?" asked Roxanne. Both women froze in place, Jazz with a long woollen scarf half wrapped around her neck, Sadie with a jar of instant coffee in her hand.

"Cancel?"

"Never!"

"Budgie would turn in her grave!" Tears welled up in Jazz Elliot's eyes. She wasn't as tough as she liked to pretend she was. "No way she killed herself," she said and rubbed at her eyes with the end of her scarf. "We were with her yesterday, all afternoon. She was in good form, considering. Dropped us off at my hotel. Said she was going home. Wanted to have an early night."

Sadie looked towards a costume rack in the far corner of the room. Budgie's silk nightgown hung at the nearest end, the newly made lace negligee draped over it. "She can't have done it," she said. "If she'd really laid herself down in the rehearsal hall to die she'd have dressed for the occasion. She'd have put that on." She pointed at the lacy confection.

"Could she have got in here?" asked Roxanne.

"Course she could." Jazz reasserted herself. "Budgie could open up the whole place. She had an old master key. It was just the outside doors that got rekeyed. Tamsin wouldn't pay to do the whole building. If she'd wanted her costume, she could have got it."

"Tell me about yesterday," said Roxanne. They sat, drinking instant coffee, and talked. Nothing had suggested that Budgie was desperately depressed. She'd eaten, drunk some wine. Loved driving her new car. She'd said she was going to tell Marla to stop sleeping over. She didn't need her there at night, now that she had the sleeping pills.

Sadie raised mascara-smudged eyes from her mug. It looked like she had wept, too. "That's another reason why she wouldn't have offed herself like that. She could have OD'd if she'd wanted to. Why would she use a knife?"

That made some sense. Gerald Blaise had been slashed. Thom Dyck had taken a knife straight to the heart, as had Budgie Torrance. All three deaths involved the use of knives.

"We need to get Tamsin back." Jazz screwed up her face like a determined beetle. She was still focused on how the production could continue. "She just had a meltdown. Stands to reason, that city cop provoked her. She'll be fine now she's had a bit of a rest. We need to get her in here before that bad little Beck bitch causes any more damage. Go ask her where she was last night." She nodded in the direction of the office that Alison Beck now occupied. Roxanne intended to do just that.

"You're not going to work today?" she asked before she left.

"Yes, we are!" Jazz replied scornfully. That was partly what they'd been fighting over with Alison Beck. "She said we couldn't rehearse. The rehearsal hall was off limits. Rubbish, I told her. Nobody's in the lobby all day. We can do scenes that don't have Lady Mac in them. There's tons of those. And meantime, she needs to get the word out. There's other theatres in this town. Maybe one of them can loan us some space. They'll help out if they can. Theatres are like that. And if not there's church halls. There's a massive ballroom at the hotel."

"She won't pay," said Sadie.

"Too bad. She'll have to. And she needs to talk to Maggie Soames right away. Get her on a plane. She's available. I've checked already."

They were interrupted by a knock at the door. A uniformed city cop poked his head around. "Sergeant Calloway," he said. "You've got company."

"I have?"

"Yeah, Detective Sergeant Jenkins just dropped by. He says he's got car keys for you."

23

COOP JENKINS STILL wore the ball cap and his eye was purple and swollen. He hadn't made it past the PTC lobby door. All the city police knew he was off sick for now. He'd tried to talk them into letting him in so he could go find Roxanne (and have a look at what was going on while he was about it), but they shook their heads ("Sorry, Sarge") and told him to stay where he was.

He waved a new set of car keys when he saw Roxanne coming his way. "I scored you an Escape this time," he said. He'd stopped in at the RCMP HQ on his way downtown. "Told them you'd sent me to get it 'cause you were so busy, that you were working on another murder. They didn't argue when they saw the state the Focus was in. Told them how I'd done you a favour and lent you my truck. Guy said he'd need to text you and verify. You didn't reply so I told him to send one to that chick that works for you."

"Izzy McBain?"

"Yeah, her. She played right along. Said they should let me have it. Called me right after. Thought it was funny and sez to tell you she's on her way in from the boonies. Boy. Some of you Mounties sure are dumb. It was that easy. That guy at the carpool hadn't a clue. He was going to give you another Focus but I talked him into an upgrade. You'll like it. It's red. You should check your messages more often."

"It's been a busy morning, Coop. You drove?"

"Sure!" he replied, rocking back and forth on his heels, his eyes roaming the lobby behind him. "Why shouldn't I?"

"How come you knew where I was? And that there was another body?" She steered him towards a table in an empty café off the lobby. It was dark and quiet there, and away from the action happening around them.

"Soon as I read that message you sent earlier about being too busy to drop off the truck, I started phoning around. I've got pals. Hey, isn't that Moran that just walked in?" Frank Moran didn't see them. He went straight upstairs to the offices.

"So, it's the Budgie bird that's dead?" He'd been listening while he waited for Roxanne to appear.

"You're off sick, Coop. It's not your case right now."

"Just asking." Coop put his cap on the table and rubbed his head. He looked like he was feeling better, even with a half-shut eye. It wouldn't hurt to let him know the basics. She described the scene in the rehearsal hall.

"You think she did herself in?" he asked.

"Don't know. Dawes sure hopes she did."

"Well, he would. Lazy kinda guy, Dawes."

"There's still the business of the missing artwork. Where is it and who took it? Budgie had no reason to steal it. It was going to be hers anyway. She didn't even want it. So, I need to find out if there's another piece missing. If we have a killer who takes souvenirs. That would prove that this definitely is another murder."

Nell Bronson began shepherding actors into the lobby. She'd brought along several boxes of tissues. There was hugging, quiet talk and blowing of noses.

"There you are." Dr. Abdur Farooq stood in the theatre doorway, watched what was happening in the lobby, then noticed them in their quiet corner. "Cooper," he said. "Aren't you supposed to be off sick for now?"

"Just hanging out with Foxy here," said Coop.

"How's that head?"

The corner of Coop's mouth lifted. "Just fine," he lied.

"Go home, Cooper," said Roxanne. "You can't do anything here right now. Thanks for getting me the car."

"Liked my truck did you?" He was stalling, reluctant to go.

"My boy did," she smiled. "Not a city car though, is it? Maybe you're really a country cop at heart, Cooper. Maybe you joined the wrong force."

"Never," he retorted. "See ya." And, finally, he loped off.

"Cops like him don't know what to do with themselves when they're off work." Abdur watched him saunter out. The uniformed city policeman who manned the door opened it for him, nodded to him as he walked through.

"Will he get reprimanded?"

"For grabbing Tamsin Longstaff's arm?" Abdur took the seat that Coop had vacated. "Maybe. Word is that he's a bit of a loose cannon. But he's got to be close to retirement. They'll be rid of him soon enough."

And he's a con, she thought, thinking how Coop had managed to convince the RCMP carpool to change the car for him. She put the keys away in her pocket and the thought of Coop Jenkins with them.

"So, Abdur. Tell me what you've got so far."

"Not much. Death happened between eight and ten last night. Single wound. You've seen it. No obvious signs of any other injury, but I'll know more after the autopsy. It's been made to look like it's self-inflicted, but I doubt it."

"Really?"

"Well." He stretched out his long legs. "There should be more blood. Not much, but there's hardly any on the hand that she's supposed to have stabbed herself with and it's more smeared than spattered. And I'd have expected more spray on the sleeve of that silk shirt she's wearing. If she'd done it where she was found, it should be there, but there's no sign of it. If someone else stabbed her she'd have fallen, then the body was rearranged. There should be some blood on the floor."

"It could have been cleaned up."

"That flooring is wood. Porous. If it's there, the Ident guys will find it. She might have been killed elsewhere. Who else could get into her condo?"

"Her PA," said Roxanne, "but she was out all night. With friends. She was dropped off just after eleven." She stopped, momentarily distracted. The dark figure of Dr. Madeleine Bissett had drifted into the lobby. Like Abdur before her, she was watching the actors. Chairs were being placed in a large circle and the cast and crew were finding seats. She glanced Roxanne's way, raised a hand in unsmiling acknowledgement and disappeared upstairs, like the board chair before her.

"Budgie could have let someone in," Abdur continued, oblivious to what she had seen. "And that person could have used her keys to bring the body over here, set it up to look like suicide, then went back and cleaned up."

"You're thinking like an investigator, Abdur."

"Comes from working with people like you, Roxanne." He'd told her all he knew for now. He'd try to get the autopsy done tomorrow and let her know if he found anything else. They got up to leave.

The actors were now taking turns to speak, telling stories and anecdotes about working with Budgie, doing their own private grieving before they got back to rehearsing the play. Jazz Elliot beetled down the stairs and through the door just as Roxanne reached it.

"God, they've started without me," she said and scurried over to join her tribe.

Upstairs, Frank Moran and Madeleine Bissett were standing in the doorway to Gerald Blaise's old study. Moran beckoned.

"You've met Dr. Bissett? She's going to be joining the board, to replace Thomas Dyck. I think she's going to be quite an asset." Moran looked at Bissett from under his hooded eyelids and smiled. She mustered a quiver of her lip.

"Did you need to talk to Alison Beck?" asked Roxanne. She expected a meeting with Alison was on Moran's agenda. "Can I have a word with her first?"

"Alison?" asked Madeleine Bissett.

"You know her?"

"Of course," said the professor, her black cloak draped on one shoulder. "Her partner, Greg, is the local theatre critic and an accomplished playwright. It's a small community, Sergeant. We all know one another. Is there anything else I can help you with?"

There wasn't, for now.

Roxanne found Alison Beck seated at her desk, tallying up figures on a calculator.

"You've been here since they found the body," she said. Alison nodded and reluctantly stopped tapping numbers.

"I have. There's so much to do. So much to figure out. Do we cancel the production or go ahead? If we do, who do we get to replace Budgie? I need to know what all the options are and the costs involved so that the board can make the right decisions. And it is all so sad…"

"You believe it's suicide?"

"Of course it is, Sergeant!" Alison Beck appeared surprised that Roxanne would think otherwise. "You saw that body? How it was arranged to look like Juliet? Budgie died in the rehearsal hall, the place where she was most at home. And the quotation, from the Scottish play? It's so…." She searched for the word. "Apt," she finally came up with. "They say that Lady Macbeth died by suicide too."

"Why would she do it?" asked Roxanne.

"Budgie was a born performer, Sergeant. She could act like things were fine, but they were not. She was a mess. Ask Jazz or Nell Bronson. They'll tell you how hard it was to get her to concentrate on the job. That's why we had to get Marla to stay over at her place and help her out. If she murdered Gerald and Thom, that explains the state she was in."

"You thought it was obvious that Tamsin Longstaff was the killer and she wasn't," said Roxanne. "Could you have it wrong this time too?"

"Don't think so," said Alison. "Think about it. *And then is heard no more.* That is about endings. Death. It's her, saying farewell."

"Where were you yesterday evening?"

Alison blinked. "Why do you ask?"

"Just answer the question, please."

"Greg and I went to listen to a band in a café. Lots of people were there. Marla Caplan was at our table."

"What time did you leave?"

"Same time as Marla. It was almost eleven." Alison Beck had an alibi. She could have had nothing to do with Budgie Torrance's death the night before.

"I've been told that you collect art?"

"We do. Greg and I like to support local artists. We often go to gallery openings. Sometimes we pick up a piece that we like." Alison sighed. "Small things, ones we can afford."

"So did Gerald Blaise."

Alison shrugged. "Well, we weren't in his league. We can't pay what Gerald could. I did like to talk about art with him, though. I miss Gerald very much." She leaned her chin on her hand. "His cremation's tomorrow and the celebration of his life happens next Monday, and now Budgie's gone and died I suppose I'll have to help take care of that too. The Monday event's going to be huge, and now it maybe needs to include Budgie." She took off her glasses and rubbed her eyes. They looked heavy. Roxanne had seen that look of exhaustion before, in the eyes of the woman that Alison Beck had replaced.

"There are no relatives?"

"No. They were both only children and they didn't have any of their own. Gerald might have wanted a child. He'd have been a good dad. His cats were like his kids. But Budgie wasn't exactly maternal."

"You didn't like her much, did you?" Roxanne said.

"Budgie? She was a handful to work with. Such a diva. But brilliant onstage. I saw her in *Medea* years ago. Unforgettable. She could be fearless, you know. I guess that's why she's done this. She must have regretted killing Gerald."

OVER AT BUDGIE'S apartment, Izzy McBain was checking the paintings and statues against the photographs that Margo had sent. They were panoramic shots of each wall. Nothing had changed. Everything was in its place.

Two Ident technicians were still at work searching for signs that a disturbance might have occurred. They had sprayed Luminol in the kitchen to see if any blood spots would show. They found some traces along the edge of the vinyl floor, but they looked old. They might not be Budgie's. Sometimes a slab of meat fell off a counter. They took samples. They'd find out later.

Izzy went into Budgie's room, plastic covers on her feet, extra latex gloves in her pocket. She smelled perfume. There was makeup on the dressing table, bottles of foundation, lipstick, eyeliner. A brush and hairspray. A hand mirror. Some jewellery, including big hoop earrings. It was all scattered around haphazardly, as though Budgie had just walked away.

The shawl that covered the safe in the corner had been removed. Its key had been among those they had found near Budgie's body. Investment papers and a will were inside. Budgie left everything to Gerald, and if he predeceased her, to the Actors' Fund of Canada. There was not a single personal bequest. Her only relative had been Gerald. Like him, she had named their accountant, Irma Friedrich, as her executor. Irma was to be reimbursed handsomely for her services.

Izzy retrieved the jewellery box from the safe, carried it over to Budgie's desk and opened it. The items it contained were wrapped in soft cloth or individually boxed. There were green earrings, a pendant with a blue stone hanging from it, an opal set in a band of wide silver, a string of perfect pearls. Apart from it, all the settings were contemporary. Were these real gems, ones Budgie had inherited from Gerald's old aunt and had had redesigned into settings that were more to her taste?

A technician spoke behind her, startling her. "There's someone here, come to collect her things." Marla hovered at the door. She pointed towards Gerald's study. "I've got stuff in there," she said. "My iPad. Clothes. Can I go get them?"

"Sure," said Izzy, "as long as you don't mind me watching, and you'll have to sign for them."

Marla was given foot coverings and gloves. She stuffed some clothes, toiletries, the iPad, into a knapsack. She was going over to PTC when she was done, she said. Alison Beck was run off her feet. Marla was needed in the office after all. She balled up the sheets from the temporary bed she had used, went through to the utility room and tossed them into a laundry basket.

"I have some money that belonged to Budgie." Marla's salary was being paid by PTC but Budgie had written her a cheque to cover expenses. Dry cleaning bills. Groceries. There was almost three hundred dollars left.

"Put them in an envelope," said Izzy. "I'll write you a receipt."

"Would you? That's great." She went back into Budgie's study, took an envelope from the desk drawer and stuffed in the cash.

"Do you think she killed herself?" asked Izzy, taking it from her.

"Well. She could get pretty sad sometimes." Marla sat on the desk chair. "The first night I was here she sat and cried in her room, sitting right there at her dressing table, great big tears rolling down her face. She missed Gerald so much, she said, kept imagining she could see him in the apartment, in the kitchen, chopping up vegetables or sitting reading in his big chair. 'It's like this apartment's haunted,' she said. That's when I decided to get her to a doctor. There's a walk-in clinic a couple of blocks away. She got a prescription for Lorazepam. That helped."

The bottle of drugs had been found in the bathroom medicine cabinet and bagged. Budgie had only taken the prescribed dose. "I didn't see her much the day she died."

Izzy sat in the big wicker chair, took out her phone and emailed Marla a receipt while she listened.

"The last time was in the morning, just before eleven. I got out the elevator here, at the ground floor, and she was going down to the parking level to get her car. She was quite cheerful. But Budgie had huge mood swings. When she was happy she was great, she could be really good fun, but when she was down she was miserable."

"Not easy to work with?"

A wry smile passed across Marla's face. "Things were never dull when Budgie was around," she said. She looked at the open jewellery box on the desk in front of her. She fingered the contents.

"Was she wearing her big diamond ring when you found her?" she asked. "She had it on yesterday."

"What big diamond?"

"It's the most valuable piece she had. She showed it to me. It had been an antique but Budgie had it made into this big, dramatic piece, two shades of gold, old yellow and a lighter one."

"We'll look," said Izzy.

As soon as Marla was gone, she and the technician listed the contents of the jewellery box and the items scattered on the top of the dressing table. There was a drawer that contained boxes of costume jewellery, rings, necklaces, brooches. They opened and closed them all. There was no sign at all of the expensive designer ring that Budgie had worn the day before, when she had driven to Cullen Village to eat Thanksgiving lunch.

24

SADIE WILLIAMS AND Jazz Elliot both confirmed that Budgie had worn a ring with a large diamond at its centre when they had eaten lunch at Roberta Axelsson's house on Monday.

"It was spectacular," said Sadie, who noticed these things.

It was nowhere to be found. Budgie's apartment was searched again, thoroughly, every rug lifted, every corner exposed. Furniture was moved, drawers pulled out and shelves emptied. Her car was subjected to the same scrutiny, as were the condo's hallways, the mirrored elevator. The search extended across the lane, into the passageways that led to PTC's rehearsal hall, where Budgie's body had been found. No gleam of gold or stab of light revealed where the ring was hidden. Like the paintings that had disappeared before it, it was gone.

"That makes it murder?" Inspector Schultz looked up at Roxanne, his laptop open at her latest report. He had summoned her to HQ to consult with him.

"The killer may be taking trophies, sir. The first two were paintings and this one is jewellery, but very artistic, I'm told."

"Someone else could have helped themselves. The PA?"

"She wasn't around when the first paintings disappeared. And she has an alibi for the time that Ms. Torrance died."

"Could the caretaker be helping himself?"

"The painting by Annie Chan's valuable but I don't think he'd would know that. Unless Gerald had told him." It was a possibility, but unlikely. Where was the motive?

"So, if someone killed her, who's your best bet?"

She didn't have one, not anymore. Budgie Torrance was dead and neither Tamsin Longstaff or Alison Beck could have been responsible for killing her. Their alibis were rock solid.

Schultz lowered his brows. They were a long way from solving this. He also wanted Budgie's murder, if that was what it was, to be the city police force's problem. The body was on their turf, and yet it had to be linked to the death of her husband and that of Professor Dyck. Two bodies found in the city, one out in the country, RCMP jurisdiction. The new case would have to be investigated by both police forces in tandem, like the murders before it, he grudgingly conceded. He'd talk to the city police force.

"So, what now?" he asked.

"Gerald Blaise is being cremated," she replied. "This afternoon."

Outside, the sun shone. That wasn't going to last long. Snow was blowing across the highways in the west of the province, icing up road surfaces and reducing visibility. The Trans-Canada Highway was closed already, just east of the border with Saskatchewan, and the storm was coming their way. The service was scheduled to start at one. With a bit of luck, it would be over before the temperature dropped below zero and the city became shrouded in wet, heavy snow.

Word that another body had been found at Prairie Theatre Centre was public knowledge already, but the police had managed to avoid issuing a name or any details to the press. That hadn't stopped word from leaking out through social media. Speculation that the well-known actor Annabel Torrance had died had travelled the airwaves across Canada already. The RCMP and the city force's communications were wrangling about shared responsibilities, stalling on having to give a response. Was it murder, the news platforms wanted to know? Neither force was willing to say. But Toby Malleson had been contacted. News was news, the bad as well as the good, and Toby was good at dropping hints. Twitter was buzzing with speculation.

Izzy McBain was waiting at Roxanne's office, impatient to see her. "We've checked the airlines. Maxwell Fergusson hasn't flown between here and Toronto recently, but he's on one today. Should be landing around now. Guess you'll see him at the funeral." She had other news. "Emilia, the missing Balfour daughter, died a couple of years ago in Nelson, B.C. She had four kids, and her obituary only gave first names, but the RCMP in Nelson have traced one of them to Surrey, B.C. They'll talk to him and get back to me, soon as they know more."

There had been some question as to whether the cremation service for Gerald should be postponed. Maybe it should. They could wait until Budgie's body was released, then send them into the fire together. But no one knew when that might be, so they decided to go ahead with the cremation as planned. The memorial scheduled for the following Monday at the theatre was intended to accommodate the whole theatre community. That could be adapted to also honour Budgie. But today, Wednesday, PTC's administrative staff, the techies and the actors, wanted to go to the funeral home to say goodbye and witness Gerald's final journey. The scheduled matinee and evening performance would go on, but otherwise PTC had closed in honour of their deceased artistic director. The cast for the show that was being performed was disappointed. They would have to stay and work. But they were mollified by being invited to present a musical number from the show at the memorial on Monday.

There was no rehearsal for *Macbeth* today. Jazz Elliot had cheered up when she learned that Maggie Soames, her choice to replace Budgie Torrance in the role of Lady Macbeth, was flying in from Heathrow, via Toronto. The board chair had listened to her plea. Dr. Bissett had supported the decision. Alison Beck had had to bow to his ruling. They just hoped Maggie would make it into Winnipeg tonight. The airport might have to close if this storm turned into a full-blown blizzard. Outside, big snowflakes were already drifting down from a leaden sky.

Izzy pulled the weather report up on her screen. "Storm warning," she said. "The highway's closed just west of the city now. It's sheet ice already."

She was looking at a video of a truck stop, the parking lot full of semis, the drivers scuttling inside, where there was light, warmth, hot coffee and Wi-Fi. There were barriers blocking all travel west. RCMP cars were monitoring the situation, lights flashing. Roxanne had been there, done that. She didn't envy them that assignment.

She'd worn dress boots with small heels today, wanting to look right for the funeral. Now she wished she'd ignored the dictates of fashion and pulled out winter ones with decent soles and a parka instead of her black wool coat. Izzy said she had a scarf and fetched it. It was pink. It didn't look great but it was better than nothing. Roxanne wrapped it round her neck and headed out into the snow.

Alison Beck stood in the foyer of the funeral home, directing guests to sign the visitors' book. A lean, dark man hovered nearby. She introduced him as Greg Baxter, her partner.

"Greg writes plays and theatre reviews," she said as she looked over Roxanne's shoulder, ready to welcome the next group of visitors. Roxanne signed as instructed, then flipped back a page to see who had already arrived. She saw Maxwell Fergusson's signature, and below it, the name of Timothy Baldwin. Gerald's young lover had travelled from B.C. to attend. Marla Caplan stood at the doorway to the hall, handing out orders of service, a tight smile on her face. Gerald's large oak coffin lay at the front of the hall, banks of white flowers cascading down either side of it. It was closed. Instead, his large photographed face was mounted on an easel. It beamed out at the growing assembly. A live string quartet was playing. The room was hushed.

Roxanne could see a leonine head of white hair, a dark one at its side, up at the front. That must be Maxwell Fergusson and Tim Baldwin. Larry the caretaker sat near the middle of the hall. So did Jazz Elliot, wrapped in shades of purple. Sadie Wilson was beside her, a brown cloche pulled down over her hair. Roxanne moved back up the aisle, looking for a spot at the side that would allow her to survey most of the crowd. Tamsin Longstaff walked towards her, released from the hospital in time to put in an appearance. She was as well-groomed as ever. She wore immaculate black clothes and clicked down the aisle in polished boots. The smile she gave Roxanne as she passed her didn't reach her well-made-up eyes. Toby Malleson turned and waved to her. He rose and made room for her beside him. They sat right behind Jazz and Sadie. Pedro Diaz, Carol Hansen, Nell Bronson and the rest of the tech crew occupied another row. Actors were ranged around them. Tamsin had rejoined her clan. Roxanne wondered how Alison Beck had greeted her when she walked in the door. Frank Moran appeared in the opposite aisle, a small, blonde woman on his arm. That would be his wife. It could have been awkward too, if Frank, his wife, and Tamsin Longstaff had found themselves face to face. But maybe Mrs. Moran knew nothing about her husband's relationship with Tamsin.

The ceremony lasted exactly one hour. No one was invited to rise ad hoc and reminisce. Anecdotes were to be saved for Monday. Lisa Storm and the two women who played the *Macbeth* witches sang together. They had good voices and harmonized well. Roxanne saw Jazz Elliot turn around and make a comment to Tamsin. There were a couple of accomplished poetry readings, one of them delivered by Danny Foyle, the actor playing Macbeth. It was more like a concert than a funeral service. Maxwell Fergusson, as one of Gerald's oldest friends, had been invited to speak.

He'd known Gerald all his life, he said. They had been schoolboys together and had remained the best of friends. Gerald had a talent for friendship. Heads nodded in agreement. He'd been a generous man, a gifted man. He and PTC had been a match made in heaven. He mentioned how Gerald and Budgie had been allies in the service of theatre. His voice went gruff when he mentioned

Budgie's name. Eyes were dabbed, lips quivered. Timothy Baldwin reached for a wad of tissue, openly weeping.

"Gerald would not want us to be sad," Maxwell reminded them. "Above all, Gerald had a gift for happiness. He wanted the plays he chose to make people laugh and smile. He liked to cook good food and share a glass of wine and a story or two. Gerald was always good company, and that is how we must remember him." He raised his open hand in the direction of his friend's smiling face in a kind of benediction that included them all.

The last song was sung lustily by the full congregation. Gerald's coffin slid from view into the furnace and a curtain was drawn discreetly over the void that was left. The crowd rose to its collective feet, ready to leave. There was no reception planned for afterwards. "We'll make it a real party on Monday," Roxanne heard someone say.

"The evening show's been cancelled." The news buzzed up and down the aisles. "They're saying we might have a blizzard. We need to get home." If PTC was closing, the weather forecast must be grim. Pedro Diaz had brought the theatre's touring van so he could drive all the actors safely home or to where they were staying. Nell, the stage manager, was driving another.

Roxanne found Maxwell Fergusson talking to Jazz Elliot in the lobby. Timothy Baldwin had retired to the washroom to fix himself up. "Poor boy's bereft," said Maxwell. He'd booked them in at the same venerable old hotel where Jazz was staying, until Monday. The time between then and now would give him a chance to have a good look at Gerald's art collection. He needed to make sure that everything was shipped correctly. He'd get that all organized and let poor Tim have a look at the place where Gerald had lived. He'd never seen it. Terrible news about poor Budgie, wasn't it, but of course Tim couldn't have come if she was still around. He, Maxwell, had sent the boy a ticket as soon as he knew. He took Roxanne by the arm. "I need to have a private chat with this lovely lady," he said and led her towards a corner.

"I have news," he announced, "that might interest you, Sergeant. There's a rumour floating around the art world that a painting by Annie Chan was auctioned in London recently. Fetched two hundred and sixty-five thousand pounds sterling."

"Really?" said Roxanne.

"I have one of those, an Annie Chan," said a voice behind them. Tim Baldwin had freshened up and returned. They both gaped at him. "It was a birthday present. I really like her work. Told Gerald, so he gave it to me. It's in my studio, on the island."

"When did you get it?"

"September. Gerald came for a visit. Brought it on the plane with him. It was the last time I saw him." He sniffed again, but this time he maintained his composure.

"Did he give you any more presents like that?"

"No," said Tim, "but he was going to come live with me. He'd have brought most of his collection with him. Now it's all going to be sold." He drooped like a sad puppy.

Roxanne turned to Maxwell. "Has he ever given away other paintings?" she asked.

"Not that I know of," said Maxwell. "It must have been a very special gift." He gave Tim Baldwin's arm a consoling pat.

Jazz Elliot was at the other side of the room deep in conversation with Tamsin Longstaff. She'd called over a young man.

"Sound technician," said Sadie Williams, joining Roxanne and Maxwell. "Now that she's heard them, she wants to have the witches sing their big scenes, maybe even sing throughout the play, like a background band. Big change and it's a bit late, but Tamsin's all for it."

Near the door, Alison Beck and her dark-haired partner were watching. "Alison isn't happy," Sadie said, looking thoroughly pleased. "Tamsin's going to be back in business, no time at all. You got a car, Maxwell? Can you give us a ride back downtown?"

Maxwell did. He'd rented one at the airport. And he'd be delighted. Maybe they could have dinner together? They waved to Jazz. Was she coming with them?

Roxanne's phone buzzed. Izzy. Many eyes followed her as she ducked back into the hall to take the call. Marla and Toby were collecting discarded sheets of paper from the aisles. Roxanne might be watching what was going on, but she was also being watched. Toby looked anxiously towards her as he tactfully walked out the hall door. Marla followed. They must all be wondering what she knew. And right now, that wasn't much.

"A guy from the RCMP in Surrey, B.C. just called," said Izzy. "He talked to Emilia Balfour's son. He has a sister in Calgary and two stepbrothers, one in Fort McMurray and one in Toronto. Their last name is Caplan."

Roxanne heard a cough behind her. Larry the caretaker stood in the aisle.

"When you're done," he said. "There's something I need to tell you."

25

ROXANNE SAT DOWN again in one of the pews. Larry slid in beside her.

"It's like this," he said. "You know that girl that just went out, the one that's been staying in Budgie's apartment?"

"Marla Caplan? Her personal assistant?"

"That's what they call it? Well, yeah, her. They had a big row, Sunday night. Her and Budgie. I heard them."

"Do you hear what they were saying?"

Larry looked sideways at her. "Bits of it. Enough." His splayed fingers rubbed his knees. He looked back to see if anyone else could hear them. There was a babble in the lobby but no one else had re-entered the funeral hall. "Remember how you and her, Marla, went down into the basement the other day? To look through all that stuff that was boxed up in that storage cage?"

Roxanne nodded, listening while her mind raced. Marla's grandmother was perhaps Gerald Blaise's cousin. Marla had shown up at PTC right after Gerald's death. She'd got the job at the theatre, had the right credentials, but that must have been luck. And then she'd wormed her way into Budgie Torrance's apartment and into her life. Had that been deliberate?

"She went back down there by herself earlier, on Sunday, when Budgie was over at PTC. I saw her. She had her phone out, taking photos. Some of the boxes were open. Looked dead guilty when I caught her at it. 'What ya doing?' I asked her and she said she was working on something for Budgie. But she looked like she'd been caught doing something she shouldn't, like she was lying.

"I was out in the hallway Monday morning, just tacking down a bit of loose carpet, and I heard Budgie yelling something about Marla snooping into her things. Budgie could be real loud sometimes. 'I don't think I want you around so much,' she said. 'I want that bed gone out of Gerald's study.'"

"How did she find out that Marla had been looking?" asked Roxanne. Larry stared out front. Gerald Blaise's face beamed back at them from its pedestal.

"Because I told her." He shifted in his seat. Then he turned back to her. "But now Budgie's dead and somebody stole that big ring she wore. So I reckoned you should know."

Marla could not have killed Budgie. She'd been at the restaurant until just after eleven that night and had called the police herself just after eleven-thirty. She would not have had time to carry out a murder, arrange the body in PTC's rehearsal hall and clean up. Abdur Farooq had said death had happened between eight and ten that evening. But still... Had she stayed at the restaurant the whole time? Could she have left for an hour or two and gone back? Was she working alone? If Emilia Balfour had had four children, there could be other grandchildren like Marla. Did any of them live in Winnipeg?

"Can you let me into that storage locker?" she asked Larry. It wouldn't hurt to go look again. She remembered Marla standing beside an open box of photographs, one held in both hands, one that showed the Balfours with their daughter, Emilia, who might be Marla's grandmother.

"Sure," said Larry. "Need to break the lock but I can do that. You want to do it today? Weather's getting bad, they say." He was going straight home, as soon as he'd cleared the snow off his car.

"I'll see you shortly," said Roxanne. Larry disappeared up the aisle. Toby Malleson appeared in the doorway as Larry left.

"We've got to get everything out of here, Sergeant," he said. Marla Caplan was right behind him, all smiles as usual, the picture of innocence. The lobby was almost empty. Alison Beck put the guest book and pen into a box and handed it to Greg Baxter, her partner.

"Don't worry, I'll fix it," Roxanne heard her say. Greg saw Roxanne. He knew she had heard that comment. Alison turned.

"We're all leaving soon, Sergeant," she told Roxanne, unfazed. Greg disappeared out the front door. Alison went into the hall, presumably to help with the final clean-up. Nell Bronson, the stage manager for *Macbeth*, was at a coat rack, zipping up a parka.

"Alison is so pissed off," she whispered through the hangers as Roxanne reached for her coat. "She was going to get Greg's play produced at PTC next year, but Tamsin says she's going to put a stop to that." She came around the side of the rack, reaching into her capacious pockets for a cap with earflaps.

Alison had been in the restaurant the same night as Marla, but had her partner, Roxanne wondered.

Nell was wrapping a long scarf around her neck, one that was right for the weather outside. "Alison's always telling people how brilliant a writer Greg is but Gerald thought he was way too edgy. Wouldn't touch what he wrote with a bargepole, he said." Nell added thick mitts to her ensemble. "It's all going to be okay, though," she added. "Tamsin isn't going to take much more time off. She'll be back real soon and we'll be rid of Alison. Tamsin will fix everything."

Roxanne walked back to the door of the hall and looked inside as she buttoned up her coat. Marla held a basket of flowers, arum lilies, white roses. She saw Roxanne and smiled again, perfectly composed, without a hint of guilt or unease. Could this cheerful young woman be responsible for three deaths? If she was a direct descendant of old Mrs. Balfour, she could try to get that old will overturned and get at least part of the fortune. It gave her a motive, but had she even been in Winnipeg when Gerald Blaise died? She had an alibi for the night that Budgie Torrance died, and why would she have wanted to kill Thom Dyck? Roxanne had been at PTC the day that Marla started work at the theatre, and it had appeared as if it was the first time she had met the professor.

Alison was talking to a man in a dark suit, a staff person from the funeral home. She had good reason to feel betrayed by Gerald Blaise. She'd been glad to be rehired at PTC, to salvage her reputation. Being fired must have hurt her. And now it seemed that Gerald had also thwarted her partner's career as a playwright. Was that enough of a motive to kill him? Thom Dyck knew the theatre community. He'd have known about Greg's aspirations. But before Budgie had died, Alison had been reinstated at PTC and she was making changes. Greg's play was going to be produced, if she had her way. Why kill Budgie and complicate things? Toby Malleson, up on the dais, was holding Gerald's framed photograph.

"You leaving, Sergeant? We've got to get out of here," he said.

Nell Bronson walked through the other door, her boots now thick with snow. "You guys coming? I've got the van running, right outside. It's coming down like crazy out there."

Roxanne followed them outside into a blinding whiteness. A van was parked close to the door, its windows almost clear of snow, fumes puffing from the exhaust. To her left, at the far end of the street, she could see the glimmer of lights and hear the purr of car engines as traffic became snarled on a main thoroughfare. Her own car was a block away in the other direction. She'd arrived too late to find a spot in the funeral home's parking lot. She could barely see where she was going. It was too early for the street lights to be on. The snow came down, thick and fast, six inches deep already. The scarf she had borrowed was only a few inches wide. She lifted it to cover her face but then snowflakes seeped down her neck, cold and wet, and still stuck to her hair and eyelashes. She pulled her coat collar closer. The boots she was wearing were useless, leaking at the seams already, the snow clumping at the heels, the leather soles skidding under her. She couldn't see where the sidewalk ended and she had to fight to keep her balance. There were few cars around on this side street. Everyone else who had parked there had already started the slow trek home.

She groped her way in the direction of the car. How far away was it? She found her car keys in her pocket and clicked the starter. Lights blinked a hundred or so feet ahead, dimmed by a screen of large white flakes. At least she could see now where it was. Sirens were wailing behind her, out on the main drag. There would be collisions on an afternoon like this. The city police would be busy. The only other sound was the hum of traffic, crawling, bumper to bumper. Otherwise, the town was quiet, silenced by a blanket that drifted relentlessly down, getting thicker by the minute. Everyone who could be was safe home already, with the doors firmly closed against the storm.

The red Escape looked like an igloo. She clicked the remote start and unlocked it, stomping her feet to get rid of the snow packed on her boots. The engine was warming up the inside. Beads of moisture were beginning to gather on the windshield under a white, frosty layer that had iced up around the edges. She slid her way to the back of the car and opened the hatch. A snowbrush lay inside. She made her way back to the front to start sweeping the snow off the roof, down over the windows. The temperature must be just below zero, not cold at all for Winnipeg, but this was heavy, wet snow and the damp made her shiver. She used the plastic scraper at the end of the brush to clear the wipers, lifting them in turn to get packed snow and ice out from under them.

She had just worked one loose when she felt herself grabbed by the hair from behind. Her head was slammed down onto the metal frame of the car, the thin scarf was yanked down, a sharp, blade held against her throat. She dropped the snowbrush, struggling to stay on her feet.

"Don't move," said a voice.

"Let go!" said Roxanne.

"Shut up." The pointed blade dug into her skin, penetrated it. The hand that grasped her pulled her upright. "Move. Back along the side of the car."

The snow fell, dense and white, wrapping them in a private, cold cocoon. Something wet and warm was trickling down her neck. Blood? She felt no pain, but she was alert with fear. The voice was male, but muffled, probably the mouth was covered. She fumbled her way along the side of the car. The hatch was slightly open, she'd left it unlocked when she took the snow brush. All her assailant had to do was lift it, slice across her throat and push her inside. She was going to die just as Gerald Blaise had done, dumped in the trunk of this car with her throat cut, her life bleeding out of her.

She felt blood seep from a cut above her eyebrow, drip down from her forehead. She blinked it away, trying to clear both eyes of snowflakes. She couldn't turn her head to catch a glimpse of her attacker because of the knife at her throat. He pushed her sideways, around the back of the Escape. The heel on her right foot skidded out below her, her hand instinctively rose. She gasped as the knife dug deeper. That hurt. Warm blood ran down her neck, mingled with cold, melted snow. The man behind her was taller than she was, and close. Roxanne could feel his breath at her ear as he released the handful of hair.

"Sorry," said the voice. "I didn't want to do this but you left me no choice."

I am going to die, Roxanne thought. She felt the weight of the man shift behind her as his left hand moved to her back, ready to push. The pressure of the blade relaxed for a second. Roxanne swung around to her left, aiming for her assailant's arm. The knife cut across towards the right side of her neck, across her jawbone, nicked her ear. She turned in time to see a whirl of snow behind the black shape of her attacker. There was the sound of a loud crack. The man's body toppled at her. It all felt like slow motion as her feet slid out below her and she fell too, bounced off the back bumper of the car, crushed by the weight of the body that sprawled over her. The head was close to hers, covered by a dark tuque, a zipped-up collar, a black scarf all the way up to the nose. The body pressed down on her. She could hardly breathe.

"Jeez, Foxy," said a familiar voice, "don't fuckin' die on me!" Coop Jenkins leaned over her. He had a baseball bat in one hand and used the other to drag the inert dark body off Roxanne. He rolled it over into the snow face up. It started to move, the eyelids flickered.

"Raise your hands where I can see them!" barked Cooper. "Or I'll hit you so hard you'll never see daylight again." Two leather gloved hands emerged on either side. "Above your head, right now." Meantime, Coop was pulling the scarf out from Roxanne's neck. He rolled it, best he could using one hand, into a wad and pressed it against the wound at her neck. "Don't think you've got a gusher," he said. "You need to do this yourself." He reached for her hand and pressed it to her throat. "Hold it tight." Then he yanked on her coat collar. Roxanne struggled to stay focused. She pushed up with her left elbow. Together they got her propped against the back wheel of the car. Coop still watched the body, bat at the ready.

"I've got my gun," she croaked, fumbling at the buttons on her coat.

"You can get it?" Coop stood over the body while he called for help. Roxanne managed to get two buttons open, reached inside the coat and the jacket under it and pulled the gun from its holster. She took wobbly aim, her eyes blurred with snow, her other hand still pressed to the blood-soaked, wadded scarf at her throat. Coop pocketed his phone and reached down to the dark shape at his feet.

"Let's see what we've got here," he said and pulled down the black scarf that covered most of the face. He seized the top of the tuque and yanked it off. Two bright, indignant eyes opened and blazed at him.

"Toby Malleson?" Roxanne recognized the face through the haze of snowflakes. She leaned against the tire, astonished, as a red flashing glow and the blare of a horn announced the arrival of a fire truck.

26

ROXANNE LAY ON a gurney in the emergency department of Winnipeg's big downtown hospital, her throat bandaged up to her chin, an IV attached to her arm. They'd try to find her a room, a nurse told her, but she might not be lucky. They were busier than usual, and this hospital was always busy. The storm had brought car accident victims and broken bones through their doors. Some people who shouldn't had tried to dig their cars out from under wet, heavy snow and had had heart attacks. Roads had iced up as it grew darker and the temperature fell. But now there was a traffic ban. Only emergency vehicles were permitted on the streets until the storm ended and snow-clearing equipment could start the job of digging out. That had allowed things to calm down. The problem was that nobody could get home either, and all the hospital beds were full.

Roxanne would have been in a hallway by now if she wasn't a cop, injured on the job and still involved in the aftermath of the case. Other police needed to talk to her privately. So they'd shunted her into a corner and pulled a curtain around her.

It had taken more than twenty stitches inside and about the same outside to close up her neck, and another three to sew up her ear lobe. "Too bad the rest of it's gone," the doctor had commented as he stitched what was left of that together. A tiny bit of flesh lay buried deep in the snow beside the taped-up red Escape, still stuck in snow on an unusually quiet city street. "Can't have been a big knife," the doctor had said chattily as he worked. "You got lucky."

The cut had not been horizontal, had missed her carotid and the jugular. It had curved up to the right as she had moved in the opposite direction, towards her ear. She had lost blood, but she had not bled out. "Try not to talk too much," said the doctor. "Whisper if you have to." That was going to be difficult. She had so many questions that needed answering. They gave her a pen and a pad of paper to write on.

They'd butterflied the gash on her forehead together, iced it to stop the swelling. Then they'd left her to get some rest, groggy and tired but far from sleepy. That was impossible anyway in this busy place where people yelled, wheels clattered, staff walked and talked, trying to create order out of chaos, coping with crises far more serious than her own.

A city police officer took her statement, said he'd forward it to Inspector Schultz.

"Who made the arrest?" he asked.

NOT ME, she wrote. She'd still been stunned into silence by the sight of Toby Malleson's face as the fire truck arrived and a firefighter with paramedic training had taken charge of her care. He'd refused to let her talk, whisked her into the cab, wrapped in blankets, as soon as he could.

"So he's ours," the officer said. Toby was locked up at the nearest city station. Sergeant Dawes would talk to him in the morning, whenever he could make it in. Dawes lived in one of the outer suburbs. It might be noon before he was dug out.

I NEED A PHONE, Roxanne had scribbled. She had to talk to Inspector Schultz herself. Using her cellphone was banned in Emerg. You can text, they told her. But Schultz himself agreed, had insisted on speaking to her: this case was a triple murder and an attempt on Sergeant Calloway's life, after all, he had informed a staff nurse, and a portable landline had been rolled to her side.

"She can't talk much," the nurse had snapped back at the inspector, in a hurry to deal with another patient.

"Hear you're going to be okay," he remarked cheerfully, "but I guess you'll be off for a while." He'd speak to the city police right away, insist on a joint interview, only right, given that she'd helped take the guy down. Might do it himself, since she couldn't.

"There's Isabel McBain," Roxanne croaked. Using her voice hurt.

"Rookie," said her boss dismissively. "Guess she could sit in on it though, since she knows the case."

Izzy had texted already. TOBY MALLESON? YOU KIDDING? Roxanne had been trying to figure that out herself. How had she missed him as a possible murderer? He had access to the theatre, had worked with Gerald Blaise and Budgie Torrance and must have known Professor Dyck. She didn't know if Malleson was gay but she expected he was. They would have socialized. At least.

She waited until Schultz was done, then called Izzy back.

"He's being very quiet." Izzy had called the station where Toby was jailed and talked to a constable there. "He's very polite, they say." That was what had put them both off. Toby had seemed so nice, so helpful, not at all capable of killing anyone, far less three people. Yet she knew now, first hand, that he could be lethal. "Coop Jenkins told them all that he made a citizen's arrest since he's laid off right now," Izzy chatted on. "How come he found you?"

Roxanne wished she knew the answer to that.

"He'll get reinstated, for sure," Izzy continued. "It's all over the news already, 'Suspended police officer saves injured RCMP Sergeant, catches serial killer.'"

Roxanne shuddered. That was not how she wanted the story told. "He's not suspended." She squeezed out the words. This time her voice sounded squeaky. "He's on sick leave." As was she. "Did they get a name?"

"Only Cooper Jenkins. Wonder who leaked it."

Roxanne could guess. Coop himself, probably. She mustered a voice again. "You did the first interview with Malleson." Izzy had, right after they had found Blaise's body. She'd questioned most of PTC's staff.

"I know!" Izzy protested. "He had me totally fooled. He was at the theatre the night Gerald Blaise was killed, watched some of the dress rehearsal, said he saw Gerald leave. But so did the rest of the cast and the crew. I didn't think anything of it. I thought he was a wuss."

So had Roxanne. A message from Schultz arrived for Izzy while she talked.

"Great," she said. "I'm going to be there when they talk to him. I'll let you know tomorrow soon as it's over. Come see you and tell you all about it. Don't know when that will be, though. The city's all socked in and Dawes is stuck out in the burbs. There's nothing moving out there except the snow. It's still coming down, there's deep drifts already. Matt's wishing that he had his Ski-Doo here. They're letting people drive them out on the streets, to help with emergencies."

Roxanne had heard about that already. More than one broken leg or pregnant mom had made it to the hospital on the back of a snowmobile.

"They think it'll stop by midnight so maybe we'll be dug out by morning. I'm going to go now. You need to get some sleep, you sound awful."

Roxanne closed her eyes, but there was too much noise and still too many questions buzzing in her head. She wanted so badly to be in that interview room tomorrow, to try to worm the truth out of Toby Malleson. That wasn't going to happen. The phone beeped again.

"You okay? All stitched up?" asked her sister Susan.

"Can't talk much," Roxanne bleated back.

"You almost died, Roxanne. We need to talk."

Roxanne knew where this conversation was going to go. Why did she have to work in the Major Crimes Unit? Couldn't she transfer out, get a desk job? Finn had already lost his dad to the

RCMP, shot through the head by a drug-addled driver with a gun, and now here was his mother with her throat cut. Couldn't she get a detachment to run now she'd made sergeant or something like that? Work regular hours? Be safer?

"Later," Roxanne croaked. "Not allowed to speak. After I get home."

"Okay. I'll come get you. The back lane should be dug out by then. Just figure out what you want me to tell Finn. He's asking."

She hung up. Roxanne picked up her own phone. She had messages from colleagues congratulating her on the arrest (Not mine, she thought) and commiserating about her injuries. There wasn't a word from Brian Donohue. She put the phone away.

The blue curtain shifted again. Cooper Jenkins nudged it aside. He held a coffee shop tray in his other hand.

"Hey, Roxy, you trying to outdo me or something?" He placed a disposable cup beside the phone. It had a domed lid. "There's a Timmies near the front door. Was going to get you a regular coffee but then I thought you might need something more than that so I treated you to a vanilla pumpkin spice."

Whipped cream swirled on the top. She lifted the pen. CAN'T SPEAK, she wrote and held it up for him to see.

"Great," said Coop. "I get to do all the talking. Hang on. I need to go find a chair."

She lifted the cup and removed the lid, sipped some of the syrupy liquid. It wasn't at all what she ever drank but after the shocks of the day she had had, she found it comforting. It came with a long plastic spoon. She scooped up some of the cream and ate it. Then she wrote: HOW COME U HERE?

He put down the chair and settled into it, read the message and picked up his own coffee.

"On police business, right? I'm back on the job. Just finished talking to the bosses. Thought I'd drop in on the way home. I brought your gun back." He reached into his inside pocket and pulled out her own weapon. "Took it when that firefighter carted you off. Nobody's asked for it. Careless." He drawled the word.

"There's a bag," said Roxanne. "Under the bed. I think." Coop looked, pulled it out. It contained the clothes she had arrived in. Her holster should be there. "Put it where no one can see it."

"Hey," said Cooper. "You spoke." She had. And it hadn't hurt. Maybe the sweet, hot drink was doing her some good. She'd drunk a third of it already. Coop noticed.

"Should have brought you a cookie as well. Guess what, I get to interview that little jerk tomorrow instead of Dawes. Me and your pal Schultz."

"And Izzy McBain," she croaked.

"That right?"

"How come you found me?"

"Well." He sat back and downed some coffee. "I was at that funeral. Went to pay my respects, like, didn't see me sitting at the back, did you? After, I went and got my truck. Had to park way past yours. Drove it back to the parking lot at the funeral home when the service was over, just to watch who was leaving, you know. Someone pulled out so I got a spot. You sure took your time, didn't you? Nobody noticed me in all that snow. It wasn't easy to see but I watched you walk by. Five feet away, never saw me, did you? Then I heard the chicks that were loading up a van outside yelling, "Night, Toby' and the Malleson guy walked into the lot, like he was going for his car, but then he turned around and walked away. Went off in the same direction as you. So I got out the truck and followed him. Wasn't hard. Just stepped in his footprints. And hey, I got there just in time."

"How long have you been following me?" Roxanne asked, and winced. Talking loudly was still not a good idea. "You put a tracker in the Escape," she whispered.

"Good girl!" Coop grinned his approval. "Dead on. That's more than my bosses figured out."

She resorted to writing again. DON'T CALL ME GIRL. She tore it off and held it up, then she wrote another: AND NEVER ROXY.

"Okay, okay." He grinned, undeterred. "See, I figured out that someone had to be following your car. Slashed your tires, scratched it up. I reckoned that they did it to put you on the wrong track, had to know that the killer used a knife, maybe knew about the Sinclairs."

She drank more of the liquid in the cup, scooped up what was left of the cream and remembered how the tech staff at the theatre had watched everything that went on around that building. They had speculated that a Winnipeg street gang had murdered Gerald Blaise. Toby Malleson would have heard that gossip.

"Whoever it was could still be following you, and I reckoned that if I caught him, I would have the killer. Bingo, eh? It worked! And I saved you while I was at it."

"Thank you, Cooper." What else could she say?

"You never guessed it was him?"

"No," she whispered. She started shaking her head, then stopped. That was not a good idea, either. "It looks like Marla Caplan was related to Gerald Blaise. I was beginning to suspect her."

"Got that wrong, didn't you?"

"You never guessed either," she retaliated.

"Nope. Never noticed Malleson much. They're telling me he's been acting real nice ever since they took him in. Says 'thank you.' 'Can you help me please, officer.'"

"Don't be fooled." Roxanne found her full voice again. "He's poison." She'd caught a glimpse of the real Toby Malleson that she wasn't going to easily forget.

"So there's nothing you can tell me before tomorrow?" There wasn't. "I'd best be off then."

"You're driving in that snowstorm?"

"Sure. No trouble at all," said Cooper. He looked sideways at her as he pushed the curtain aside. "Too bad they used black thread on the ear. And that eye's gonna turn black. You'll look as bad as me."

27

BY NINE THE next morning, the main arteries of the city had been unclogged. Large snowblowers filled the backs of waiting trucks that then carted their heavy load to the dumping ground near the city limits. It was slow work as roads were cleared one by one and the mounds of dirty snow piled up. The ban on nonessential traffic still stood. Offices were closed for the morning at least, and Roxanne Calloway was staying where she was until she could be picked up.

Jazz Elliot sat in her hotel dining room and munched on toast and marmalade. Rehearsals couldn't begin again until after one, but it looked like Maggie Soames would make it in on a plane from Toronto around then. Once she had Maggie, they would work fast. And meantime, the sound techie had spoken to a musician in town. He composed, had worked with the theatre before, and had been happy to spend time while the snow blew working up some music for the witches to sing. Preliminary recordings should be in her inbox as soon as she had finished breakfast.

"Have you heard the news?" Maxwell Fergusson took the chair beside her. Tim Baldwin followed at his heels. "They've arrested someone for the murders. That policewoman from the RCMP almost got killed. Must have happened yesterday, right after Gerald's cremation."

"Did they say who they've got?"

"Not a word." Maxwell beckoned to a server. Jazz searched her many pockets for her phone. She opened up Facebook. Her newsfeed was full of comments about the arrest. One was from Alison Beck.

"Was at Funeral Home at 3:40. Sgt Calloway left just before. Was fine."

"So she didn't do it. Too bad they're not going to lock her up," said Jazz.

"I'm having the full breakfast," said Maxwell. "How about you, Timothy?"

Tim Baldwin shook his head. He was vegan. And still too sad to eat much.

IZZY MCBAIN'S PARTNER, Matt, owned a big Ford truck. He'd had snow tires installed last week. Izzy drove to the city police station in plenty of time for the interview with Toby Malleson. They showed her to the interview room. There was a table with four chairs and another solitary one in a corner, presumably for her. She tucked the bag she was carrying under it, draped her parka over the back, took her place and waited.

Toby Malleson was escorted in just after nine. The city constable who guarded him looked at Izzy, said nothing and stood by the door. Toby looked in good shape, although he held himself stiff and straight. Coop Jenkins' baseball bat had cracked a couple of ribs. He wore the suit that he had been arrested in, a bit creased for being slept in, but he had shaved, his hair was neatly combed and his tie was straight. A lawyer bustled in behind him, not one of the high fliers who had attended Tamsin Longstaff and Budgie Torrance when they had needed legal support, but she looked experienced and her manner was efficient. She appeared to be confident, as did her client.

Seconds later, Coop Jenkins and Inspector Schultz arrived. They stood looking down at Toby Malleson. Toby half rose, stretched out a hand.

"Good morning, gentlemen," he said with a bright smile. They both sat without shaking it, announced their names and status, switched on the recorder, and began. Schultz went first, a bullfrog in full throttle. Cooper leaned back, watching to see how Toby reacted. The swelling had subsided on his damaged eye. He could see through it just fine.

"You are charged with attempting to murder RCMP Sergeant Roxanne Calloway yesterday afternoon at around fifteen hours twenty." Schultz had photographs at the ready, one of the gash to Roxanne's neck, others showing blood spatters on the side of the car and in the snow, a Swiss Army knife with a two-inch open blade. "Sergeant Jenkins witnessed the scene."

Coop described seeing Toby follow Roxanne though the snow to her car, and what he saw when he got there. "You had your hand raised, holding that knife." He tapped the photo of the knife with a finger. "It had blood on it. You were holding Sergeant Calloway with your other hand. She was sliding down the side of the car, she'd just turned her head to look at you. I saw the blood at her throat. I took action to stop you, using a baseball bat. You fell to the ground and dropped the knife in the snow. Swiss Army knife, open. Forensics say that the same type of blade was used to cut the throat of Gerald Blaise."

"Stop right there." Toby Malleson's lawyer held up her hand. "You need to hear what my client has to say with regard to this charge." She sat back, folded her arms and nodded to Toby.

"You've got it all wrong," said Toby Malleson, a gentle smile on his lips, his eyes sorrowful. "Let me tell you what really happened."

"I did follow Sergeant Calloway from the funeral home. I had to. I needed to speak to her, urgently. You see, I knew who was responsible for those murders. I'd been figuring it out for a while but it was only after the service yesterday afternoon that I was absolutely sure."

Coop's good eyebrow rose. So did the corner of his mouth. He looked skeptical. Toby continued, undeterred:

"Alison Beck, our acting general manager, had good reason to hate Gerald Blaise. She had worked for us previously. She had been fired back then. She told people that she blamed Tamsin Longstaff, but that was not true. I know that because she called me the night after they did it, took her keys and marched her out of the building. She was so humiliated. She blurted it all out, how she'd wanted Gerald to produce a play that her partner, Greg, had written, instead of the one we have up right now. Pushed hard. Challenged the whole playbill Gerald had lined up for this season. Told Gerald he needed to get more in tune with the times or he wouldn't get his contract renewed. She went too far, said she'd drunk some wine that night with Gerald, got careless. It took a lot to piss off Gerald, but she did it. He told Tamsin, she told the board that Alison was a problem and that was it. She was history. And what totally got to her was that Gerald made sure he was out of town when they actually let her go. He left it to Tamsin and the board chair to do his dirty work. Was too much of a coward to face her himself.

"By the next day she was telling a different story, how she thought Tamsin was responsible. Everyone loved Gerald, no one would have wanted to believe her, so she shifted the blame. But in her heart, she hated him for what he had done."

Inspector Schultz had folded his arms. His head sank into his shoulders as he sat, reptile-like, listening.

"I couldn't believe it when she got reinstated, but I guess we needed her at the time. We had lost both our bosses and Alison had only been gone a few weeks. She knew the ropes. And maybe some of the board agreed with her about how Gerald had been getting stale. So she was rehired, temporarily. She's been making all kinds of changes while she can, but that's about to end, because our real GM is coming back. Tamsin told Alison and Greg in the lobby after the service. I heard her. She said she'd pay Alison off and Greg could forget about PTC producing his play. She'd be putting a stop to that. Then she walked away and I saw the look on Alison's face. Pure venom, officers. And I thought, they are the killers! Alison had an alibi for the night that Budgie was murdered, but where was Greg at the time? She's the boss in that household. She could have made him do it.

"Tamsin left shortly after that. Said she was going home, and I saw Greg leave right after her. And I knew that Tamsin was in danger. I needed to talk to the sergeant, but I couldn't get to her, she was always busy talking to other people, and Alison was still there. But when the sergeant left, I was able to follow right after her. The snow was coming down thick and fast, but I could see her footprints. She was wearing heeled boots. I knew which ones were hers." Toby was gesticulating with his hands, telling his story as convincingly as he could.

"I caught up to her at her car. She was struggling to get her key into the lock. It had iced up and of course neither of us had any de-icer, but I did have my Swiss Army knife in my pocket. I reached around her to try to poke it into the lock, to try to pry it loose, and that is when she slipped. Those silly heels, you know. One of them just slid out below her and she fell. Her head caught my arm. The knife was still in my hand, open, and her neck landed right across the blade. It happened so fast. I couldn't have stopped her. And that's when you, Sergeant Jenkins, arrived on the scene and jumped to entirely the wrong conclusion. I wasn't trying to kill Sergeant Calloway. I was trying to help her. It was a complete accident." He looked at both men in front of him, indignant. Then he said, "Has anyone checked up on Tamsin Longstaff? Is she safe?" He sounded quite heroic.

Schultz pursed his lips in disbelief. Coop Jenkins glanced towards Izzy, incredulous. The constable at the door tapped a message on his phone. Tamsin Longstaff would need to be contacted, just in case any of this was true.

"I don't believe a word of it." Coop Jenkins leaned forward on his one good arm. "I spoke to Sergeant Calloway last night at the hospital. And I've read her statement. You attacked her from behind."

"So sad, isn't it?" Toby Malleson shook his head, "That the police are under so much pressure to make an arrest. Three deaths already. Sergeant Calloway must be desperate if that's what she's saying."

"You accusing Sergeant Calloway of perjury?" growled Inspector Schultz.

"I'm telling the absolute truth," said Toby Malleson, all wide-eyed innocence.

"Well," said Cooper Jenkins, "the way she tells it, she'd already unlocked the car. Got out a snowbrush. If our Ident Unit finds that brush in the snow beside the car, that'll prove her right."

"Not necessarily," said Toby Malleson. "The back hatch might have not been frozen. And the driver's door could have thawed by the time your forensic people got to it. She'd started the engine with the remote."

Schultz and Jenkins left the room to consult. They were stymied. It was Malleson's story against Roxanne's. His seemed absurd. Perhaps the angle of the cut to her neck would tell the truth, but the medical report they had so far did not prove Roxanne's case. They returned to the room, ready to try another approach. They ignored Izzy McBain, sitting quietly in the corner.

"Where were you the night of October 2?" asked Schultz.

"The night poor Gerald died?" Toby answered brightly. "That was a Wednesday. There was a dress rehearsal. I watched part of it. There's so much work for me to do the night before a season opening. I was in the office, mainly. Gerald watched it all, I believe. He popped his head around the door to say goodnight. He was happy. He liked the show. Said that he thought it would do well. He was looking forward to the following night. Gerald loved openings. It's so sad that he didn't make it. He said, 'Goodnight, Toby,' and disappeared off down the corridor. It can't have been long past ten. That was the last time I ever saw him."

"How long had you known him?" asked Cooper.

"Oh, years. Fifteen, maybe? I worked for a smaller theatre company before I got the job at PTC. That was just over eight years ago. Gerald was a great boss. We all miss him."

"How friendly were you?"

Toby smiled back at him. He knew where that question was leading. "We were colleagues, Detective Sergeant. Gerald had other interests in that regard. He and I had a good professional relationship. Nothing more."

"Not so!" said a loud, clear voice from the corner of the room. Izzy McBain reached down into the bag at her feet, lifted out a small, blue notebook and held it high. "This," she said, "is Gerald Blaise's address book. A special one. Where he kept the names of all the people he had sex with. And see?" She flipped it open and pointed. "Ty Malleson. And your phone number. I know it's yours because I called it. Got your answering machine."

"Let's see that." Inspector Schultz held out a hand. Izzy walked over and handed it to him. He peered at the scribble inside. "You sure?" he asked.

"Yessir," said Izzy. "See that bag?" She pointed towards it. "I've got Gerald Blaise's diaries in there. They go back years. He mentions a guy called Ty a lot. I got most of those transcribed last night." She walked back to the chair and took a folder from inside the bag.

"The last entry was on Tuesday, September 29, the day before Blaise died. It says, 'Tell Ty? Tomorrow?'" She opened the folder and laid it in front of Inspector Schultz. "Sorry I couldn't let you know before this, sir. I got it all during the night and you were stuck at home in the storm.

Schultz took the printout, sent by Dr. Margo Wishart, at 3:24 am. Izzy stood at the end of the table. Toby Malleson's face had paled, his mouth tightened.

"You were crazy about him," Izzy said quietly, taking the opportunity while her boss read. "Weren't you? Did you go out with him after that dress rehearsal? You'd been in a relationship with him. Did he tell you he was ending it? Leaving you for another, younger man? Is that why you killed him?"

She watched tears begin to well up in Toby's eyes. And she watched him blink so he didn't shed a drop.

"So how did it happen?" Izzy asked.

Toby Malleson took some time to think before he replied. When he did, he spoke quietly, as if he was talking to himself while he remembered.

"He didn't say goodbye at the theatre," he admitted. "We left together. Went to the Riverbank Grill. We liked to go there. It isn't far but Gerald hated to walk. He insisted on taking his car. Said he'd drive me back to PTC after." He looked up, not at them but into the corner of the room where Izzy's empty chair still sat, the incriminating dairies under it.

"He told me he was leaving. Me. PTC. Winnipeg. Everything. Was going to go and live with that young guy in B.C. And he wasn't sorry. Not at all. He was happy. He couldn't hide it. Went on and on about how he'd be free to concentrate on collecting art, go travelling with Timbo." His voice grew bitter. "That's what did it. Got me really upset. I'd always known I was special to him because he called me 'Ty.' It was his private name for me. Gerald only gave names like that to people he really cared about. Like calling Annabel 'Budgie.' He was the person who first called her that, you know. He told me so.

"When I heard him say 'Timbo' I knew that this new guy mattered. That I'd been supplanted. It really was over." He raised his eyes towards them, miserable. "I don't know what got into me. I wasn't sad. I was so cold inside. Chilled. I got so angry. Fifteen years we'd been together. There were others, for sure, but none of them threatened what he and I had. And now he was ending it as if it had all been nothing." He was so quiet now that they had to lean in to hear him. The recorder was sensitive, though. It would pick up what he said.

"He lifted the bill and said it was his treat. What a joke. I followed him out to the car. And when I put my hand into my jacket pocket, there was my Swiss Army knife. It was dark. Late. No one else was in the parking lot. It was all over in a matter of seconds." Another long silence followed. They waited. Toby took a deep breath. Now his voice had a harder edge to it.

"I drove him back to PTC in the trunk of the Audi. My car was still parked outside the theatre, in my usual spot. And I thought, 'What the hell, he gave that Baldwin guy the Chan?' He'd told me that, you know, popping peanuts in his mouth, like it didn't matter. He'd never given me a present that was anything like as good as that. I had his keys in my hand. So, I let myself into the condo and helped myself to a couple of paintings I've always liked. I put them in my car, put Gerald's keys back in the ignition of his and left him there." He stopped speaking. He looked exhausted.

"Why did you kill Professor Dyck?" asked the Inspector.

"Thom? He knew all about me and Gerald. We hang out together sometimes. Thom was a good listener. Gerald told him things. So did I. Sometimes you just need someone to confide in. He was in the theatre for a meeting not long after they found Gerald's body. The place was crawling with police. He passed me in the hallway and he gave me this look, like he knew. So he had to go. I knew he jogged most mornings. I took along a kitchen knife, just in case I needed to leave it with him."

"And Annabel Torrance?"

"Budgie could be such a bitch." For a moment, Toby looked more like his usual self. "She figured it out, too. Well, not quite but close enough. She'd come over to the theatre after hours one night to bawl out Alison Beck. Alison always worked late and Budgie had heard that she'd been in touch with Maggie Soames, to find out if she'd be available if Budgie had to be replaced. She was furious about that. She bumped into me in the corridor right after. She was still in a filthy mood. Poked me with her finger. 'What about you, Tobe?' she asked. 'Missing your old buddy Gerald? Did he tell you he was going to drop you for some bit of muscle on the West Coast?'

"And she must have seen something in my face. 'How come the police aren't asking you their stupid questions?' she asked. 'Maybe you're the one who did him in,' and off she went, cackling. Jazz should have had her play one of the witches," he added bitterly. "She'd have been a great hag."

He'd called on Budgie on the Sunday night. He'd told her that he needed to get into the rehearsal hall to check Nell Bronson's latest rehearsal schedule. No one else was around, but Budgie had a master key. Could she let him in?

"She was a different person when she was happy," he said, almost wistful. "She walked over there without a single suspicion of what I had planned. I'd taken along another knife from my kitchen. It was so simple. She had no idea. I cleaned up a bit, got a mop from the cleaning closet, and cloth so I could wipe things down, then I laid her out on her back, like she was Juliet in her tomb. You know she last played that role when she was almost fifty? And she was brilliant. You could almost believe she was a teenager. I wrapped her hands around the handle of the knife. And I had this moment of inspiration, that I could make it look like she'd killed herself, and I could use the words from *Macbeth*. There was a script on the table, and markers. I used those and then I was done." He raised his hands, open, towards them. He was finished.

But Coop Jenkins was not. "You scratched up Sergeant Calloway's car. Slashed her tires. What was that about?"

"She suspected Tamsin!" Toby looked indignant. "I couldn't have her blamed for something she didn't do!"

He'd also been worried that Sergeant Calloway would eventually think about him and start asking awkward questions, he said. He'd thought using it to divert attention to some street kids was smart, but it didn't last long. He passed the RCMP building on the way home, the day after she arrested Tamsin, drove into the lot and found her RAV4. He'd stabbed each of the tires, then he'd waited to see what she would do. It had taken a while but he'd eventually seen someone bring a Ford Focus to the door and watched her get in. He'd followed her. Got the number.

"And then," he told Jenkins, "I was in the Forks that weekend, doing some early Christmas shopping, and there you were, walking into the coffee shop. It didn't take long to find out where she'd parked the Focus. I thought I was being quite cunning, but it didn't work."

He folded his hands, rubbed his knuckles, looked down at them. "She figured it out anyway. She stood in the door of the funeral hall after the service, watching me clearing up, with this suspicious look on her face, and I knew she was onto me. I needed to do something. So I followed her."

"So you did try to kill her," Jenkins said.

Toby shrugged like it didn't matter.

"Well then," said Schultz. "I think we've got enough here." He nodded to the city constable to come and take Toby away. "All right, McBain," he added. "Let's see what else you've got here."

Izzy fetched her bag, happy to oblige.

28

"IT WAS A slam dunk!" Coop Jenkins popped the cork on a bottle of Prosecco. He'd dropped in at the liquor store on the way to Roxanne's apartment. "Izzy nailed it. Thought she was going to make him cry."

Izzy was lifting food containers out of a bag. "I got you soup," she said. "You can try mushing up the wontons."

"I can swallow." They were in Roxanne's kitchen. Traffic outside was moving again. Her sister had finally managed to drive to the hospital. She'd planned to take Roxanne to her own house and put her in the spare room, where she could take care of her.

"No way," Roxanne had said. "I'm going home." Susan had reluctantly agreed. She'd be back later, with the boys and groceries.

"Get some rest," she had said. That had seemed like a good idea but it hadn't lasted. It hadn't taken long for Izzy and Coop to wrap up the case with Inspector Schultz after Toby Malleson had been led away. They'd called to find out where Roxanne was. And then they'd brought lunch. Roxanne picked up a wonton and swallowed it.

"See," she said, "I'm doing fine." She'd given up on whispering and writing down what she wanted to say. The painkillers were doing their work. Izzy held up a fizzy glassful of wine.

"We're celebrating," she said. "You want some?"

Roxanne took it, drank a cold mouthful. Why not? She could sleep for days after, if she wanted to. She was off sick.

"We got him for all three murders, and the attack on you. He'll be put away for years." Cooper downed half of his glass. "That was brilliant, how you got him to confess, Isabel." He passed Izzy a container of lemon chicken.

"I am a pro and don't call me Isabel." Izzy swatted him with the back of her hand. Roxanne had already been told the gist of the story, but she wanted to hear more about Izzy's part in it.

"He got it wrong when he said I suspected him," she said. "I never imagined it was him. How did you figure it out?"

"Well, after I talked to you yesterday on the phone, after they'd finished stitching you up, I thought, Toby Malleson had to be having it off with Gerald Blaise. He was just the type to fall for Gerald, wasn't he? And Gerald didn't sound like he was the kind to say no. I knew the three notebooks that we had, the ones Gerald wrote, were still in your office. So I got the truck out and drove to HQ."

"Hadn't they ordered everyone off the roads by then?"

"Sure. But I was on police business, right?"

"My office was locked." Roxanne scooped up some fried rice and chewed. It went down okay.

"Used my credit card. It was easy. Those locks are such garbage! You'd think HQ would have better ones," said Izzy. "Anyway, I found the notebooks and looked up the M's in the one with the addresses. I thought I could make out T and M but I wasn't sure, so I called Margo Wishart."

"The art prof," Roxanne explained to Coop. "She can read Gerald's handwriting."

"And I know her from Cullen Village," said Izzy. "So, we got together on Skype and I held up the page so Margo could see it and she read 'Ty Malleson.' And Margo said she'd seen that name before, just the 'Ty,' in Gerald's diaries and she still had the transcription of the book we gave her before in her computer, so she looked it up. And there he was. Then she said, 'This diary just goes back through this year. Gerald had to have other ones. He's not the kind to have thrown them out and wasn't he keeping stuff so he could write a memoir sometime?'

"So I asked her if it was okay if I hung up and called her back later, then I got hold of Larry Smith at the condo building and asked him to go down to that storage unit you told me about and see if he could find them. Didn't take him all that long. There was a whole boxful of them. So I got back in the truck and drove over there and picked it up. Got to say it was pretty freaky out by then, so I went straight back to HQ and decided to stay there until morning. I knew they'd get dug out sooner than our apartment building would and I thought I might need the copier or something like that anyway.

"I was online with Margo half the night, figuring out what the rest of those diaries said. First mention of Ty was fifteen years ago. He and Gerald had been really hot back then. It had cooled off a bit but they still were a pair, right up until the night that Gerald Blaise took him out for a drink and told him it was over, like it was no big deal. What a jerk."

"Who, Blaise?" Cooper Jenkins had emptied his plate and reached for more. Roxanne had progressed to bits of chicken, cut up small. "You think so?"

"Sure," said Izzy. "He played them all for suckers. Not just Toby Malleson. Budgie. Tamsin Longstaff. Maxwell Fergusson. Even Alison Beck."

"Still, he didn't deserve to get his throat cut, did he?" Roxanne fingered the bandage at her throat. "He died in the trunk of that car while Toby drove him back to the PTC parking lot."

"Suppose not." Izzy reached for the bottle. "You want some more?" Roxanne did. Izzy topped up their glasses. "Schultzy's pleased with me. Said 'Well done, McBain.' Says I'm a keeper."

"Good," said Roxanne, sipping the cold wine. Izzy was headstrong but she had good ideas and she was willing to act on them. In this case she'd done everything right.

"You're not going to be leaving Manitoba, are you?" Izzy asked.

"Who, me?" Roxanne put down her glass.

"Yeah. To go to Ottawa."

"Ottawa?" She was perplexed.

"To live with Inspector Donohue. That's what the guys at HQ are saying."

Roxanne tried not to show her surprise. It didn't work.

"You didn't know? He went there for an interview. They're all saying he's probably going over to CSIS. He's really interested in all that intel stuff, right? He was supposed to be back yesterday but he got stuck because of the storm."

That explained why Brian hadn't called. He probably knew nothing about what had happened to her. If he was planning to move, that could be why he'd wanted to talk to her earlier. CSIS was Canada's international intelligence branch. A job like that would be exactly what Brian would want. Would she want to go live in Ottawa? Was it going to be an option or was this when Brian Donohue would dump her? Coop Jenkins listened to the whole exchange with that sardonic, one-sided smile of his.

"Donohue?" he said. "Good-looking guy? Dark hair? I've met him, when he was still a sergeant. We were at a conference."

They heard the front door open. Finn and his cousin Robbie ran into the kitchen. They both stopped dead in their tracks when they saw Roxanne, bandaged up around her neck, black stitches at her ear, her forehead taped and bruised and a plastic shield covering one eye.

"I know what I'm going to be for Halloween this year," she said. "What about you?"

Halloween was less than two weeks away. She'd still be off work. This year she could go trick-or-treating with Finn, for sure. The job wouldn't get in the way, for once. She'd still be on leave.

Coop Jenkins got to his feet.

"Time I was off," he said.

"You going already?" she asked.

"Sure. Got things to do. See you around, maybe." And Coop disappeared out the door. He almost collided with Susan, Roxanne's sister, a grocery bag in each hand.

"Who was that?" Susan asked as she hoisted the bags up onto a kitchen counter.

"Just a guy we've been working with," said Roxanne.

MARGO WISHART OPENED her eyes to meet those of her dog, staring at her. She knew that look. Bob needed out. She'd opened the door for him just before four in the morning. He'd waded through the snow to the nearest shrub, then loped back inside and Margo had gone to bed. She looked at her bedside clock. It was dead. The power was out. The house was cold.

She got out of bed and went to the back door. She could just push it ajar against the weight of the snow, enough for Bob to squeeze out. Then she opened her iPad. 12:05, it said. She'd slept the whole morning away. Her cellphone was half charged up. There were messages from Roberta and Sasha. The whole area was without power. Trees, weighted with snow, had fallen and taken out hydro lines. She looked out the window. Laden branches were bowed down almost to the ground. The snow was fresh and new, the sky bright blue. She could see dark shapes moving out on the surface of the lake. Canada geese, hundreds of them. The day the snowline reached as far south as Cullen Village, they'd be off, skein after skein, honking their way south. And they hadn't left yet. This snow would melt. There would be a few more weeks of fall weather yet, if they were lucky. She let her dog back in and opened the fridge door. She couldn't make coffee. Some juice would have to do.

She read the newsfeed on Facebook. The police had made an arrest. They didn't say who, but Margo knew who it was. Her cellphone rang.

"You heard? They've got the murderer! Wonder who it is?" Margo tried to sound surprised. She needed to keep quiet until the news that PTC's marketing director was the killer became official, or leaked out.

"I got an invitation from Jazz Elliot to be her guest at the opening night of *Macbeth*," said Roberta. That solved a problem.

Margo could take Sasha along. "Do you need help digging out?" She did. "I'll phone Sasha, see if she's okay. I've got the stove going. We could all come here and warm up after. Eat sandwiches for lunch."

Margo smiled. Everything was returning to normal in her part of the world.

THE NEWS THAT Toby Malleson had been arrested rippled through the hallways of Prairie Theatre Centre.

"Our Toby?" said Nell Bronson. "I can't believe it!" Pedro Diaz shook his head in disbelief.

"Little shit," Sadie Williams muttered into a box of buttons. "He sure had us fooled."

Jazz Elliot stood in Tamsin Longstaff's office. Tamsin had reinstated herself.

"I'm going to need a live band," Jazz said. "Come listen."

Jazz had her priorities right. Work had to go on. Tamsin clicked her way to the rehearsal hall.

"Double, double toil and trouble; Fire burn, and cauldron bubble," the witches sang with gleeful malice.

"Okay," said Tamsin. "We can do that." She wasn't worried that she couldn't meet costs now. The pall that had hung over the theatre had lifted and word was out that the famous Maggie Soames was on her way from London, England, to play Lady Macbeth. She'd been held up because of the storm but she'd be in Winnipeg by the end of the day. Ticket sales were booming. Tamsin was going to have to hire a new marketing director but the next play up, *A Christmas Carol*, was an easy sell. She could take her time doing that. Meantime she'd get Marla Caplan to fill in.

"Nobody noticed until now that Gerald scheduled the Scottish play to open right around Halloween?" Danny Foley asked. He was dressed as Macbeth in a greatcoat over a tailored suit, a kind of contemporary battledress. "Witches and all? I tell you, the guy was brilliant."

Gerald Blaise was rapidly acquiring legendary status. Pedro's crew had found old archival tapes. They would splice some together and show them on Monday at the memorial for their beloved dead AD. They'd do a montage of shots from Budgie's career too. Maxwell Fergusson was staying on so he could attend, but Tim Baldwin had booked himself on a plane home to B.C. later in the day.

"I couldn't bear it," he had said. He hadn't been able to see where his dead lover had lived after all. The condo was all sealed up, the wills probated.

"At least he's got the Chan," Maxwell had said over breakfast. He and Jazz had started to make a routine of those. They enjoyed their morning chats. "Sooner or later everything will have to be sold and I'll get my cut."

"Everything is back under control," Tamsin told her board chair, Frank Moran, by phone early afternoon. She'd paid off Alison Beck, no problem. Alison was going to apply for a job at the art gallery. PTC would give her a decent reference. "Are you free tonight? Dinner at my place?"

"I could do that," said Frank Moran.

MARLA CAPLAN SAT in the apartment of her cousin, Chloe Delaney. "I don't think I'll take the job," she said. "I need to put some distance between myself and PTC. I'll give them two weeks' notice, stick around for the opening of *Macbeth*, then I'll go back to Toronto. I miss living there and my old boss at the Arts Council says a job's coming up at Young People's Theatre. I'd like to work at that place. You can keep an eye on things from here?"

Chloe nodded her pretty head.

"I called the lawyer who represented Tamsin Longstaff when she needed help. He said he doesn't handle cases like ours but he gave me the name of someone who does. We've got an appointment next week."

The contents of a large brown envelope lay strewn on the coffee table in front of them, photographs of the artworks in Gerald's collection, of the boxes in the storage unit open to show the contents of the ones that contained antiques. Marla had found a photo of the old Rosedale mansion.

"Can you believe that Gramma Emmy walked away from all of that? Raised my mom and your dad dirt poor, while Gerald Blaise got everything he wanted."

There was one photo that was not a copy, the one that showed the Balfours with their daughter, Emilia—their grandmother. Marla had helped herself to the original.

"Look how pretty she was. You look just like her, Chloe."

She'd also taken a man's hairbrush, with Gerald Blaise's initials engraved on the back and several hairs embedded in the bristles, DNA evidence to prove they were related. And a ring, large, sculpted and gold. Chloe picked it up and slipped it on her finger. The large diamond caught the light.

"Too bad we have to get it melted down," she said. "It's a great design."

"Nobody's missed it yet. Budgie had left it lying on the dressing table in her room. It was easy to pocket it. Then I told the police that it was gone, because I didn't want anyone to suspect me and they needed to know about it. They thought Budgie might have killed herself. If the ring was gone, they'd know something else had happened to her. They've forgotten that it's gone, for now, but that won't last. Best that we get rid of it, plus we could use the money," said her more practical cousin.

Chloe took it off. "Guess so," she said. "You think we'll get it back? Our inheritance?"

"Maybe not all of it." Marla wrapped the ring in a piece of soft cloth. "But some, for sure. I'd best get back to work."

Acknowledgements

A big thank you to my publisher Karen Haughian and her team, including the able and patient Ashley Brekelmans, her marketing assistant; Terry Gallagher of Doowah Design for the cover; and Douglas Whiteway, my editor, for his thorough and insightful work.

Thanks also to my daughter, Kirsty Macdonald, who did a first edit and always makes the right suggestions.

David D'Andrea and Andrew Minor advised me on all things to do with policing. It was David who suggested that the RCMP could investigate a murder that happened in the city as long as the body was found outside Winnipeg's perimeter. That helped get this story started. Ann Atkey read a draft later in the process and gave me some great feedback. Above all, thanks to everyone for your support and for the conversations!

About the Author

RAYE ANDERSON IS a Scots Canadian who spent many enjoyable years running theatre schools and delivering creative learning programs for arts organizations, in Winnipeg, notably at Prairie Theatre Exchange, and in Ottawa and Calgary. Her work has taken her across Canada, coast to coast, and up north as far as Churchill and Yellowknife. She's also worked as far afield as the West Indies and her native Scotland. She has two daughters and one granddaughter.

Now, she lives in Manitoba's beautiful Interlake and is part of a thriving arts community. *And Then Is Heard No More* is Anderson's second novel featuring RCMP Corporal Roxanne Calloway, who made her debut in *And We Shall Have Snow*.